THE TALISKER DEAD

A D.I. DUNCAN MCADAM MYSTERY

THE MISTY ISLE
BOOK 3

J M DALGLIESH

First published by Hamilton Press in 2024

ISBN (Trade Paperback) 978-1-80080-365-7
ISBN (Hardback) 978-1-80080-301-5
ISBN (Large Print) 978-1-80080-467-8

Look out for the link at the end of this book or visit my website at **www.jmdalgliesh.com** to sign up to my no-spam VIP Club and receive a FREE novella from my Hidden Norfolk series plus news and previews of forthcoming works.

Never miss a new release.

No spam, ever, guaranteed. You can unsubscribe at any time.

SCOTTISH NAMES
PEOPLE AND PLACES

Characters;
 Èibhlin - (Eve-leen)
 Eilidh - (Ay-lee)
 Mhari - (Vh-ari)
 MacEachran - (Mack-Eck-ran)
 Marsali - (Mar-ser-lee)

Places;
 Portree - (Por-tree)
 Fiscavaig - (Fis-car-vaig)
 Tarskavaig - (Tars-car-vaig)
 Kensaleyre - (Ken-sal-ayre)
 Sligachan - (Slee-gak-an)
 Trotternish - (Trott-er-nish)
 Waternish - (Water-nish)
 Minginish - (Ming-in-ish)
 Quiraing - (Kir-ang)
 Raasay - (Raa-see)
 Isay - (I-say)

Airdrie - (Air-dree)
Mallaig - (Mall-aig)

SCOTTISH PHRASES AND SLANG

Slang;

    Wee - (Small)

    Cannae - (Cannot / can't)

    Dinnae - (Did not / Didn't)

    Disnae - (Does not)

    Nae - (No)

    Blether - (Chat / conversation)

    Braw - (Good)

    Weans - (Children)

    Bairns - (Children)

THE TALISKER DEAD

PROLOGUE

THE VOICES ARE MUFFLED. Both of them are trying to keep from being overheard. Is that for my benefit? Probably. Mum seemed off when she picked me up after school this afternoon. She asked me how my day was, much as she always does, but something was different with her today. She was quieter. In general, recently, she is quieter.

The thin shaft of light stretching out from between the door and the jamb hurts my eyes as I peer through into the front room. The fire is lit. I can't see it, but I can smell the peat and feel the warmth leaving the room and mixing with the cold air in the draughty hallway where I'm sitting. My toes are already numb. I should have brought my duvet, or a blanket, but then they'd know I was here. I definitely should have worn my slippers. Dad will be upset if he finds me out here, listening. I should be in bed at this time on a school night.

"We can't go on like this!" Mum says. I can hear the tension in her voice. That isn't just a comment; she really means it. "We had another letter through this morning."

"From the bank?"

My mum is looking tired. I mean, she always looks tired

but now it's not just the usual fatigue of a normal day… it's more world-weary, worn out. As for my dad, he's himself. He doesn't say much at the best of times. Gran said he was always like that. How did she once describe him to me? Removed. That was it.

"We're falling further behind…"

"I know."

Tension in his voice now too. This never ends well.

"On the mortgage and the—"

"I bloody well know, woman! What do you expect me tae do?"

"Pay it!"

My dad is exasperated. He's up… pacing the room.

"How can I pay it when we don't have any money?"

Mum is on the brink of tears now. I know. She cries when dad is out on the boat sometimes, always at night, and only when she thinks I'm asleep. Oftentimes, I'm just pretending though.

"Can we… try something different?"

"Different how?"

Mum is shaking her head. She's clutching at straws now.

"I don't know… maybe we could modernise—"

"Modernise?" Dad says with a dismissive laugh. "What with?"

He's becoming angry, or as angry as he gets at any rate. He's giving her that look; the one he does when he's feeling uncomfortable and wants to exert control over the conversation. He's frightened. It's not something I see routinely in him but it's there, even if he won't allow himself to show it openly.

"We're not bringing in enough to cover our costs as it is. You know I've had to let wee Connor go already."

"I know… but you have to do something!"

"The big ships are coming in and trawling everything in

sight. We're having to go out to deeper waters... it's dangerous and we have to spend longer out—"

"I know all that but—"

"But nothing! After all this time, you still don't get it, do you? The stocks have been decimated. There are too many of us going out after the same catch. Something's got to give. We all need to row back on the take."

"And how are you going t' feed your family if you do that? We're your priority – or should be – and not the bloody North Atlantic."

"I'm well aware of my responsibilities."

Dad looks straight at me. I swear he can see me through the crack in the door. I'm holding my breath. If I move, he'll see, if he hasn't already.

"Things have to change... for everyone, not just for us," he says quietly.

"Do you think the rest of them will accept less? Don't be so naive!"

"Change is coming to this industry, whether we like it or not. I cannae hold it back, no matter how much I might want to."

"But you don't, do you?"

"What?"

"Want to. You think it's time for people to come away from the sea, don't you?"

Dad is looking at her. He doesn't want to say so – fearful of her reaction, I suppose — but she knows what he is thinking. He's talked of little else for ages.

"Aye. Things have to change. Like it or not."

"Then... what are we going to do?"

I've heard frustration in her voice a lot recently, tension, even a little anger but now she is scared. That's both of them.

"A lot of the boys... are talking about heading down to the

docks. There's still good work to be had in the yards on the Clyde."

"The shipyards?"

"Aye."

"What do you know about building ships?"

"I've spent ma whole adult life at sea—"

"In a boat, not building one."

She's angry now. He's not though. What is that expression? I've not seen it on my dad's face before. He looks like the boys at school did when the fourth goal went in at the weekend; accepting their fate that it wasn't going to be their day. Resignation, that's it. Dad is looking away from me now, away from Mum too, and out into the darkness. During the day you can see all the way across Loch a' Ghlinne to Rùm and the Isle of Canna beyond that, but now, all that can be seen is darkness, with the rain striking the window in earnest. It seems like Mother Nature is keen to reflect my parents' mood.

"I dinnae know what else to do. I really don't."

"And what about us? Do you expect to drag us down to Glasgow as well?"

"It'll be grand."

"For you maybe. But what about—"

"I said… it'll be grand. The bairn will adjust."

"She's never known anything but the island. It's a big ask at this age…"

"Aye… well, sometimes I wonder if we'd all be better off if I wasnae here at all!"

"Don't say that…"

I've heard enough now. I don't want to leave my friends, my home. I don't even want to leave my school, and I hate school. There's the sound of movement from the room. They must have heard me, so I hurry back upstairs, avoiding the squeaky floorboards with the skill and poise of a professionally trained Scottish dancer and I'm back into my bed, under the covers, before I hear a single footstep on the first squeaky tread at the base of the stairs.

My door creaks open a few moments later and I lie facing the wall, away from the door, keeping my breathing slow and measured. It's my mum. I know it's her. She has a reassuring presence that I can feel by sense alone. She is always the one to check in on me. The door closes and I am alone again. For the first time in as far back as I can remember, I feel something I haven't in a long time.

Now I'm scared too.

CHAPTER ONE

THE AREA in front of the community hall was already filling up as he parked the car. When his sister, Roslyn, had first suggested he might like to join them at the Staffin Burns Night celebrations, he'd been hesitant. However, as the day drew nearer, Duncan found himself rather looking forward to a night of tradition and nostalgia celebrating the life of the national bard.

A lone figure, kitted out in full ceremonial Highland dress, stood off to the left of the main entrance playing a traditional piece of music to greet the arrivals. Duncan knew from memory that the piper was wearing the traditional garb of the 77th Regiment of Foot, more commonly known as the Montgomerie Highlanders, a regiment raised in the mid to late 1700s from several Scottish Highland clans, not least the MacDonalds, the Lords of the Isles.

Staffin's Burns Night dinner was so well regarded in the area that it was attended by invitation only, and you needed to know someone in order to receive an invite. Roslyn was such a person, and a large part of what made the event such a success every year.

Duncan nodded to the piper as he passed, entering the building and finding the hall packed with people, chatting and catching up with one another before the event really got underway. A gregarious old boy was holding aloft a bottle of scotch and offering anyone who came within three feet of him a wee dram. Four lines of tables were arranged across the hall, filling it to capacity, and a rough count must place the attendees numbering almost several hundred. As usual, one table was placed on a stage at the far end of the hall, adjacent to the others, and always earmarked for local dignitaries and committee members.

He was running slightly later than planned and so the majority of people were already present, many of whom were already taking their seats. Duncan found himself scanning the guests for Becky Mcinnes and her family, her son Callum, in particular. For several months now, Duncan had been wrestling with what he should do about the news she'd given him and indeed whether he should act on it at all.

Having left Skye as a teenager, he'd returned years later only to discover that Callum Mcinnes was in fact his son, a secret kept from him until very recently. His eyes searched for the fifteen-year-old... or might he be sixteen now? The thought came to mind that he didn't even know his own son's birthday. As for his son, Callum didn't know who his biological father was. As far as the lad knew, Davey Mcinnes, the abusive man who'd raised him, was his father.

Having steered clear of Becky and her family over the festive season, allowing everyone the opportunity to breathe, including himself, he was finding his mind ruminating on numerous curiosities. What was Callum like, what was he interested in and whether, despite his lack of a presence in the boy's life, the two of them had any shared characteristics? He certainly hoped, if they did, that the boy was more focussed than himself, and therefore less likely to drift through life like he had done so.

"Duncan!"

He turned to see Ros striding towards him. He almost didn't recognise her, all dressed up as she was. Roslyn was a crofter's wife and more commonly found outdoors grafting. She flung her arms around him. "You came!"

Holding her at arm's length, he grinned. "Of course, I came. Did you think I was going to miss this?" He looked her up and down. "You scrub up well, Mrs Macdougall."

She waved away his compliment, but she blushed beneath her make-up and that made him smile. She was as uncomfortable with praise as he was. Not that he received a great deal of that. His gaze drifted past her and back across the assembled guests, more of whom had already taken their seats. He still couldn't see Becky, for it wasn't only Callum he was looking forward to seeing.

"She's no' here, Duncan."

"Who?" he asked innocently, arching an eyebrow at his sister who smiled and shook her head.

"Who indeed? Honestly, you'd think the two of you were twelve years old again."

"I dinnae know what you're on about," Duncan said, protesting half-heartedly along with a smile of his own.

"Come on, we'd better take our seats," Ros said, gesturing towards the piper who was taking up his place inside now at the back of the hall. "We'll be getting underway any minute, otherwise the food will be dry."

"Where are we sitting?" Duncan asked.

"Where do you think, you daft sod?"

Duncan had no idea, so he allowed her to take the lead and he fell into step behind her as they weaved their way through the throng. The large hall was so full that passing between the line of tables was almost impossible once people had taken their seats, leaning back to speak to those behind and beside them. The general noise level was high.

Surprised to find Roslyn mounting the steps up onto the stage, he hesitated. She must have sensed he wasn't following and turned, encouraging him to join her. Reluctantly, he mounted the steps and came alongside her as he scanned the room before them.

"I shouldn't be up here."

"Nonsense. You're my family, and if Ronnie can have his kin at the table, then so can I."

Duncan could see Ros's husband Ronnie sitting at the table deep in conversation with a brunette. Duncan hadn't seen her in a while, but as he approached, she broke off her conversation with her brother and got up before bounding across the stage to give him a warm embrace and a big smile.

"Duncan!"

He reciprocated the hug, smiling down at her. "Mo Macdougall, how are you keeping?"

"All the better for seeing you, Duncan. And it's Bates now."

"Ah… married… of course. I should have known you'd not be single for long."

"Someone who didnae know you might take that as a slight on my morality, Duncan McAdam! Is it good to be back?"

He knew Roslyn's sister-in-law well enough that she'd see through a lie, so he chose to be truthful. "It's nice, yes… but there have been a few surprises along the way."

"Life would be dull without them, Dunc! I'll look forward to hearing all about it."

"Mark my words, you don't want to get drawn into it."

Over her shoulder, he saw Ronnie staring at him with that

deadpan expression he always had whenever the two of them made eye contact. Duncan must have wronged the man in a previous life because since his return, Ronnie had been cold with him, and he still didn't understand why.

"I see you and Ronnie are getting along famously," Mo said, seeing their exchange.

"Better than ever," Duncan said. "You can't have a word with him, could you?"

"And say what exactly?"

"I don't know… ask him not to be such an arse?"

"That'll be going against his core sense of being though, wouldn't it?" she countered. "A tree is still a tree, even if you trim its leaves."

"Aye, but you can chop a tree down though, eh?"

Mo playfully took a swing at his face, and he swayed away from her to avoid it, grinning.

"You two!" Ros said, hurrying up to them and pointing at a man standing by a lectern on the far side of the stage. Duncan recognised him as Donald MacArthur, the chairman of the local committee and master of ceremonies this evening. Duncan and Mo hurried to the table and took their seats, pretty much the last in the hall to do so, as MacArthur began reading the Selkirk Grace, sticking to the *Covenanters' Grace* in *Lallans*, the lowland Scot's dialect, rather than the Standard English version later given at a dinner to the Earl of Selkirk by Robert Burns himself.

> *"Some hae meat and canna eat,*
> *And some wad eat that want it;*
> *But we hae meat, and we can eat,*
> *Sae let the Lord be thankit."*

. . .

AT THE CONCLUSION of the grace, the piper started up with a traditional rendition of Robert Burns's song, *A Man's a Man, For A That,* and a small party stepped out of the kitchen area to the rear bearing a silver platter with a massive haggis placed upon it. They formed a processional line and slowly made their way to the front of the hall, at all times accompanied by the tune from the lone piper.

The guests were engrossed in the spectacle, draped as it was in tradition and Duncan felt a flutter of pride in his chest as he watched the approaching group. The man bearing the platter set it down in the middle of the table, barely three feet from Duncan. Donald MacArthur came around to the far side of the table, facing the guests and theatrically hefted a large dirk into the air, preparing to deliver the *Address to the Haggis.*

The guests looked on in anticipation as Donald began.

"Fair fa' your honest, sonsie face, Great chieftain o' the pudding-race! Aboon them—"

Duncan's mobile sprang into life and all eyes turned towards him as he scrambled through his pockets trying to find the device and to silence it as quickly as possible. It took a few attempts before he managed to do so. Feeling his face reddening, he caught Ros glaring at him. He shrugged apologetically. Donald MacArthur continued with the address, albeit slightly thrown by the untimely interruption. Behind him, Mo was looking over at Duncan trying very hard not to laugh at his discomfort. Her brother didn't find it amusing, though. Ronnie shot daggers at him.

The mobile vibrated in his hand and Duncan got up from the table as carefully as he could, trying hard not to draw attention away from the speaker. He failed miserably, the legs of his chair scraping on the wooden stage and shrieking.

Several people in the audience tutted at him and others sighed. Realising that all hope of a dignified exit was lost, Duncan hurried to the edge of the stage, descended and quickened his pace to the nearest exit only to find it locked. He had to walk the length of the hall to the entrance, feeling disapproving eyes upon him.

Once outside, he felt the stiff breeze coming in off the water and shivered. Drawing his coat about him, he clicked on the tab to return the missed call.

"Sir, it's Angus—"

"Yes, I got that from your name coming up on the screen, young man."

"Sorry to bother you, sir," Angus said. "I hope I didn't disturb you."

Duncan glanced back into the hall just as cheering and applause erupted. MacArthur must have finished the address, and Duncan pictured him driving the blade of the ceremonial dirk into the haggis.

"No, you're all right, Angus. I... wasn't up to much anyway. What's going on?"

Angus appeared to be leaving a room, his voice echoing more as he switched locations wherever he was. He also lowered his voice.

"I've got a missing child, sir. I'm at the parents' house just now and it's all getting a bit frantic, you know."

Duncan checked his watch. It wasn't particularly late in the day.

"How old is the... boy or girl?"

"Fifteen, sir. His parents say he left the house at the usual time to catch the bus into town, but he didn't come home when he should have."

"Wouldn't be the first teenager to slope off with his pals for a bit after school. Has he got a girlfriend?"

"No, no, the parents have thought of that. They've been ringing round all his pals. No one has seen him all day. They called a friend of theirs who works at the high school and the lad never turned up for morning registration. None of his pals have seen him either."

Duncan took a deep breath. None of them is admitting to seeing him, which isn't necessarily the same thing.

"Okay, where are you?"

"Bracadale," Angus said. "Well, between there and Coillore anyway."

The township of Bracadale was on the west coast of the island alongside Loch Beag, an inlet of the greater Loch Harport. It would be a solid hour before he could get there.

"Text me the address and I'll make my way over."

"Okay, great. Sorry to bother you with it, sir. It's just—"

"It's no bother, Angus. I'll be about an hour. Keep talking to the parents; get us a list of his friends, where he likes to hang out, what he's been up to recently… that type of thing."

"Okay, will do."

"With a bit of luck, the lad will beat me home."

"Aye, let's hope so, eh?"

Duncan hung up and put his mobile away. The doors to the hall opened and Roslyn walked out with a face like thunder.

"You cannae just turn up and be respectful like normal people, can you?"

He blew out his cheeks. "That's a bit harsh, sis. If work calls, what am I supposed to do?"

"Maybe silence your damn phone for starters."

"Aye, I should have done that," he said, embarrassed. "I'm sorry. Timing, eh?"

"You couldn't have done it any better," she said, her stance softening. "Do you have to go?"

"Aye, sorry. We've got a missing kid."

"Oh no!"

"Ah… it's probably nothing. He's likely gone to a friend's or something and his parents are spooked. I'm sure it'll be fine."

She nodded solemnly, and he turned to leave, half expecting her to return inside but she lingered with an anxious expression.

"Something up?" he asked.

"No… well… aye…"

Confused, Duncan raised a solitary eyebrow in query. "Which is it?" he asked with a smile.

"It's just… look, I know it's none of my business, but you and Becky—"

"Aye, you're right. It's none of your business," he said firmly.

"I know! It's just… you and her have fallen out."

"We have?"

She fixed him with a stern look, and he relented. "We have, aye. It'll get sorted."

"I couldn't help but notice things were awkward between you and Davey—"

"Yeah, well, Davey and I—"

Is it about wee Callum?"

Duncan was surprised and failed to mask it. "And… er… what do you know about Callum?"

She was nervous now. "Aw… nothing. Forget I mentioned it."

"No, go on. What do you mean?"

She shrugged, self-assured now. "I know they have trouble at home… Becky and Davey. Callum just gets caught in the middle sometimes, that's all." The door to the hall opened and a head poked out, glancing at both of them in turn, flushing red at interrupting them.

"They're waiting on you, Roslyn."

"I'll be right there," Ros said, and the woman nodded before retreating back inside. Ros turned to Duncan, taking his hand in hers. "You're a forgiving man, Duncan."

"Thanks."

"And you've grown as a person, I can see that. And you're right, you are an arsehole."

"Again… thanks," Duncan said, and they both smiled. "I really need to go."

"Text me later?" Ros said. "Let me know you're safe?"

"I will."

She leaned in and kissed his cheek before giving his hand a gentle squeeze then letting go and heading back inside, calling to him over her shoulder as he crossed to where he'd left his car. "Don't be expecting an invite to next year's Burns Night, though!"

Duncan laughed but said nothing.

"Aye, you laugh but when they don't let me back either, you'll be for it, Duncan, I tell you now. I'll haunt you."

"A year is a long time on this island, Ros," Duncan said, glancing back with a wink. "Dinnae worry."

"And folk have long memories too."

"Aye, right enough."

CHAPTER TWO

DUNCAN DROVE BACK DOWN to Portree and then turned
towards the west and cut across the island through Glengrasco
before arriving on the shore of Loch Beag on the west coast of
the island. Pausing at the junction with the A863, Duncan's
headlights illuminated a number of small sailing boats laying
at anchor in the loch, gently bobbing on the swell. Although
cold, the breeze was gentle here tonight and the thick cloud
cover offered respite from the severe overnight frosts they
were used to at this time of the year.

He turned left onto the main coast road that wrapped
around the loch, crossing the causeway before taking the next
left and leaving the main road which continued on around the
headland down the Minginish peninsula, skirting Loch
Harport. Duncan saw Angus's car parked in front of a single-
storey, lime-rendered property situated in an elevated position
overlooking Loch Beag.

Getting out of his car, he drew his coat about him as he
walked to the front door and rang the bell. Grateful for the
lack of a strong wind, he still felt the chill in the January night

air. Snow was on its way, he knew it without the need of hearing a forecast. It was Angus who opened the door and he seemed relieved to find Duncan standing before him.

"Oh… it's you…" Angus said before quickly adding, "Sir."

"Who were you expecting?"

"Ah… hoping it would be wee Finn," he said, apologetically. He shrugged. "You know… forgot his key or something."

"No word then, I take it?" Duncan asked. Angus shook his head and stepped aside to give Duncan room to enter. The hallway was narrow, and Angus had barely managed to close the door behind him before a woman appeared from the front sitting room.

She was restless, wringing her hands before her, ashen faced.

"This is Mrs MacGregor," Angus said, introducing them. "She's Finn's mother."

Duncan glanced at Angus, who was stating the obvious but rather than point it out he simply smiled at the woman.

"Have you any news?" she asked, nervously.

"No… I haven't," Duncan said, wanting to quell any expectation formed from his arrival. "I'm DI McAdam… Duncan… and I'm here to help find your lad."

Another figure appeared behind her, a man, and Duncan guessed this was Finn's father.

"Mr MacGregor?" Duncan asked.

"Aye, Anthony MacGregor," he said, casting a stern eye over Duncan.

"I'm pleased to meet you, but not under these circumstances."

"Aye… come through," Anthony said, steering his wife back into the sitting room. Duncan and Angus followed. "You sit yourself down there, love," Anthony said, helping her sit down on the sofa. Without the wind blowing a gale outside and with no television on, the house was deathly quiet with only a ticking clock mounted on the far wall to punctuate the silence.

"So... can you tell me the last time you saw your son?" Duncan asked. He could easily take Angus aside and get the information without having them repeat it but the parents were clearly on edge and anything that occupied their minds might help ease their worries.

"You saw him this morning, didn't you, Marsali?" Anthony asked, looking at his wife. She nodded.

"Yes... Finn left for school... at the usual time."

"When was that?" Duncan asked.

"A little after seven. He has to get down for the school bus and it's a wee while to Portree."

"In his uniform... with his backpack?"

"Yes," she said, nodding firmly. "I gave him a few pounds to buy his lunch because I hadn't had time to make his sandwiches this morning—"

"Aye, staying too long in your bed..." Anthony said. Marsali glared at him but he didn't seem to notice.

"I–I've not been sleeping well recently... and it's all become such a rush first thing in the morning."

Anthony scoffed but didn't comment.

"That's okay, Mrs MacGregor. We can all relate, I'm sure."

Angus nodded furiously. Duncan saw Anthony's microexpression flash across his face, suggesting he disagreed but didn't voice it.

"We've been onto all his pals from school and none of them has seen him," Anthony said.

"I figured he'd be with one of them and just had an afterschool club or something."

"He's not interested in any after school clubs... he doesn't like the sports and he's—"

"Aye... well, whatever. He's not here and that's the main thing, isn't it!" she snapped back, and Anthony looked away. They were both tense, which was suggestive that Finn wasn't one to stay out unannounced.

"And am I right in thinking that you've been in touch with the school directly?" Duncan asked.

"Aye," Anthony said. "We spoke with Rona... and she said Finn never turned up to the school this morning."

"And who is Rona?"

"His head of year," Marsali said, nodding towards Duncan. "She and I go way back. We were at school together."

"Did any of his friends see him? On the bus perhaps?" Duncan asked. Both parents shook their heads. Duncan turned to Angus. "Let's find out who was the scheduled driver this morning, just so we can confirm whether he was on it or not."

"Why would his pals lie?" Anthony asked, frowning.

Duncan sucked air through his teeth. "Kids... they don't always tell the truth... especially if their pal has asked them not to."

"Why would Finn do that?" Marsali asked.

"We don't know that he has," Duncan replied. "We'll just cover all the bases, just in case."

"It'll be wee Raymond," Anthony said. Duncan looked at him quizzically. "Who was driving the bus. It's always wee Raymond."

"Is he young?" Angus asked.

Anthony shook his head. "Nah... he's just quite short, you know? It's just a little earner for him as he winds down to retirement. The weans call him Raymondo... because he unbuttons his shirt and wears a little gold chain and a medallion, like it's 1986 and he's in Miami or something. But he'll have been driving."

"And he knows your son?"

"Oh aye… no doubt," Anthony said.

"Okay, I asked DC Ross here to collate some information regarding Finn's pals and interests—"

"Aye, that didnae take long," Anthony said. "He's not into much… and only has a couple of pals to speak of."

"Girlfriend?" Duncan asked.

"Nah… not that one would be interested."

Marsali glared at her husband. Anthony shrugged.

"Well, you can give me the stink eye if you want, lass, but it's true. He's no' interested in the girls."

"You said he has a couple of friends," Duncan said. "Who are they?"

Marsali nodded. "He's friendly with Cammy and Callum."

"Aye, the Mcinnes boy in particular," Anthony said. "Thick as thieves, those two."

"Right," Duncan said, feeling a pang of something in his chest at the mention of Callum's name. "Cammy?"

"Cameron McGinn," Marsali said.

"Dougal's boy," Anthony added.

"From Drynoch?" Duncan asked.

"Aye, you know them?"

Duncan shook his head. "No, not really but I know the name. Dougal is a building contractor, isn't he?"

"Aye… and if you hire him expect your hoose to fall doon in the coming months. The island cowboy. If it weren't for the incomers, he'd be bankrupt within a month, I swear to God."

Marsali shook her head. Duncan half-smiled.

"Thanks for the tip." Duncan quickly glanced around the room, spying a photograph hanging on the wall, framed, front and centre above the mantelpiece. It was a family shot, a young boy with Marsali's arms draped around his shoulders, her hands interlocked at his chest. Anthony was also in the photo, standing awkwardly to one side with a rather odd expression on his face. Perhaps he wasn't one who enjoyed being in front of the camera. Many didn't.

"That was three years ago," Marsali said, following Duncan's eyeline. "Sgarasta Mhòr Beach."

"Harris?" Duncan asked. Marsali nodded. The beach was unspoiled, and the water looked a clear turquoise. Beyond them, in the background, the Atlantic Ocean stretched away under an almost clear sky with a few sparse white clouds scattered around to break up the blue; the next landmass across the water would be Greenland. "A lovely spot for sure."

Marsali smiled politely, but it was as if recalling the family break only brought her pain. Duncan shifted tack.

"I would like to speak about your son more, but before I do, may I see his bedroom?"

Anthony MacGregor nodded solemnly, and Marsali led the way, taking Duncan back into the hall and towards the rear of the property. Finn's bedroom was the last door on the right and his mother opened it, hesitating to enter. Duncan touched her elbow and she looked up at him – she was a diminutive figure, a few inches over five foot tall – and he smiled reassuringly.

"I can take it from here, if it's all a bit much for you?"

She seemed flustered, perhaps feeling guilty about not wanting to enter her son's room, Duncan couldn't tell, but his smile was enough to calm her. She nodded, stepping aside to make room for him to pass.

The door swung to behind him and he sensed Marsali's reluctance to rejoin Angus and her husband in the sitting room. Duncan turned his focus to the teenager's room. He was pleasantly surprised. Recalling his own room when he'd been a similar age, the contrast couldn't be starker. He expected piles of unwashed or even clean laundry, strewn about the room, the carpet only visible in patches beneath clutter and teenage debris.

The reality was very different. Everything was ordered, clothes folded neatly, a desk beneath the window with a writing pad set down alongside a laptop with a separate keyboard and a large monitor. Beside the monitor was another family photograph of the three of them. This one looked more recent than the one on display in the sitting room, Finn looking older, leaner, with finely chiselled features. Although older, Finn was still not much taller than he had been in the photograph taken three years previously, his father towering above his wife and child. At only fifteen, it was surprising to see, although Finn possibly drew more heavily from his mother's gene pool than from his father's.

The young man seemed happy enough in the photo, as much as you could tell from a still image at any rate. Anyone could fake it, but genuine smiles usually shone through, and his seemed like one of those to Duncan.

The presentation of the room in general reminded Duncan of the boarding house at high school when they had an open day for parents and prospective pupils to look around the facilities. A far cry from what was generally the norm would be seen on that day. This bedroom didn't seem particularly lived in, and besides the posters on the walls, he didn't appear as if Finn MacGregor had put his stamp on it.

The bed was made, the duvet folded up to the pillow. It wasn't quite military regimen, but not a bad effort for a young lad. Was it his choice or did one, or both, of his parents insist on such tidiness? The walls were lined with posters as one might expect, but they weren't depicting footballers or bands. Finn MacGregor had an interest in wildlife and scenery, by the looks of it. Two of the posters must have come from the *National Geographic*. They had creases, as well as staple holes, where they'd been folded to fit into the now defunct publication. One was an image of bottlenose dolphins, often visible in the waters around Skye, along with common dolphins, harbour porpoises and the odd basking shark.

A framed landscape print hung above Finn's single bed. This was easily recognisable as one of Skye's iconic snow-capped landscapes; the Cuillin Hills taken from Elgol, across Loch Scavaig. It always felt eerie to Duncan, picking through another person's belongings, turning over their private space. In the mind of a teenager, their bedroom was often the only safe space they had that they could call their own.

Moving to the desk, Duncan opened the top drawer and inspected the contents, which were also arranged tidily.

"Seriously… who is this kid?" he said quietly to himself. Moving onto the next drawer, he found a mix of books and magazines, again focussed on nature, but nothing of any notable interest. The third and final drawer had several boxes in it, one was a selection box of men's toiletries and the other a watch box, Seiko branded. Duncan made to close it, but something caught, preventing him from doing so. Dropping to his haunches, he peered into the drawer to see what he'd disturbed that might be blocking the runners and preventing the drawer from closing fully.

Realising that the problem was not in the drawer itself, Duncan used the torchlight function on his mobile to peer into the space behind the drawer where he could see something was wedged against the runner. It took a minute for him to contort himself in such a position to put his hands to the back and grasp a smooth, leather-lined box and tease it out without dropping it. He examined it. It was a presentation box, high-quality lambskin leather or similar, soft to the touch with neat stitching along the lines.

"Well, well, well..." Duncan said, opening it to reveal a velvet-lined interior. The box should have contained a sgian-dubh, a small knife traditionally used for all manner of things; anything from cutting rope, material, preparation of food and even for defence. Nowadays, it was much more of a ceremonial blade worn as part of traditional Highland dress along with a kilt, and commonly tucked into the top of the sock on either the left or right leg depending on the wearer's preference. Where the blade would have rested though, Duncan found only a space for it beneath a purple, transparent folder not much larger than a child's pencil case with a single button clasp on the folding flap. He set the box down on the cream carpet and took a couple of photographs with his mobile. The bedroom door opened, accompanied by a gentle knock, and DC Angus Ross entered.

"Have you found anything interesting, sir?"

"I'd say so, young Angus," Duncan said, pointing to the folder. "What do you think?"

Angus came over and looked at the folder. "Whoa... how much is there?"

Duncan cast an eye over the mixture of ten and twenty-pound notes inside the folder. "Two... maybe three hundred pounds. I've no' counted it yet though."

"Where does a teenager get that kind of money from around here?" Angus asked.

Duncan shook his head. "No clue. He doesn't want it known though, judging on where he kept it stashed away."

"Looks clean and crisp."

"Aye," Duncan said, nodding, "but it's all this new plastic polymer stuff now, so it always looks new."

"Right enough. When your mum puts it through the washing machine, it's no' ruined like it used to be either."

"Aye, is that right?" Duncan asked, arching an eyebrow as Angus flushed. "I'd keep that snippet of information away from the ops room, if I were you, young man... or you'll never hear the end of it."

CHAPTER THREE

TAKING the box and the folder containing the cash with them, Duncan and Angus went back to the sitting room where they found Anthony MacGregor sitting alone in an armchair, staring out of the window across Loch Beag, the twinkling of lights visible from the houses on the far shoreline all that punctuated the darkness. He looked up at them as they entered, his expression clouded and became as dark as the exterior.

"Mr MacGregor," Duncan said, holding the folder aloft, "do you happen to know how your son came by this?"

Anthony sat forward, his forehead creasing as he eyed the money. Shaking his head, he slowly stood up and came closer. Marsali appeared from the kitchen, observing them.

"No… where on earth did he get that from?" Anthony asked.

"Does Finn have a part-time job?" Duncan asked. "Maybe after school or on the weekends?"

"No, he doesnae have time for anything… by the time he gets back from school there's not much left in the tank, if you know what I mean?"

"Tired?" Duncan asked.

"Aye... and he's lazy with it too," Anthony said, which triggered Marsali to enter both the room and the conversation.

"He's not lazy! He puts in a lot of effort—"

"He's a lazy wee shite, woman," Anthony said in a measured tone. "He doesnae rise from his pit on the weekends until gone nine o'clock in the morning and he's cuttin' around the house for much of the day."

"He gets tired... you know that," Marsali said, looking between Duncan and Angus.

"Tired... my arse," Anthony said. "This generation don't know they've lived. Back in the day, at his age, they'd be in the army... or out on the trawlers—"

"Like your father... not like you," Marsali said. Duncan couldn't help but think this was a regular discussion the two of them would have, and he guessed neither of them ever came out on top with a definitive win.

"How about you, Mrs MacGregor. Do you have any idea where Finn would have got this kind of money?"

She frowned, thinking hard. "Maybe he saved up his pocket money—"

"Pocket money!" Anthony said, snorting a laugh and pointing at the cash. "That there is a about ten years' worth of pocket money."

"Maybe he's holding onto it for someone... one of his friends perhaps?" Marsali countered.

"Aye... one of those no-good friends of his," Anthony said. "Where did you find it anyway?" he asked, turning to Duncan.

"It was in one of his drawers," Duncan said, keen not to feed into an established narrative. "What about this?" Duncan asked, holding up the box for the sgian-dubh.

Anthony's frown deepened. Marsali came over and studied it.

"I've never seen it before," she said, curious. "Finn has been saying for a while that he wanted a particular sgian-dubh, but… I didn't think he had the money."

"This looks like an expensive one," Duncan said.

Anthony snorted, shaking his head. "One of his pals… up to no good, I'm telling you."

"You mentioned his friends," Duncan said. "You've spoken to the parents, right?"

"Aye, most of them," Marsali said.

"Most?"

"Oh, well, whichever one answered the phone, you know? I meant I hadn't spoken to every parent."

"He's a bright man, Marsali," Anthony said. "You don't need to be so particular."

"Maybe I should have been more particular when I chose who to marry," she snapped back. Anthony sneered at the retort but stayed silent.

"You said that Finn is closest to the two boys, Callum Mcinnes and Cammy McGinn, right?"

"Aye," Anthony said before Marsali could answer. "Cameron is an interesting lad… and when I say interesting, I mean a couple of sandwiches short of a picnic, you know? He's not very clever, and I dare say he bores easily."

"Callum is a much better influence," Marsali said. "I think that's what my husband is trying to say."

"I know exactly what I was saying. Cammy is a head case." He nodded towards Duncan and Angus. "No doubt you'll be coming across him very soon in a professional capacity. As for the Mcinnes boy… Marsali is right in saying he's a better influence… but since all that business with the stolen car, and turning it over at the side of the road… I think it'd be best for everyone if Finn found a new set of friends. The lad's been drifting."

"You've been saying that for years," Marsali said. "No one is ever good enough for you…"

"What's that supposed to mean?"

"It means you're always finding fault with people."

"*He stole his mother's car* and stacked it at the side of the road! He nearly killed his wee sister, too. What do you want me to do, adopt him?"

Marsali shook her head and Duncan found something rising within him, a natural instinct to defend his son perhaps, but he quelled it. No one knew the reasons behind Callum's decision to steal the car that night; to take him and his sister away from the violence of Davey Mcinnes, only for it to end in tragedy. Duncan knew, but Becky, Callum's mother, couldn't face airing the family secrets in public. It was a decision that Duncan wholeheartedly disagreed with but could understand why she couldn't do it. He only hoped that it wasn't a choice she'd regret at a later time.

"Did you speak to Callum's parents?" Duncan asked.

"I did, aye," Marsali said. "I spoke to his mum, Becky. She's so lovely. She spoke to Callum, and he said he'd not seen Finn all day."

"Did he have any idea where he might have gone to?"

She shook her head. "Becky said he had no idea."

Anthony scoffed in the background. "More lies."

"Tony!" Marsali said.

"Well… he's a liar. Same as Cammy. You cannae trust either of them." Anthony wagged a finger at Duncan. "Speak to them yourselves. They'll know. If anyone does, it'll be them."

Duncan nodded. "We will, don't worry. Tell me, how has Finn been recently, in himself, at school, that type of thing?"

This time, it was Marsali who spoke first. "He's been a little preoccupied recently, but he's a good boy and all his teachers like him. He's very clever. They think he could make it to St. Andrews once he's finished his schooling—"

"Aye... he'll no' fit in to a posh place like that," Anthony said. "His place is here on the island—"

"There's more to this world than the Isle of Skye!" Marsali said.

"Aye... and most of it is plain awful. He doesnae need to go to somewhere like that... warping his views of the world!"

"He can make something of himself," Marsali said, exasperation in her tone.

"He can be plenty good enough by staying here on the island."

Duncan sought to steer the conversation back to the present. "But he's doing well at school? There are no problems, behavioural or with any of his classmates?"

"Only that he's falling asleep in class—"

"He's not *falling asleep* in class," Marsali said. "He just gets tired."

"Staying up all night on his mobile phone... chatting with his pals," Anthony said. "He'll not survive at St. Andrews if he cannae get out of his bed in the morning."

"You're not aware of any bullying... or anything like that?" Duncan asked. Marsali shook her head.

"His grades have slipped a bit recently, that is true," she said, tentatively glancing at her husband, who chose not to add any more detail. "We don't know why... but as I said, he is a little preoccupied... distracted, might be a better description."

"Distracted by what?" Duncan asked.

"I don't know really," she said. "He's been troubled by the state of the world, sure enough."

"The state of the world?" Duncan repeated.

"Yes. Finn is passionate about the environment... about ecology and nature."

"Aye, I saw the posters in his bedroom," Duncan said. "It makes a change to being into hip hop and football like most bairns his age."

"True," Anthony said, "but he does get himself worked up about things he cannae control... like what gets dumped into the sea... climate change and all of that. I mean, it's not like we can do anything about it from Bracadale, is it?"

Angus frowned. "We all have to start somewhere though."

Anthony looked at him, much as Duncan assumed he would look at his son whenever he said something similar, with disdain, if not utter contempt.

"Aye... well some of us cannae afford such moral attitudes, young man. The world was here for billions of years before we got here... and it will be here billions of years after we've left it."

"True enough..." Angus said, "although it might be uninhabitable by then... but..."

Duncan arched an eyebrow and Angus took the hint and dropped it.

"So, that's Finn's passion is it; the environment?"

"Yes, very much so," Marsali said. "It's all he talks about. His favourite subject is science at school, and he relates it to the island and the natural world as a whole."

"Sounds like he's a great kid," Duncan said.

Marsali beamed at him. "He is, yes."

"Head in the clouds," Anthony said.

"Forgive me for being blunt, Mr MacGregor," Duncan said, masking his irritation, "but you don't seem as concerned as your wife about your son's whereabouts. Why is that?"

Anthony fixed his eye on Duncan, stone faced. "Because

I'm not concerned. He'll be up to something, and I have nae clue what it is, but he'll be back as soon as he's good and ready. If that's not today, then a cold night out some place will be enough to bring him home in the morning. I dinnae doubt it."

Duncan nodded and turned to Marsali. "You disagree though?"

"I do. This isn't like him. He's been out of sorts recently… not sleeping well… tired all the time. He's just not been himself." She looked on the verge of tears and finally, her husband seemed to notice how worried and upset she was, coming to stand alongside her and putting a supportive arm around her shoulder, pulling her into him.

"He'll be all right, love. I'm sure of it. Like you said, he's a bright boy. He'll be home soon enough."

In most cases, Anthony would be correct. Teenagers who skip a day of school would be hanging out with friends or a girlfriend, perhaps older children who'd already left school, and oftentimes they'd be doing something they know their parents would disapprove of. This would keep them away, firstly because of what they were doing and, secondly, fearful of what they would face when they came home. However, there were other cases, granted, a minority of cases, where something altogether more sinister had occurred.

Looking at the worried face of Marsali MacGregor, Duncan hoped this was not one of the latter cases.

"Your son has a computer," Duncan said. "Do you happen to have access to it?"

"Aye, of course we do," Anthony said, removing his arm from around Marsali. She looked disappointed by the action, preferring the physical comfort and support. "We wouldn't let him have a secret online life, you know?"

Marsali nodded vigorously. "You hear such stories… about

online grooming and the like, don't you? It's not safe these days."

Duncan could appreciate their concern; it was a known problem with children being online so much, but the risks were often overblown, particularly in such a remote part of the country as here on Skye.

"I understand," he said.

"We only let him have the thing in his bedroom because of those daft games he's always playing with his pals," Anthony said. "They spend hours in a – what do they call it? – a *virtual world* playing *Mind Craft*."

"Minecraft," Marsali said, correcting him.

"Aye, that's what I said, Minecraft."

Marsali rolled her eyes, but her husband didn't notice.

"It's such a waste of a life," Anthony continued. "There's a whole world outside to explore, and it's real!"

"Not that you'll let him explore it," Marsali said. "Unless you mean keeping to the boundaries of the island…"

"There's nothing on the mainland that will be better for him that he cannae find on this island." Anthony was matter of fact. Again, his wife showed disdain for his opinion but didn't comment further.

"Does he spend a lot of time outside?" Duncan asked. "Exploring the island?"

"Oh yes," Marsali said. "He's out and about a lot of the time… when he's got the energy. As I said, it's his passion, nature and the environment. I swear he'd leave school completely if he could spend the time outdoors."

Anthony looked on the verge of going off on yet another rant, but he caught Marsali's eye and must have thought better of it.

"Could he be doing that just now?" Duncan asked.

The parents exchanged a glance, but neither seemed sure either way.

"Don't worry, we'll put the word out," Duncan said, smiling.

"You'll start searching for him?" Marsali asked, fear edging into her tone. "It's just that you hear about the police waiting for twenty-four hours before they can begin an investigation—"

"Don't believe everything you hear," Duncan said. "Out here, we look after our own... and we'll no' be leaving a young lad out there by himself if we can help it. We just need to narrow down where we start looking."

Both of them seemed relieved, even Anthony, who up until now didn't seem too worried but it was possible he was using bravado and optimism to mask his feelings from them, particularly from his wife. Duncan glanced at Angus.

"Finn's mobile phone," Duncan said, "could you give us the number?"

"I've been phoning and phoning," Marsali said, "and he doesn't pick up."

"He could be out of range of a tower," Duncan said. "With the number we can try and track him through the GPS signal the phone gives out. Even if you can't make calls, sometimes the signal will still get through. At the very least we will be able see where he's been heading throughout the day as his phone connects from one mast to the next."

"What if he's switched the damn thing off?" Anthony asked.

"With modern phones that doesnae matter," Duncan said.

"Aye... big brother is always watching and listening, eh?" Anthony muttered.

"Which might help locate your son," Duncan said. Anthony nodded begrudgingly.

"Would you mind furnishing DC Ross with the password for Finn's laptop and allowing him to have a look around on it?"

Anthony shrugged, looking at Marsali who was happy enough. "I dinnae see why not. What do you expect to find?"

Duncan smiled reassuringly. "Bairns today... it's all social media, streaming and gaming. It could tell us who he's been speaking to—"

Marsali gasped, eyes wide. Duncan held up a hand.

"Most likely, he's just been speaking to his pals, don't worry unduly. Finn will probably say things to them that he wouldn't voice to his parents... and maybe not even say aloud, if you know what I mean?"

Anthony put his arm around his wife again, giving her a gentle squeeze. "It's probably nothing, love. He'll be home... I believe it in my bones."

"That's usually the case," Duncan said, trying to muster as much confidence as he could without offering false hope. He'd been bitten in the arse that way many times before.

"What happens now?" Anthony asked, looking at Duncan.

He checked the time. It was late, and there would be little they could do until the following morning. This was not what the parents would want to hear.

"We'll reach out to the parents again," Duncan said. "I know you've already done so, but when the police call it can sometimes loosen tight lips, if you know what I mean. Especially where weans are concerned. DC Ross will make a start on Finn's laptop, searching his emails and social media posts and we'll look to build a picture as to what he may be up to —"

"Up to?" Anthony asked, almost accusingly.

"If he had plans today that no one was aware of," Duncan said, and Anthony appeared to accept the explanation. "First thing tomorrow, we'll be onto Finn's mobile phone service provider, looking for the GPS data and any call records they are prepared to share with us without a warrant. If we need one, I dare say we'll obtain one quickly enough under the circumstances. Then, once we have narrowed down where he was today, if Finn hasn't reappeared that is, we'll begin a search. I'll also speak to the school myself and see what they have to say about him."

Both of them looked relieved, almost as if they were expecting to be palmed off whereas Duncan was offering them a lot of action, although he knew that there would be little progress overnight. Even if they did have a general idea as to where Finn might be, there was nothing they could do in the darkness of a January Skye night.

"Thank you, DI McAdam," Anthony said, nodding appreciatively.

"Duncan, please," he said.

Anthony nodded again. "Is there anything else we can do?"

"Stay home, keep the phone line clear just in case Finn calls," Duncan said, also taking out one of his contact cards and passing it to Marsali. "If you think of anything, have a question… or just need an ear, call me on that number. I don't care what time it is, okay?" She smiled at him. "We'll do everything we can to find your lad. You have my word on it."

CHAPTER FOUR

A BELL SOUNDED, reverberating against the solid walls and polished floors of the corridor. The general hubbub of a few hundred children carried to them; they were gathered in the playground, just through the nearby double doors. Moments later the doors flew open and the teenagers came bundling through en masse, filling the corridor, laughing and joking as they made their way to their classrooms for registration. None of them paid any attention to Duncan or DS Alistair MacEachran, who was standing beside him.

"You know," Alistair said, frowning, "I swear they get younger and younger in schools these days."

"That's because you're getting older, Alistair," Duncan said, with a wink and a smile.

"Aye... you're turning out to be quite a detective, you know?" Alistair said drily. "You might be able to make a career out of this job after all."

"Thanks, Al. Very good of you to say so."

Alistair cocked his head. "Aye, who says you need a personality as well as the ability, eh?"

The conversation ceased as they were approached by Rona

MacAllister, Finn MacGregor's head of school year. She had excused herself to find someone else to cover for her at the morning assembly that would be taking place after registration. Finn's disappearance had gone through the school like wildfire, as gossip tends to do, and the school administration wanted to nip any rumours in the bud. Duncan knew it wouldn't work; Finn would either have been murdered or kidnapped by aliens before mid-morning break.

"I'm sorry about that, Mr McAdam," Rona said, smiling as she joined them, a sheen of sweat on her forehead. Duncan guessed she had to physically seek someone out rather than use the internal phone system. "It took longer than I thought."

"Nae bother, honestly," Duncan said. "Were you able to find the boys?"

"Yes, they'll register and then they'll both be brought down to my office, and you can speak with them there."

"Great, thank you."

Rona led them along the corridor, much more open now that the majority of children were in their respective classes although there were still a number of stragglers, latecomers or those who purposefully held off making it to class on time.

"Er... Neil..." Rona addressed one young lad who was probably no more than thirteen, toying with the lanyard around her neck as she spoke, "you should be putting your phone away and getting yourself into registration, young man."

The boy glanced at her and quickly secreted his mobile phone into his pocket, looking at her innocently as he passed.

"Sorry, Miss."

"Don't be sorry, be on time," Rona said sternly.

"I will, Miss. Sorry."

The boy, Neil, rounded the turn in the corridor behind them and Duncan saw him already reaching into his pocket for the mobile, shooting a quick glance towards them to see if Miss MacAllister would notice. She didn't. Neil had his little victory. Rona took them to a door halfway along the corridor where her title, but not her name, was stencilled on the opaque glass.

Inside the office were a desk and several filing cabinets and the only natural light came from a rectangular window fitted horizontally into the wall. It was narrow, obscured and with a steel mesh lining cast within the glass. All of this gave the office a dingy outlook. Rona noticed Alistair looking around.

"I know. I drew the short straw," she said. "All my colleagues call this the vitamin D room…"

"Aye," Alistair said quietly, "as if we dinnae have trouble enough seeing sunlight at this time of the year as it is."

Rona smiled. "It comes from being the last one promoted into a head of year position."

"Well, you'll just need to get yourself up the ladder a bit more then," Alistair said. Rona agreed, offering them a seat by gesturing to the two fabric-lined chairs in front of her desk. Both of them sat down. "So… Fionnlagh MacGregor," she said, sitting forward resting her elbows on the desk and clasping her hands together.

"Yes, what can you tell us about him?" Duncan asked.

Rona was thoughtful. "He is a student who has demonstrated a lot of promise, academically."

"That's what his parents told me, his mum in particular."

"She's right. Finn can go anywhere and do anything…" she paused, reflecting. "I mean, within reason. He's not a genius, but in the past he has been studious and attentive to his studies. He hasn't reached his level yet, and I think he'll do well in higher education."

"You said, *in the past*," Duncan said, picking up on the hidden meaning. "How has he been recently?"

"Well, it would be remiss of me to say that there aren't issues at present," Rona said, clearly reticent. "His attendance is down this school year and his grades have slipped."

"What do you put that down to?" Duncan asked. "Is he struggling with the material this year?"

Rona shook her head without hesitation. "No, I would find that hard to believe. Finn is an intelligent child. As I said, he hasn't found his ceiling yet and I think he'll be far beyond the confines of this school when he does. No... I would say it is more to do with attitude than with anything else."

"Attitude?" Duncan repeated, and Rona nodded. "Is he a disruptive child?"

"No, I wouldn't say so. In the past month or two," she said, her forehead creasing in concentration, "perhaps back in November and then more so in the run up to Christmas... he became... distracted."

"His mother said the same thing," Duncan said.

"Yes, well I'm not surprised. It has been very clear to us all at the school."

"Any idea what you might put that down to?" Duncan asked.

Rona considered the question. If she had an answer, then she wasn't sure of it. "We have yet to get to the bottom of it. I said Finn wasn't disruptive in class, not like some of them, but has become quite argumentative. The troubled teen years... some would say, but this has been something different. I've been teaching long enough to know when it's more than just adolescent angst."

"I see. What was he argumentative about? Anything specific?" Duncan asked.

"Not specific, no, but he is a passionate child... and he has formed his core values at an earlier age than some others."

"Weans are always quite full-on when they pick a cause,"

Alistair said. "It's only when they get out into the real world that they realise an ideology doesn't necessarily work in practice."

"You're not wrong, DS MacEachran..." Rona said, although she pronounced his name Mac-eech-ran, which Duncan knew would irritate his detective sergeant no end, and Duncan would swear he saw Alistair's moustache twitch as Rona said his name. "...but engagement with the issues of the day is very high among this generation of children, which is a positive thing. However, with Finn, he does seem to have taken things to a deeper level... some might say obsessive. It is almost as if..."

"Almost as if what?" Duncan asked.

"As if... he's finding other causes in which to channel his... rage... anxiety... his frustration at the world."

"He sounds like a bairn with anger issues," Alistair said.

"Anger is usually a method of venting by someone who feels out of control," Rona said.

"Aye... and not just with the weans," Alistair said.

"Have you spoken to his parents about this?" Duncan asked.

"Not directly," Rona said. "There have been letters home though. And Marsali has replied."

Neither Anthony or Marsali had mentioned any of this to Duncan or Angus, as far as he knew, the night before which he found odd.

"Tell me, what was their reaction?" Duncan asked.

"Calm," Rona said after considering her reply. "Marsali assured me that there were no issues at home and that Finn was probably going through a phase."

"Standard," Alistair said. Duncan glanced at him. "If you dinnae want to discuss something in public you'd rather keep within the family, that's what you say."

Duncan thought that a cynical take, but Rona was inclined to agree.

"In my experience, that's correct, DS MacEachran." Alistair's eyes narrowed at the second mispronunciation of his surname. Duncan feared he might explode once they left the office. "I must admit that I was surprised though. They've always been a tight-knit family, but I never had the thought of anything untoward happening at home. Finn is a lovely lad, but something has changed in him."

"Are you saying that you think something is going on at home?" Duncan asked.

"I see nothing in school that would contribute to a shift in Finn's attitude. He is engaged with his subject matter, he has friends and there is no bullying that we have been made aware of... so there is likely an exterior push beyond the ascent of adolescent hormones. That's not to say that I'm speaking of abuse or neglect, but only to say that whatever has affected him this academic year is beyond the school gates."

"I see," Duncan said. "I appreciate your candour. Can I ask you about his friends, Cameron and Callum in particular?"

"Of course. They are his two closest friends... they are referred to as the three musketeers in the staff room."

Duncan smiled. "What are those boys like? Are they steady influences on Finn... similarly passionate..."

"Not as passionate about the issues as Finn, no. That's not to say they don't care but are less engaged and certainly less vocal. Callum Mcinnes, in particular, is a quiet lad."

"How is his general wellbeing?"

Alistair glanced at him, and Duncan pretended not to notice.

"Callum?" Rona asked and Duncan nodded. "Well... he's had a rough few months. He got himself into a spot of bother—"

"We know," Duncan said.

"Right, yes of course you would," she replied. "Since he's been back, he's got his head down. Callum isn't one to feel comfortable as the centre of attention. He finds it difficult. He'd much rather be the grey man."

"What do you put that down to?"

Rona shrugged. "He isn't the most confident of children. That business at the end of last year didn't help matters either."

"Any problems at home?"

Again, Alistair looked sideways at him, arching a quizzical eyebrow. Duncan felt the intensity of the stare.

"None that I am aware of," Rona said. "Why do you ask?"

Duncan shook his head. "I'm just building a picture of... Finn's relationships, that's all. So, you would say the three of them get on well?"

"Oh yes, very much so. They share many of the same classes, although I believe Finn's ceiling is higher, from an educational point of view."

"Right, good to know."

There was a knock on the door and it cracked open. A young teaching assistant poked her head through the gap, looking between them all.

"I have the two boys for you, Miss MacAllister," she said quietly. Both Duncan and Alistair smiled at her, and she returned it with one of her own.

"Thank you, Kirsty," Rona said. "Can you have them wait outside and I'll come and get them in a moment."

Kirsty nodded and retreated, closing the door behind her. Duncan turned back to Rona.

"These letters you sent home to the MacGregors."

"Yes?"

"You said Marsali replied?"

"She did, yes."

"In writing… over the phone or in person?"

"In writing," Rona said. "I've had two letters from her."

"Aye, right," Duncan said, thinking on it. "And… you're sure it was Marsali MacGregor who replied?"

Rona chuckled. "I know a child's handwriting when I see it, Detective Inspector. I've seen many an excuse written by pupils to get out of exams, swimming lessons or PE on a rainy day, to know the difference. Besides, Finn… and his little cohort… have terrible handwriting. Trust me, it's obvious."

Duncan smiled. "Great, that figures."

"Would you like to meet the boys?"

Duncan's chest fluttered and he nodded. Both he and Alistair got up from their seats as Rona MacAllister went to the door and opened it, beckoning the two boys to come in. They entered, Callum a step behind his friend, and both looked nervous. To be fair, whenever Duncan had been summoned to a senior staff member's office during his school days – which was often in his case – it seldom ended well.

Duncan did his best to reassure the boys with a smile. Alistair did the same but managed to come across like a deranged scout leader about to hurl them off a cliff face. The two boys sat themselves down, Rona taking a position off to their left, close enough to offer support and let them know they were not alone with the police, but deferential enough to let them know the policemen were in charge.

"Do the two of you know why we've asked to speak to you this morning?" Duncan asked.

"Is it about Finn?" Cameron asked, sitting forward and seemingly moving beyond any nerves he may or may not have held about the meeting. On the other hand, if Callum had been able to retreat any further into his seat, then he'd have passed through it and fallen off the back.

"That's right," Duncan said to Cameron before glancing at Callum who averted his eyes from Duncan's gaze, looking down at his hands in his lap. "Now, it's important that the two of you know that, despite us being policemen," he gestured to Alistair, "DS MacEachran and I are only interested in making sure Finn gets home safely. My name is Duncan…" he said meeting Cameron's eye and then glancing at Callum who lifted his gaze to meet his, "…McAdam. I know I've… met you before, Callum."

Callum nodded, pursing his lips under Duncan's gaze.

"How are you?" he asked Callum.

"I'm all right, thanks."

"Good to know," Duncan said. "You've had one heck of a few months."

Callum nodded glumly. "I've had better, it's true."

"Can either of you tell us anything about where Finn might be?"

Both of them immediately shook their heads, Callum looking away, back into his lap where his hands were firmly clamped together. Cameron seemed the most responsive.

"What about you, Cameron?"

"I prefer to be called Cammy," Cameron said.

"Okay, no problem," Duncan said. "Cammy, has Finn said anything to you recently about any plans he had… any issues that were bothering him?"

"Och no… none that I mind anyway."

"And you, Callum?"

Callum looked up at Duncan, briefly meeting his eye and then shook his head as he looked away again.

"When did you last see or hear from him?"

Cammy sat forward, keen to answer first. "I spoke to him the day before yesterday, at school like, you know? He was all good then. Giving it a good bit of banter, you know?"

"He didn't seem troubled?" Duncan asked.

"No, far from it. We shared a chat on Discord that night as well."

"Discord?" Alistair asked.

"Aye, Discord," Cammy said. "It's a chat app, you know?" Alistair looked at Duncan. Neither of them had heard of it. Cammy was incredulous. "You've never seen Discord! Yous lot are so behind the times."

"Was he okay… on Discord?" Duncan asked.

"Oh aye, he was grand. Up for the craic as always."

"Callum?" Duncan asked.

Callum glanced up and then shook his head. The boy didn't have much about him. That disappointed Duncan, but he couldn't understand why that was.

"Have you heard from him since yesterday, after you realised he hadn't made it into school?"

Cammy shook his head. "Nah, I texted him, but he hasn't come back to me. Where do you think he is?"

"We were hoping you could help us with that," Duncan said.

Cammy shrugged. "No, cannae. Sorry."

Duncan looked at Callum, but he didn't lift his head.

"Okay boys…" Duncan glanced at Alistair and then looked across at Rona who seemed embarrassed by how unforthcoming the boys had been, "I guess we will leave it there for now, but we may wish to speak to you later."

Cammy seemed disappointed but Callum looked at Miss MacAllister and she nodded.

"You boys should return to class," she said and both of them stood up. "No dawdling, straight to class, okay?"

Callum went straight for the door without looking back, although Cammy did pause at the threshold, turning back to Duncan.

"I kinda fancy joining the bobbies one day," he said with a grin.

"Oh, do you, aye?" Alistair asked.

"I can see masel' with the old blue lights and sirens going as I'm gunning away doon the road, eh," Cammy said, smiling.

"Aye, it's just like that," Alistair said, stone faced. "You'll fit in well."

Duncan said, "Well… we can always have a chat about that some time, if you'd like to know more about how to apply?"

Cammy's face lit up and his head bobbed enthusiastically. "Aye, I'd like that very much, thanks!"

"Off to class now, Cameron, please," Rona said. Cammy backed out of the room and Rona followed, likely going to make sure the two boys headed off in the right direction rather than hanging around to discuss the meeting and delay their attendance of classes. Duncan and Alistair were alone.

Alistair sighed. "I'll say two things. First, young Callum knows way more than he's letting on."

"He'd have to know more. He didn't say a thing, did he?"

"Aye, right."

"And the second?" Duncan asked.

Alistair shook his head. "The day that Cammy walks into Portree Station in uniform, is the day I'll be handing in my bloody warrant card." He shook his head. "What a state the world has come to."

Duncan smiled, but his thoughts drifted to his son.

CHAPTER FIVE

DUNCAN'S MOBILE RANG. It was Caitlyn. He'd tasked her with taking the morning briefing so as he and Alistair could make their way over to the school prior to registration.

"Good morning, DC Stewart," Duncan said. "How did the team handle your—"

"I'm not at the station, sir," Caitlyn said. Duncan could hear the wind through the mouthpiece as she raised her voice. He could hear what sounded like waves breaking in the background too.

"Where are you?"

Alistair cocked his head, his brow furrowing with curiosity.

"I'm out at Talisker... on the beach. I think you need to get out here," Caitlyn said, her tone grave. Duncan had a sinking feeling. "We've got a body at the foot of the cliffs."

Duncan checked he and Alistair were still alone in Rona's office. The door was closed.

"Is it Finn MacGregor?"

"No... well, not unless he's aged twenty-odd years over night... and had a sex change while he was at it."

Duncan didn't know whether to be relieved or disturbed. He looked at Alistair and nodded towards the door. Alistair stood up just as the door opened and Rona MacAllister entered, smiling at the two of them. The smile faded as she read their serious expressions.

"Has… er… something happened?" she asked.

"Nothing for you to worry about, Miss MacAllister," Alistair said. "I'm afraid we have an unrelated matter to attend to."

"Oh… right."

"We'll be in touch," Duncan said, covering the mouthpiece with his hand. "If the children come forward with any information, please can you give us a phone?"

She nodded and Alistair handed Rona one of his contact cards. He casually pointed at his name. "If you cannae get me on the mobile, just ring the station and ask for DS MacEachran."

He emphasised the pronunciation of his surname, but it was clear Rona hadn't caught on. She smiled, accepting the card.

"Thank you very much. I'll do that."

They left the office and made their way to the car park. Duncan glanced sideways at Alistair.

"Do you think you get a little hung up on how your name is said sometimes?"

"No," Alistair replied. "It's not hard."

"It is though."

"MacEachran has three syllables – three – the same as yours."

"But the spelling makes it complicated," Duncan argued playfully, unlocking the car as they approached it.

"The only thing making it complicated is an inability both to listen and to read," Alistair countered. Duncan smiled and they both got into the car.

From Portree, they headed south on the A87, turning off at Sligachan beside the famous old arched bridge which drew tourists in their droves every year. The road doubled back on itself, and they continued on towards Merkadale and Carbost. The Cuillins were off to their left in the distance, the snowy peaks of the northernmost Munros in the Cuillin range, Bruach na Frìthe and Sgùrr nan Gillean, partially visible beneath the veil.

Approaching Carbost, the road split with one path heading down towards the township lying on the shore of Loch Harport whereas they took the left fork, heading up and then across towards Talisker. The route climbed into the hills along a single track and again they came to another fork, left towards Eynort and Grula or continuing on towards the bay. The lack of traffic using this road became obvious due to the tarmac breaking up in places. Talisker itself sported a farm bearing the same name, and a light scattering of houses, but it was a largely unspoiled area of the island, wild and remote.

Eventually, they crested a rise and the road started down towards sea level. Thousands of years ago, a glacier must have cut through this valley, forming high mountainous ridges to both sides where the remnants of the glacial path was now only marked by the River Talisker, tracking the road to the south before ultimately joining the sea in the bay bearing its name.

The tarmac road terminated at the farm. A small green sign directed them towards the beach along an unmade track running beside a drystone wall, used to access Talisker House. They set off down the mud track, arriving moments later at the house where Duncan found Caitlyn's car parked alongside a liveried patrol car. They also parked there and then headed onto the footpath down to the bay. They could hear the sea breaking on the rocks in the distance, the easterly wind carrying the sound towards them. It was bitingly cold now, the wind funnelled straight at them by the lay of the surrounding land.

The bay was breathtaking. The beach was encased by high-sided cliffs to the north and south. On one side was a spectacular waterfall cascading over the rugged basalt cliff face but the wind was so strong it almost reversed the flow of water, blowing it up into the air and away from the rock. To the south side was another steep cliff with the picturesque Talisker Stack rising up out of the water, marking where the cliffs finally ended in the sea. The waves were breaking upon the rocks at the foot of the southern cliffs which was where they could see several figures, two wearing hi viz jackets, and the other's hair was flapping in the wind; Caitlyn.

Caitlyn moved to meet them, joining them halfway between the beach access and the foot of the cliffs. She greeted them before falling into step alongside, guiding them to where the body lay.

"Any idea who she is or what she was doing out here?" Duncan asked, raising his voice to be heard above the wind noise.

"No, she's not carrying any ID that we've been able to find," Caitlyn said. "She's dressed for the outdoors, mind."

"Hiking?" Duncan asked.

"I'd say so, aye," Caitlyn replied as they got closer. "She's at the foot of the cliffs there."

They reached the two police officers, two of the Macdonalds, Ronnie and Fraser. Both of them greeted Duncan and Alistair with grave expressions.

"How are you doing, fellas?" Alistair asked.

"Aye, braw," Fraser said. "How's yourself?"

"Be all right if this weather holds off," Alistair said as Duncan dropped to his haunches to examine the body. The woman was in her forties, he guessed, judging from the crow's feet at the corners of her eye and the grey streaks in her red hair. She likely dyed it to maintain the original colour but hadn't done so recently.

Casting an eye over her clothing, Caitlyn was correct. She was well dressed for the conditions. She wore sturdy synthetic walking boots and trousers, both of which would easily stand up to the worst of the wet and cold weather Skye would throw at her. She appeared to be wearing several layers of clothing on her upper body, two thin layers along with a thicker knitted turtle-necked jumper with a bright yellow, hooded waterproof coat over the top.

Alistair also examined her. "Could she be a fisherman... woman..." His brow concertinaed in thought "...fisherfolk... is it?" he asked, glancing at Caitlyn with a raised eyebrow. She laughed, breaking the sombre mood.

"Watching you navigate the realms of political correctness is something of a favoured hobby of mine, sarge," she said with a sideways smile.

"Aye," Duncan said absently, glancing up at the two of them, "it's like giving a horse an etch-a-sketch."

"Oh... is that right, aye?" Alistair said. "I'll have you know I am a modern figure of a man."

Caitlyn's smile broadened. "And by modern, you mean the turn of the nineteenth century, right?"

Alistair laughed.

Duncan turned back to the woman's body, sprawled across the rocks at the base of the cliff face. Everyone's focus turned serious. Duncan looked out to sea beyond the famous solitary stack at the bay's mouth.

"Looking at her hands, she's not come off a trawler," Alistair said, standing behind Duncan. "I've seen a Scalpay fisherman's fingers, and they look more like sausages than pinkies. Link sausage, not square, obviously."

"Thanks for making the distinction," Caitlyn said.

Duncan frowned, thinking hard. "She's not come off any passing boat dressed like this. She's kitted out for climbing a Munro, not for sailing."

"You think she might have been hiking," Caitlyn said, "and fell?"

They all looked up at the summit above them. The cliff face on this side of the bay wasn't as sheer as its counterpart on the north side, but it was still steep. It wasn't unheard of for people to get too close to the edge of such a promontory in search of the perfect photograph only to lose their footing or catch a gust of wind that knocked them off balance, pitching them to their death.

"Once you're over the edge," Duncan said, "the only thing stopping you will be the water... or the rocks below when you hit them."

The dead woman had suffered a massive head injury, not surprising considering the impact if she had fallen from above. Duncan glanced at Ronnie and Fraser.

"Have either of you been up there yet?"

They glanced at one another before looking at Duncan and shaking their heads. Clearly, neither man wanted to be tasked with hiking up to the top and seeing what they could find.

"I'll go," Caitlyn said, glancing at the two uniformed officers who seemed relieved, "but one of yous is coming with me."

"I'll come," Ronnie said, begrudgingly. Fraser stifled a satisfied smile, clearing his throat as Duncan caught his eye.

"Well... I was about to volunteer like, but seeing as Ronnie is up for it, I'll stay down here."

Duncan broke the eye contact, much to Fraser's obvious relief.

"I think it's more likely she fell than she was washed in on the tide," Duncan said. "Her clothes are dampened by the sea and the spray, but she's not been fully submerged as far as I can tell."

"By the colour of her skin, I doubt she's been here for very long either," Alistair said. "What do you reckon, a day?"

"Aye," Duncan nodded, "two at the most. Get onto scenes of crime and have them send a team out here. Until we're sure what happened to her, we'll have to treat it as an *as yet, undetermined death*."

"I'll give Craig a call as well," Alistair said, referring to their on-call forensic medical examiner, reaching for his mobile and stepping away. Duncan looked at the woman again. The nails of her fingers were neatly manicured, but she wasn't wearing any nail polish or varnish. The skin of her palms was rough, but not rough enough to suggest she worked with her hands. He doubted she was in white collar employment either. She could be well used to camping or outdoor recreational activities though. Similarly, she didn't appear to be wearing make-up which added weight to his notion that she was here either on a walking holiday, out for a hike or simply camping wild. He was keen to know what she may have left atop the cliff above them, assuming his theory was correct.

"Anyone reported missing or late back in the last thirty-six hours?" Duncan asked.

Caitlyn shook her head. "No, I checked. It doesn't mean someone won't be calling it in, in the next day or two."

Duncan nodded. "You said she's not got any ID on her, right?"

"Yes," she said, "although I did find this in her pocket."

Caitlyn produced a transparent evidence bag from her internal coat pocket, neatly rolled up to protect the contents. She passed it to him. "I didn't want to give it to you until you'd had a chance to look at the body."

Alistair hung up on his call and walked the short distance back to join them. "Aye, aye, what's all this then?"

Duncan unfurled the bag to see a page of lined notepaper inside. It had a rough edge on the left-hand side where it must have been torn from a pad. The wind caused it to flap in his grasp, and he pulled it tight whilst holding it up to the light, so he could better read the handwritten scrawl across the page. He saw a mobile number.

"I wonder who that belongs to," Alistair said.

"I don't," Duncan replied flatly.

Alistair raised his eyebrows quizzically. "You don't?"

"I already know," he said, meeting Alistair's eye. "It's mine."

CHAPTER SIX

BACK IN THE operations room at the station in Portree, Duncan found Angus hunched over a laptop on his desk, a large cup of takeaway coffee beside the machine, as he studied the screens.

"Is that Finn MacGregor's laptop?" he asked. Angus glanced up and nodded, his forehead creased in concentration. "How are you getting on?"

"I'm doing okay... but the lad is a bit..."

"A bit what?"

Angus paused, taking his hands away from the keyboard and picking up his coffee. "Messed up."

"What's that you say?" Duncan asked.

Russell, DC McLean sitting in the background, piped up. "He's a little nutter... to coin a phrase."

Duncan frowned. "Be more specific."

"He's a full-on environmentalist," Angus said.

"Mentalist is right," Russell added. "An eco-warrior... the likes of which the island has never seen... or needed, for that matter."

Duncan moved to stand behind Angus who turned back to

his screen. "Russell is on the right lines," Angus said, "albeit articulating Finn's interests in a… boomer-esque kind of way."

"Who are you calling a boomer?" Russell said. "I'm Generation X… just about."

Angus laughed. "You wish."

Russell feigned indignation before reaching into the bottom drawer of his desk's pedestal and taking out a packet of crisps. Duncan noted his enforced diet appeared to have gone out of the window a couple of weeks before Christmas, around the same time as they refilled the office tuck box with confectionery for the holiday season. Duncan leaned on the desk, looking over Angus's shoulder.

"What have you got?" he asked.

"Finn has book marked multiple sites in his browser… as you do when you are interested in subjects. He has quite a varied range from the environment to history, much of it associated with Scotland, Highlands and Islands. That sort of thing. A lot of them are your mainstream, Heritage Scotland, Historic Environment Scotland…"

"So, he's quite proud of his roots," Duncan said, glancing at Russell, munching his way through a bag of pickled onion Monster Munch. "Nothing wrong with that."

"Aye, you wait and see," Russell replied.

Angus continued. "Now, these sites… marine conservation sites… Greenpeace… are all normal, right?"

"Aye, go on," Duncan said.

"All book marked at various points over the last couple of years—"

"Probably coinciding with him getting a phone or a computer for school," Duncan said.

"Aye, right. However, these past three to four months… he's been visiting pages that are shadow banned by search engines—"

"Back up for me," Duncan said, placing a hand on his shoulder. "Shadow banned?"

"Oh... erm... sort of restricted viewing," Angus explained. "They are still there on the internet but search engines, platforms sort of... restrict their reach, so you really have to search for them through other platforms."

"Ah... so banning them by choking off their views, but not actually banning them?" Duncan asked.

"Right. They are there, but in the shadows..."

"Hence the term *shadow banning*," Russell said, through a mouthful of crisps.

"Aye, thanks, Russell," Duncan said. "What would I do without you?"

"You're welcome," Russell replied, failing to detect any hint of sarcasm.

"Why would these sites – presumably they are sites – require shadow banning?"

Angus glanced up at Duncan. "Hard to say, but a lot of platforms these days are wary of being perceived as taking any side in a contentious issue—"

"And every subject feels like a contentious issue these days," Duncan said quietly. "What are these sites?"

"Blogs and forums mainly," Angus said.

"Fora," Russell said over his shoulder. Feeling Angus's eyes upon him, Russell turned his chair to face them. "The plural of forum is fora... not forums. Didn't you do Latin in school?"

"No," Angus said. "That's why I'm a polisman. What's your excuse?"

Russell grinned and Duncan gestured for him to turn his chair around and get on with his own work.

"The subject of these blogs and *forums*?" Duncan asked.

"Environmental issues, climate change… raging against fossil fuel backers, corporations and the like. Eco-activism."

"And doing right by the climate gets you shadow banned, does it?" Duncan asked.

"No, I don't think so. But some of these activists are not simply sitting down in the middle of a busy street and stopping traffic. They are encouraging much more direct action."

"Hard core activists then?"

"Aye, kinda like the difference between PETA and the Animal Liberation Front back in the day."

Duncan exhaled. "To what extent is Finn immersed in all of this?"

Angus shrugged. "As far as I can tell he's just reading the source material. I've read a few bits that he accessed, and although I can agree with a lot of the subject matter, there is the touch of tin foil hat going on."

"Any suggestion that he was looking to get involved in anything; demonstrations, events… or attacks?"

"Not yet," Angus said, "but I can keep digging."

"Please," Duncan said.

"You think this might be related to his disappearing act then?"

"I don't know, to be honest. The school and his parents think he was distracted by something… and we have nothing else to go on. Is there anything going on around the island that might draw the ire of eco activists?"

"Not my area of expertise," Angus said. "I'll have a nose about though, see what I can find out."

Duncan patted him on the shoulder just as Alistair entered the ops room.

"Did they find anything on the cliff above the bay?" he asked.

Alistair shook his head. "Nothing related to the body, or

anyone else. The wind is fierce up there though, so bad that if it weren't staked out it'll likely be across the other side of the island by now."

"What about the scenes of crime team?"

"All done," Alistair said. "There wasn't a great deal for them to do to process the scene. Craig Dunbar has the body on its way to the morgue now. The postmortem will begin this afternoon."

"Early thoughts?"

Alistair shrugged. "Much the same as us; the body probably lay there overnight... perhaps since as early as this time yesterday, but the night air temperature can skew things. Craig said he'd get back to us as quickly as he could once he knows more."

"Still no report of a missing person matching her description," Russell said.

Duncan nodded. "Can you start contacting people on the mainland, widen the parameters a bit. Maybe she came onto the island recently and no one knows she's missing yet?"

"Is there a car abandoned anywhere nearby?" Russell asked.

Alistair shook his head. "I've asked Ronnie and Fraser to look around, but there was nothing obvious."

"Aside from the route we took to get there, which direction could someone come from?" Duncan asked. It wasn't a part of the island he was overly familiar with. A couple of visits to the distillery in Carbost was about as much involvement as Duncan had ever had with Talisker.

Alistair picked up a copy of the Ordnance Survey map of the area, unfolding it and laying it out across his desk.

"Here's the bay," he said, tapping his finger on the beach and then tracing it back to where they'd parked their car at Talisker House. "You can come in from the north side, coming down a track from Fiscavaig way... but you'd be walking it."

"How far is that do you think?" Duncan asked.

Alistair thought on it. "Depending on whether you're walking to Talisker itself and then cutting west towards the sea or if you're heading for the cliff top... it's around three miles or so, if heading for Talisker itself, I'd say. Less if you cut across the moorland to see the waterfall from above, although off the track it gets a bit soggy underfoot."

"And from the south?"

Alistair sucked air through his teeth. "There's no path that way, but if you're into hiking then there's no reason not to. It's remote... untouched by man nor beast, you might say. To the southeast is Eynort, and I guess if you're taking in the sights you could walk around the headland. The views are stunning."

"You'd have no other reason to be out there though," Duncan said.

"None that I can think of, no."

"If you had a campsite, it'd be hard to come across it if you weren't specifically looking for one," Duncan said.

"Which daft sod would want to be camping out there at this time of year?" Alistair asked.

Duncan smiled. "It takes all sorts, though, doesn't it?"

Alistair frowned. "Does that mean I need to press gang some volunteers into walking the headland?"

"Let's hold off on that until we've tried the obvious first."

"So..." Alistair said, perching himself on the edge of a nearby desk and folding his arms across his chest, "have you remembered her yet?"

Duncan shook his head. "I've never set eyes on her before."

"You're sure?"

"Och… yes, I'm sure… I think I'd remember giving some random woman my number."

Alistair's brow furrowed. "So where did she get your number from?"

Duncan was at a loss. Picking up the evidence bag, he studied the piece of paper. It had been folded into a neat square at some point, the creases in the paper were still visible. The one edge was jagged, where it had been torn from a larger pad, and the other corners were now dog-eared because it had been loose inside the coat pocket of the dead woman. However, it was still in good condition overall, indicative perhaps that it hadn't been removed from the pad for long. Maybe a couple of days ago, although that was just his instinct rather than anything scientifically conclusive.

Alistair's mobile rang and he answered it. Angus looked over at Duncan, catching his eye.

"Sir… have you got a moment?" Angus asked. Duncan crossed to the young DC's desk.

"What is it?"

"An email exchange," Angus said. "You know I've been looking at these *fora*," he looked at Russell, seeing the big man's ears prick up but he said nothing, "and Finn has been commenting on a few threads."

"Aye, go on," Duncan said.

"Well, he's had a bit of an exchange here and there, but one account in particular seems to have had a lot of interaction with his handle."

"His handle?" Duncan asked. "I suppose you can't come on these sites and just be called Dave206?"

Angus laughed. "Aye, that's right. Some do… but others seem to want something…"

"Way cooler," Duncan said, and Angus nodded.

"Finn is *Eco-F35*."

"Catchy."

"Aye, probably linking to the fighter jet… nae much cooler than that is there, in the mind of a teenage bairn anyway?"

"Very environmentally friendly too," Duncan said. "Those jets run on biofuel, after all."

Angus grinned. Not even he was gullible enough to fall for that.

"And who is he talking to?"

"Don't know… someone going under the name of Eve… bunch of numbers."

"A bot perhaps?"

Angus shrugged. "Maybe, lots of numbers usually signals that, doesn't it? But in this case, I think not. They are having a bit of back and forth across multiple threads. I think it's a real person… they have a lot in common… views and that."

"Is there any way we can find out who that is?"

Angus was reflective. "I can contact the forum admins and ask… but they're likely based outside of the UK and therefore immune to our legal requests… and these types are probably not very trusting of the police…"

"Fair point," Duncan said, "but no harm in finding out the details and asking the question. If they are UK based, then we can force it."

"I can always set up an account of my own," Angus said. "Maybe they will interact with me?"

"Good idea," Duncan said. "Go the official route first and if that fails, we can have a crack at that." Alistair hung up his call and Duncan was about to rejoin him and had a thought. Turning back to Angus, he said, "How far back does the interaction between Finn and this other account go?"

"I don't know," Angus said. "I've been starting with the most recent and working backwards."

"When you find out, let me know, yeah?"

"Will do. Are you thinking someone might be grooming him?"

Duncan didn't want to think so, but it was plausible despite almost dismissing the likelihood when speaking to Finn's parents. Duncan walked back to Alistair, whose expression was grave.

"What's up? Did your monster truck fail its MOT or something?"

Alistair shook his head. "That was Craig on the phone."

"He's keen."

"He just thought we should have the heads up. They're about to get to work on the deceased... and she was stabbed."

"What?"

"Aye... a single stab wound to the chest... straight through the heart, Craig reckons. She was lying on her left side... and with the thick coat she was wearing... the shallow sea water rinsing the coat clear of the blood... means we missed it."

"Stabbed?"

"And that's all we know, for now," Alistair said. "Maybe the fall killed her... but someone helped her along the way."

Duncan exhaled forcefully. "Right, let's get a description out to the islanders. Have someone mock up a drawing of her, that might help jog people's memories. We need to know who this woman is... and we'll go from there."

"And you're sure you dinnae know—"

"Aye! I'm sure."

Alistair cocked his head. "Just asking, you know?"

CHAPTER SEVEN

DUNCAN PULLED his car into the side of the road, taking a moment to settle himself before he reached his destination. The afternoon had been a blur of meetings, phone calls and briefings, culminating in a press conference to officially announce the discovery of the body on Talisker Beach. The press conference had been swiftly concluded, with the gathered journalists chuntering their disapproval due to the scant detail provided besides the artist's impression of the deceased.

Open to taking questions, Duncan had answered each one as comprehensively as he could, although it didn't satisfy the assembled people who continued to ask the same question but in a different way, seeking the more salacious details. Duncan wasn't being deliberately obtuse; they really knew very little. He left out the stab wound and also the slip of paper with his telephone number on it.

The phones in the newly formed incident room were ringing as he left, Alistair handling the process with the full team of detectives manning the lines. Duncan was confident they'd get something from the coverage. The island wasn't densely populated, and strangers stood out, perhaps less so in the peak tourist season but at this time of the year, lone hikers drew attention. At least, he hoped so.

The wipers scraped across his windscreen, and he looked out into the darkness as the rain fell. It had started snowing earlier before drifting into sleet and now falling as rain. With a bit of luck the cloud cover would remain and all of this standing water wouldn't freeze overnight.

Putting the car into gear, he pulled away from the verge and made his way up into the hills towards Maligar. The Mcinnes' house was the last in the line of houses making up the little township and Duncan saw the lights of the house were on as he approached, turning into the driveway and pulling up beside Becky's car. There was no sign of Davey's pick-up, which was something of a relief.

Approaching the front door, he hesitated before knocking. Alistair had offered to make this trip, but Duncan had told him he wanted to speak to Callum again, to try and get more out of him than they'd managed in Rona MacAllister's office that morning. Speaking to Callum unofficially, and in the safety of his own home, he hoped would help him to speak freely.

All of this was true, but Duncan would be lying to himself, as opposed to everyone else, if he didn't admit there was another reason. Ever since learning that he was Callum's father, he'd found himself wondering what the young man was like; did they share interests, mannerisms... and could they forge any form of bond in the coming months and years? Would they be allowed to?

The door opened and Becky was startled to find Duncan standing in front of her.

"Duncan?" she said.

"Aye, it's me."

She looked past him, to both the left and right. "I thought I heard someone on the drive."

"That was me," he said. "I was about to knock—"

"What are you doing here?"

He was surprised by her aggressive tone. "I need to speak to Callum."

She made to object, but Duncan cut her off, anticipating what she was about to say.

"It's about Finn MacGregor's disappearance, that's all."

"Oh… right, of course," she said, her stance softening. "Has he no' shown up yet?"

Duncan shook his head. "But we're still looking."

"Well… Callum said he spoke to the police at school this morning."

"Aye, that was me."

Her eyes narrowed but she didn't comment. It would appear Callum hadn't said who'd spoken to him at the school. Becky eased the door open, beckoning Duncan to come inside.

The hall was cramped with a coat rack on the wall behind the door and numerous items of casual footwear scattered beneath the hanging overcoats. These old croft houses were practical in their construction. Many properties had been added to over the years, but not this one. People lived an outdoor life in these parts and the creature comforts of modern living were not as common as they might be in the central belt of the mainland.

"You'll have to take us as you find us, I'm afraid," Becky said, leading Duncan through the house. "It's all a bit of a mess."

"Ah… you should see mine," he said.

"How is it going with the refurb?"

Duncan wrinkled his nose. He'd been patching up the old McAdam family house since he'd decided to stay on the island after returning to work on a case towards the end of the previous year. Progress had been slow and then gathered real pace before grinding to a halt as his focus slipped onto other matters, notably his work.

"It's getting there."

"Are you out of the caravan?" she asked, entering the kitchen and adjusting the flame beneath two pans on the stove, before turning to face him and leaning against the counter, folding her arms across her chest.

"No... still there."

"Must be... bracing?"

Duncan smiled. "Aye, I was chipping the ice off the inside windows until recently."

"Did you buy a bigger heater?"

"No. I just stopped—"

"Chipping off the ice," she said, smiling.

"Aye," he said, grinning. His expression turned sombre as their eyes met. "How have you been, you know, since—"

"All good, Duncan," she said, breaking eye contact and turning away from him to stir whatever it was she was cooking. Clearly, she didn't want to discuss their particular situation. Hearing movement from the sitting room, he turned to see a teenage girl enter the room, leaning heavily on a crutch in her left hand.

"Something smells good," Duncan said, smiling at Eilidh, Becky's daughter, a couple of years younger than her brother, Callum.

Eilidh cast a suspicious eye over Duncan but returned his smile with a polite one of her own.

"How long will dinner be, Mum?"

"About a half hour," Becky said, glancing at Duncan. "Your father should be home by then.

"Right, thanks," Eilidh said, looking at Duncan again.

"How is the recovery coming?" he asked her.

She inclined her head. "Slower than I'd like, but... the physio says I'm doing grand."

"Well... you're young, you'll get there," Duncan said supportively. Eilidh nodded and made her way back into the sitting room, allowing the door to swing to behind her. "How is she doing?" Duncan asked. It had been a few months ago where Eilidh had been severely injured as a passenger in a car driven off the road by her brother.

"It's slow progress," Becky said, "even considering how quickly they heal at this age. The consultant is confident she'll make a full recovery."

"That's good to hear." Duncan paused, Becky's eyes flicking across at him and away again. "And you, you're okay?"

Becky made a show of getting on with her food preparations, but it was clear to him she was avoiding answering the question. Since that night when she'd told him he was Callum's father, they'd barely seen each other except maybe in passing once or twice. They'd been avoiding each other, making this moment even more awkward than it might have been.

"Bex?" he asked.

She threw the wooden spoon she was holding down onto the work surface. It startled Duncan. Becky took a deep breath and turned to face him.

"What is it you're looking for from me, Duncan?"

He didn't have an answer for her. He hadn't really considered what he was going to say. All he knew, was that he wanted to get to know his son a little better.

"I..." He frowned. "I... don't know."

"Well, it's good that you've gathered your thoughts these past couple of months."

Duncan was confused. "I thought you wanted me to keep my distance?"

"Aye… that's true… keep your distance, but not disappear completely."

"I thought it for the best, what with Davey and all—"

She sighed. "Davey… aye, well he's something else entirely."

"Is he behaving himself?" Duncan asked. Spotting movement in the corner of his eye, Duncan looked across to see Callum entering the kitchen. He nodded towards Duncan, but looked like he'd immediately thrown up his guard. "Callum," Duncan said, smiling.

"Mr McAdam," Callum replied. Becky glanced at Duncan and then at her son, smiling.

"Are you okay, love?"

"Hungry."

"You're always hungry," Becky said. "Dinner will not be long." She glanced nervously at Duncan. "Detective Inspector McAdam has come to speak with you."

Callum seemed alarmed and Duncan moved to assuage his fears. "It's okay, Callum. I just wanted to speak to you about Finn a bit more, if you don't mind?"

Callum nodded but didn't appear happy about it. "I've still not heard from him, if that's what you're going to ask me?"

"That's okay," Duncan said, glancing at Becky who was making herself busy. He looked past her to see the moonlight reflecting off the snow outside. There was a break in the weather. It would take a prolonged period of warmer, wetter weather to get rid of the snow that had fallen in the last couple of days. "Shall we step outside for a moment?" Becky twitched involuntarily. "If that's okay with your mum?" he asked.

Becky acted as if she hadn't been listening, looking over and shrugging. "Of course, if Callum is okay with it?"

Callum also shrugged. "I'll get my coat."

They went out the back door, the cold air hitting Duncan like a hammer to the chest when he drew breath. Callum zipped up his coat, thrusting his hands into his pockets. They walked a short distance away from the house, neither speaking, and Callum wouldn't make eye contact.

"Do you like being outdoors?" Duncan asked.

"Aye, it's all right. Sometimes I prefer it," Callum said. "If I'm not on my computer."

"You into your gaming, are you?"

He nodded, but still didn't meet Duncan's eye.

"Finn spends a fair bit of time online," Duncan said. Callum didn't comment. "One of my detectives is going through his laptop just now."

At the mention of this, Callum's head shot up and they finally made eye contact. Was that worry he saw in the boy's expression.

"He doesn't seem to be into playing games though."

Callum looked glum. "Nah... he used to be, but recently... not so much."

"He spends a lot of time on forums and stuff, doesn't he?"

Callum shrugged. "Aye... he's always on about a lot of things."

"He does seem to be, aye," Duncan said. "He's passionate."

"Goes too far though."

"In what way?"

Callum looked away, perhaps concerned he'd said too much.

"Callum?" Duncan pressed.

"Ah, you know... he can go on a rant every now and again."

"On the environment?"

Callum shrugged.

"Has Finn got himself wrapped up in something that maybe he's lost control of?"

Callum looked at him, his eyes narrowing. "What do you mean by that?"

"You tell me." Callum shook his head, shifting his weight between his feet. Duncan realised he was losing the feeling in his cheeks. "This is important, Callum. Your friend is missing, and you don't seem overly worried—"

"I don't know where he is, all right?" Callum bit back.

Duncan frowned, allowing a moment to pass where they could both settle down. Maybe he was pressing the lad too much. "Who would Finn go to if he was in trouble?" Duncan held his hands up. "Just... hypothetically, if he was in trouble, where do you think he would go?"

"He... he'd come to me, I reckon."

"And has he; come to you?"

Callum looked away, then shook his head.

"What about Cameron?" Duncan asked. "Apparently, the three of you are inseparable."

Callum smiled. "Cammy is an all-right guy, but... no, Finn wouldn't go to him in a crisis. Not unless he wanted things to get much worse, anyway."

Duncan smiled. "Good to know. Can you tell me about Finn."

"What do you want to know?"

"How is he at the moment? Apparently, his grades have slipped... and his teachers think he's not quite himself."

Callum looked away into the darkness. The moon was

obscured again, and Duncan felt a few spots of rain beginning to fall again.

"Aye, he's… all right."

"How is he getting on at home?"

"With his parents?"

"Aye," Duncan said. "His dad seems a bit… of a character."

Callum snorted a laugh. "Yeah, you could say that. I thought my old man was a pain in the arse."

Duncan refrained from asking more about Davey. "Does Finn not get on with his father?"

"Not recently, no."

"Why is that?"

Callum shrugged. "They just don't get on, that's all."

Duncan knew there was more to it than that, but he didn't feel he could apply any more pressure. At least he had the boy talking.

"Is it bad enough that Finn might want to run away?"

Callum baulked at the comment. "No. Not at all. It's nothing like that."

"Then… what is it like?"

Callum looked down at the ground. He wasn't going to elaborate. Duncan eyed him in the little light emanating through the kitchen window, searching out any features that might remind him of himself. Callum looked far more like his mother though. He had the same skin tone, hair and eye colour as she did along with his mother's finely sculpted cheekbones. He was even built more like her, slight, rather than thicker set as Duncan was himself. That could change as he grew obviously. Duncan thought he'd make the most of this time they had where they were alone.

"What… are your plans after you finish school?"

Callum shrugged. "I'm probably going to work with my dad."

"On the croft?" Duncan asked, failing to mask his surprise. Callum looked at him, his eyes narrowing.

"Dad says it's an honest living."

"Aye," Duncan said, "that's true, but... have you thought about staying on in education? Maybe doing A-Levels and then university?"

"Nah... my dad won't have it. I'm not suited to it."

"Says who?" Duncan asked. "Your father?"

Callum tilted his head to one side. "Aye."

"And what does he know about it?"

"About what?"

"Life... what's out there beyond the confines of this poxy island..." Callum was watching Duncan now, with an expression of both amusement and surprise. "Ah... sorry. It's not for me to say... but there's more to the world than what you'll find here on Skye."

"You came back."

Duncan looked at him. "What?"

"You came back, didn't you? Mum said you were away a long time, and then you came back."

"Aye... that's true."

"Then... if it's so good away from the island, why did you come back?"

"Erm..." Duncan frowned, unsure of what he should say. "It's complicated. That's what happens when you become a grown up... life becomes...er..."

"Complicated," Callum said.

Duncan nodded. "Aye."

The rain was falling steadily now, more like the sleet of earlier in the day. Callum was studying Duncan, much as he had been the young lad previously. He felt uncomfortable under the teenager's gaze.

"Come on, let's get back inside."

They walked the short distance back to the house, Duncan seeing the beam of headlights as a vehicle turned into the drive at the front of the property. Davey Mcinnes was home. They entered the kitchen and Callum hurriedly shook off his coat and disappeared out into the hall.

"Dinner will be in about ten minutes!" Becky called after him.

"Aye, fine," Callum shouted over his shoulder. Duncan heard his footfalls on the stairs as he hurried back up them. Becky looked at Duncan expectantly.

"What?" he asked.

"Did you get what you wanted?"

Duncan hadn't gleaned a great deal from the conversation about Finn MacGregor, but he'd learned a bit about his son.

"What's this about him leaving education?"

Becky glared at him, glancing towards the sitting room where the sound of a television carried to them. Duncan moved across and closed the door.

"It is what it is, Duncan," Becky said. "Not everyone is suited for academia."

"He's bloody sixteen…"

"I know full well how old he is," Becky said, keeping her voice down so as not to be overheard.

"In this day and age, you cannae be ditching your education… to—"

"To what?" she asked accusingly.

"To work on a croft."

"Why not?"

"*Why not?*"

"Yes… what's wrong with working the land, Duncan?"

He frowned. "Nothing… but…there's more to life—"

The door opened and Davey Mcinnes walked in, taking off his coat and hanging it on the back of a chair at the head of the dining table.

"More to life than what?" Davey asked, resting his hands on the top of the chair and looking between them.

Duncan drew breath.

"Than what?" Davey repeated, now looking directly at Duncan, staring at him sternly. "Out with it, Duncan. You're never shy in speaking your mind usually."

"Duncan thinks—"

"I'm asking Duncan what he thinks," Davey said, interrupting his wife. "He doesnae need you speaking for him."

Duncan held Davey's gaze. "I think it's wrong for the lad to be quitting his education so early, that's all."

"Aye… wrong, is it?" Davey asked, raising one eyebrow inquisitively.

"I think so," Duncan said. Becky was anxious, Duncan could see her getting flustered, wanting to intervene but Davey had already chastised her once. Some things… some people, didn't change.

"Well… good job it's not any of your business then, isn't it?" Davey said flatly. "What brings you all the way out here to see *my family*, anyway?"

"I came to speak to Callum."

Davey glanced at Becky, who kept her back turned, making ready to begin serving out, and then he looked back at Duncan.

"What business have you got speaking to my son?"

Duncan felt his chest tighten. "His friend, Finn, is missing… and I wanted to ask him about it."

"Ah… right. And have you done that?"

"I have, aye."

"Then perhaps it's time you set off home," Duncan," Davey said, pointing at the table with knives and forks set out for the evening meal. "As you can see, my family is about to have their supper."

Duncan nodded. "I'll see myself out."

"No need for that," Davey said, as Eilidh poked her head around the door from the sitting room, sensing supper was ready. "I'll see you out."

Duncan glanced towards Becky, momentarily catching her eye. She pursed her lips and looked away, evidently keen not to make any expression that could be misconstrued.

"Thank you for letting me speak to Callum," Duncan said. Becky smiled and nodded before turning away. Duncan smiled at Eilidh and then made his way through to the hall, Davey Mcinnes a half-step behind him. As Duncan reached the front door, Davey put a hand on it to stop him from opening it. The two men were up close to one another.

Davey spoke in a whisper. "Is there any reason why it had to be you who came out here today?"

"It's my case," Duncan said flatly.

"And detective inspectors interview teenagers about their friends who have done a bunk often, do they?"

Duncan held Davey's eye. "On occasion, they do, aye."

Davey nodded, a wicked gleam in his eye. "Well now, there shouldn't be too many more occasions coming up any time soon, right?"

Duncan wouldn't be intimidated. "We'll see."

Davey stared at him for a few seconds before releasing his hold on the door and allowing Duncan to open it. He walked out into the falling sleet. Davey leaned on the door frame, watching him walking to his car.

"Mind how you go in this weather, Duncan. It's treacherous out there."

He closed the door before Duncan could look back. Reaching his car, Duncan looked back at the house. He saw a figure in an upstairs bedroom, back lit by the light coming through from the landing because the room itself was in darkness. It could only be Callum. He fought the urge to make him aware that he'd seen the boy, instead getting into the car. By the time he'd put his seatbelt on, pushed the start button and looked up once more, he saw Callum had gone.

CHAPTER EIGHT

DUNCAN ROSE to a fresh layer of snow. To make matters worse for him, the gas canister fuelling the heating in his caravan had run out overnight and the spare he kept for this occasion seemed to have a dodgy valve. He was unable to get it connected. It was a fierce-looking Duncan who met DS MacEachran at the mortuary to go over the postmortem results with Dr Dunbar.

Craig Dunbar was his usual eccentric self as he welcomed them in the lobby before leading them down to where the body was stored. The room was maintained at a consistent temperature which Duncan found warm despite having driven across the island with the heaters on in his car almost at the maximum until the cabin temperature made him feel nauseous.

The deceased woman was laid out on a mortuary slab, a blanket covering her entire body. Dr Dunbar pulled the sheet back to reveal her head and the top of her shoulders, folding the sheet at the base of her neck.

"We won't trouble you for long, my dear," he said quietly as he retrieved his file and opened it up to the summary page.

Glancing between Duncan and Alistair, he put his glasses on to read. "I've emailed copies of this across to you both. However, I thought we should discuss some of the—" he paused, frowning "—more peculiar aspects of this particular case."

"That sounds ominous," Alistair said, sipping at his take-away cup of coffee he'd brought with him. Duncan glanced at it and Alistair read his mind. "If you'd said, I'd have picked one up for you too."

"So, we shall start with the more straightforward details," Dr Dunbar said. "We have a woman—"

"You don't need a medical degree for that," Alistair said. Duncan shot him a withering look and Alistair arched his eyebrows. "I was just saying."

"Thirty-five to forty years of age," Dr Dunbar said, looking at Alistair over the rims of his glasses. "Death was by way of a single puncture wound, directly to the heart which severed both the left and right pulmonary arteries as well as punc-turing the aorta." He paused, glancing down at the body, glumly. "I'm terribly sorry, my dear. There was no way you would have survived, even if it were not for the ensuing fall from height."

"You think she definitely fell from atop the cliff?" Duncan asked.

"Without a doubt," Dr Dunbar said. "Whether she fell or was pushed, I can't say, but the damage to the skull, her right shoulder blade and left femur are all indicative of a severe impact consistent with falling from height. Either that or she was run over by a lorry."

"No' many lorries running up and down Talisker Beach, doc," Alistair said.

"Well, quite so, Alistair. Therefore, the fall it was."

Duncan cast an eye over the red headed woman lying on

the mortuary slab. "You said she wouldn't have survived, even without the fall?"

"Undoubtedly not, no. The stab wound would have seen her bleed out in a matter of minutes. With such a significant wound, the victim could do so within minutes." He nodded towards her. "And this was such an injury."

"What can you tell us about the weapon used?" Duncan asked.

Dr Dunbar thought on it for a moment. "A lockable blade, no more than three inches in length… I would suggest with a sharpened cutting edge to one side and a serrated or saw-tooth edge on the opposite. A blade width of an inch or less, but certainly no more." Reaching down, he grasped the edge of the covering sheet and drew it back until the upper torso was revealed. Setting the sheet down, he leaned in to where the small wound could be seen. It was narrow, slightly more than an inch wide, but that could easily have been made wider as the blade was withdrawn and the victim either moved or fell away, widening the incision. "I believe the blade entered directly like this—" he made a forward stabbing motion in the air, "—and then either the blade was angled upwards or the poor lassie pushed away from the attacker, or fell away, and that motion carried the blade higher and through the aorta and into the right pulmonary artery. Very unfortunate."

"But only the one stab wound?" Duncan asked. Dr Dunbar nodded. "That's unusual, wouldn't you say?"

"Oh… I don't disagree, but in this case that was all that was needed."

Duncan nodded. "What else can you tell us?"

"She was likely dead when she landed at the base of the cliffs or died very soon afterwards. Judging by the time of death – which I estimate as being approximately fourteen to sixteen hours before she was discovered – we can determine that she spent some of that time in the water. The tide will have carried her further from the base of the cliffs, bringing her up the beach to the place where she was found. However, there is no seawater in her lungs, so I can say with confidence she died before entering the water."

"Time in the water will mean a distinct lack of trace evidence," Duncan said, failing to hide his disappointment.

"Not that I expect there will have been much to be had in any event," Dr Dunbar said. Duncan looked at him quizzically. "There are no signs of her having been bound, no indication of any defensive wounds, no skin samples beneath her fingernails – which were kept short, not manicured, but short – and, before you ask, no indication of any kind of sexual assault."

Alistair scoffed. "So, you're telling us that she was out in the arse-end of nowhere and was attacked, stabbed once... died and then left to be discovered... and she didn't see it coming?" He looked at Duncan and Craig Dunbar, shaking his head. "You'd see someone coming to kill you from a mile away out there... not to mention you don't just bump into people on the headland there. It's wild... especially at this time of the year."

"All extremely valid contributions, Alistair," Dr Dunbar said. "However, I deal in medical fact and not speculation. Whether she was there alone or with her killer, I do not know, but that is my interpretation of what came to pass."

Duncan looked closer at the stab wound. One end of the incision was ragged, likely caused by the retraction of the blade with the saw-tooth edge that Craig spoke of. Dr Dunbar looked at him as Duncan stepped back, silently asking permission to re-cover the body. Duncan nodded and the sheet was replaced.

"Onto the peculiarities then?" Duncan asked and Craig smiled.

"Indeed. And they are peculiar, I assure you." He retrieved his file, tracing his notes with his forefinger. "She was in fairly good shape, clearly exercises on a regular basis. Having studied her, I would say she spends a fair bit of time outdoors, likely an accomplished hiker; the muscle definition of her legs and her lean body mass backs that hypothesis up."

"And that she was dressed in hiking kit," Alistair said out of the corner of his mouth. Dr Dunbar ignored him.

"The contents of her gut indicate she was a vegetarian, or at least had been eating a non-meat diet for some time prior to death—"

"I could go with a bacon sandwich right now, I must say," Alistair said quietly whilst Dr Dunbar continued unchecked.

"And by this age, a consistent meat-eater will likely have several pounds of undigested red meat in their bowels—"

"Or maybe not..." Alistair muttered, frowning.

"She was previously a smoker... and a heavy one too based on the tar lining her lungs. Even a twenty a day habit for twenty years wouldn't generate this level of coating... so I would suggest she either lived abroad where the tar and nicotine content are far less well-regulated or she may have had access to cheap imported contraband cigarettes, here in the UK."

"We haven't found any of her possessions yet," Duncan said. "We don't even know her name."

"Well, I can't help with that directly," Dr Dunbar said, "but..."

"But?"

"This brings me to the real peculiarity that I am struggling with."

"Go on," Duncan said, intrigued.

"I need to do some research but there are abnormalities in this woman… that I am at a loss – presently – to explain. She was suffering from pigmentary retinopathy; a salt-and-pepper pigmentation in the retina that can affect one's vision."

"And that's unusual?"

"It is rare… a sporadic disorder that involves the degeneration and atrophy of the retina, particularly at the level of the photoreceptors. Often, this is a genetic condition which is passed down from parents to children."

"Okay," Duncan said. "That is interesting."

"Oh, there's more. As you know, I run all manner of toxicological analysis of the blood looking for legal and illegal substances… also assessing conditions and the like that may have been a factor in the death of my patient—"

"And?" Duncan asked, keen to head the doctor off before he went full-on medical and left both him and Alistair behind.

"Well, I go over and above what is usually deemed necessary in a postmortem examination, just to keep myself interested in my work—"

"And you found something," Duncan said.

"Oh, he definitely found something," Alistair said.

"I did, yes," Dr Dunbar said with a gleeful smile. "Your victim's cerebrospinal fluid protein concentration came in at 100mg/dl."

Duncan and Alistair exchanged a look. Neither man had a clue what that meant.

"English please, Craig," Alistair said. "Or Gaelic, if you prefer… anything but medical speech, please."

Dr Dunbar smiled. "44mg/dl is the cut off point for most people… that is for those who are not suffering from diabetes or prediabetes. It is quite possible for someone who is fasting overnight to generate a level of 99mg/dl or lower, which would be quite normal. 100 to 125mg/dl would be indicative of a prediabetic condition and anything above that level would strongly imply the person was diabetic."

"You said she was in good health," Duncan said.

"Which is indeed the peculiarity that I mentioned, Detective Inspector. Our young lady here shows none of the signs of being diabetic or prediabetic. Now, these anomalies could indeed have other plausible causes."

"For example?"

"Multiple sclerosis," Dr Dunbar said. "Someone suffering from MS can indeed have these same protein concentrations... but, I have looked and there is no scarring of the nerves to indicate such a condition. As I said, she was in good health."

Duncan took a moment to think about it. "So, what are you telling us? Is this something that could help us to identify her?"

"Possibly... if I can figure out what condition she had, presuming there is one." Dr Dunbar's forehead creased in thought. "I need to do some more tests... maybe re-run them and then reach out to some of my colleagues. But – and I must stress this is only a possibility – such a condition would need to be treated and not by a general practitioner, but someone with in-depth knowledge."

"A specialist," Duncan said.

"Find the specialist, name the victim," Alistair said.

"I only hope it doesn't prove too difficult to narrow down," Dr Dunbar said. "I've not come across results like this before. What you have here, Duncan, is a good old-fashioned mystery."

Duncan glanced at Alistair. "Tell us something we don't already know, eh?"

Alistair cocked his head. "And you're sure—"

"If you're about to ask me again if I'm sure I don't know

this woman, I swear to the almighty I'll have you writing parking tickets by sunset," Duncan said.

"No... Detective Inspector Touchy, I wasn't."

"Really?"

"All right, I was... but are you sure you dinnae know her?"

Duncan sighed, nodded towards Dr Dunbar and turned to leave. Alistair looked at Craig who suppressed a smile. Alistair shrugged.

"I was only asking."

CHAPTER NINE

THE MINGINISH COMMUNITY Hall was a rectangular, timber-clad building in the small village on the west coast of Loch Harport, sitting in the shadow of the nearby Cnoc Glas Heilla, a small mountain summit of only three hundred and forty-one feet, according to the maps.

The volunteers began gathering inside at first light, and soon the numbers had swollen to such an extent that the briefing had needed to be moved outdoors into the car park. Despite the news of a woman's body being found on the beach at Talisker, there was still the small matter of a missing school-boy. Several reports had come into the station of a teenager matching Finn MacGregor's description seen in the area after he went missing. Follow-up requests and interviews with locals had failed to identify who it was, and so Duncan had made the call to begin a search of the area.

The bulk of the CID presence in Portree was still focussed on identifying the woman lying in a fridge in the mortuary, but Duncan had assembled as many of his uniformed counter-parts and any locals who were willing to help in the search at the local community hall. The staff had done a wonderful job of providing cups of tea and coffee to those who arrived, and a local hotel had arranged for freshly made sandwiches and snacks for those who turned out.

Each group of six volunteers had a police officer between them and the next group, with strict instructions not to pick up anything they might find and simply to alert their nominated police officer to what they'd found. Everyone was ready to go, with the local area split up into a grid pattern with groups methodically set to walk their area.

If the sightings were accurate, then Finn was very much alive and nearby. Thus far they'd failed to find any sign of him. Although Duncan thought that Callum Mcinnes was still holding back, he doubted whether Finn's friend knew exactly where he'd gone to. If he did, then he was an accomplished liar. Duncan doubted it. Callum didn't seem like the type. It was possible his own emotional link to the boy could be clouding his judgement. However, he pushed that thought to the side for now.

Walking out into the car park at the front of the hall, Duncan saw both Fraser and Ronnie Macdonald setting off at the head of their respective groups. Fraser was tasked with walking the northern side of Ardtreck Burn between the stream and Loch Harport. Ronnie was taking the south side, heading up to the headland point and the Ardtreck Lighthouse. They each had a dozen volunteers between them, and all were experienced hikers or locals who understood the land. The last thing anyone wanted was to have to send out rescue parties for a turned ankle, or worse, whilst out searching for young Finn.

The mountain rescue teams were also present, although they'd been tasked with tackling the higher ground where a slip or trip could see someone falling into a gully and be more life threatening. Duncan was unsure of how successful this search would be, but he had to do something to find Finn. With each passing day, the fear in everyone grew that something negative had befallen the young man.

Duncan was joining Caitlyn's group – Caitlyn being the only other CID officer who was involved in this operation – as they walked south of the Minginish Community Hall, across towards the mountain. How long he would stay in attendance, he was unsure. If there were developments in the Talisker Bay case, then he might be needed.

Caitlyn nodded to Duncan that they were all set, and he signalled for them to make a move.

"Can I join you?"

Duncan turned to find Becky standing behind him. His mouth must have fallen open because she smiled.

"I can go with another group if you'd prefer?"

"No… no, it's not that," he said. "I'm… just surprised is all."

"Finn is Callum's best friend. Of course, I'm going to help."

"Aye, of course."

Becky fell into step alongside him as the group headed out, clambering over a nearby fence ringing the hall to keep the sheep out. The search would start there, and the group spread out, a few feet from one another, forming a line and started walking slowly, examining the ground at their feet as they went.

"Do you think he's out here?" Becky asked, lowering her voice so only Duncan would hear her. They were on the end of their search line and had already drifted away to be a few steps behind the others as well.

"Honestly, I don't know," he said, stopping momentarily and looking around them and then up to the heavens. Fortunately, there had been no further snowfall overnight. If there had been then the search would have been even harder, not only covering anything they might find, but also making the ground far more treacherous than it already was.

"You think Callum knows more than he's letting on, don't you?"

Duncan took a moment to choose his words carefully, as they both moved off again.

"Aye. Don't you?"

She tilted her head almost imperceptibly. "Yes."

"What's he said to you?"

Becky shook her head. "Nothing. And that's why I think he knows more than he's saying. Where those two boys are concerned, they're always talking. If something is going on with Finn, then I'm sure Callum will know something about it."

"Then why isn't he talking to us?" Duncan asked, stopping and turning to face her. "I mean, maybe not to me, but to you."

"I think you're overestimating how much willingness a teenager has to discuss his friend's secrets with his mother, Duncan."

Duncan smiled. "Aye, I suppose you're right. Loyalty and all that."

"Yes, something like that," she said. Nodding towards Marsali MacGregor, also a member of Caitlyn's search team, Becky said, "I'm surprised you let her join you out here."

"Marsali?" Duncan asked and Becky nodded. "I asked her not to, but…"

"Aye, she's quite a formidable character, isn't she?"

"You know her well?"

Becky shrugged. "No, not really. Only through Callum and Finn being friends… the odd chance meeting at school, parents evening or a Christmas social. Apart from that... we don't have much to do with the MacGregors."

Duncan picked up something in her tone, but he couldn't quite tell what she meant by it, if anything.

"Do you know Anthony?"

She looked away. "I don't."

Again, there was that tone. He'd heard it enough in their shared history to know there was something she wasn't sharing with him.

"Davey then?"

She nodded. "They are mates. They go out drinking together... watch the rugby, that sort of thing."

"Speaking of whom, you didn't answer me the other night."

She turned to face him, the wind blowing her hair across her face. She moved it aside, tucking some behind her ear to try and stop it but the breeze was stiff, and the action made little difference.

"What question was that?" she asked innocently.

"Davey, is he behaving himself?"

She pursed her lips momentarily and nodded. "He's been better. It's almost like a switch was flicked within him before Christmas."

Duncan nodded. It might have been Duncan flicking that switch, suggesting he'd launch him off a cliff if he laid a finger on Becky or her children ever again.

"Aye, that's good to hear."

Becky smiled weakly. Duncan knew that leopards didn't change their spots, and domestic abusers wouldn't cease attacking their victims. It was only a matter of time.

"He's been going to counselling sessions," Becky said. "He goes across to Kyle once a fortnight."

"That's good."

"He's trying, Duncan." She met Duncan's eye. "He is, you know? He's trying to face his demons. I'm sure it's hard for you to believe that—"

"It's got nothing to do with me," Duncan said. "I don't care what he gets up to, as long as he doesn't come at you or the bairns, you know?"

She smiled at him, and the years seemed to fall away from her face. The lines around her eyes, the ones formed by a harsh and stressful life, softened momentarily and she looked much as she had done twenty years earlier when they were childhood sweethearts.

"I wish we could go back a way," he said quietly. "I'd do things differently."

Becky's smile faded. "Don't do that, Duncan."

"Do what?"

"Say things that just aren't true… and even if they were, it's impossible… unless you've invented the ability to time travel in the last couple of months."

He felt hurt. He meant what he said.

"I would do it differently," he argued. "I'd have been there for you and the little man—"

"Duncan, you couldn't wait to get shot of me… and if you'd known about Callum, why would it have been any different to the first pregnancy?"

"That's not fair! I didn't even know you were pregnant the second time around—"

He'd raised his voice and the nearest person to them, an elderly local who Duncan didn't know, glanced over at them. Duncan lowered his voice.

"You didn't tell me…"

"And you know why, Duncan," she said. "We've been over this."

"I know we have but—"

"There is no *but* in this case, Duncan. I didn't want to... I wanted to keep this one, and had I told you then you might have talked me out of it."

"I know that, but—"

She held up her hand. "No... there's no but in this."

"There bloody well is," Duncan said, anger rising in him. "I didn't get to choose. You made the damn choice for me!"

Becky sighed, drawing a deep breath and rolling her eyes.

"No, you're going to listen this time," he said. "You don't get to just dismiss me as if... as if..."

"As if what, Duncan?"

He gritted his teeth, trying to calm himself so as not to say something he'd regret.

"What?" she repeated.

"As if my feelings dinnae count, that's what."

"Of course, they count!"

"Well, they didn't when you made the choice to keep Callum from me, did they?"

"I told you why I did that—"

"It was the biggest decision of my life," Duncan countered, "and you took it away from me! That wasnae fair... and that's on you!"

Becky started at the tone in his voice; far more aggressive than he usually was, even in the heat of the moment. Becky cocked her head.

"That's... a fair comment," she said quietly. Duncan felt guilty then, his anger dissipating.

"Sorry... I didn't mean to be so..."

"That's okay," she said, reaching out and taking his hand in hers and giving it a gentle squeeze. "And you're right. I robbed you of the chance to be... a father to Callum, to see him grow into the lovely young man that he has become."

"And I still can't do it now, either."

She released his hand and it fell limply to his side. The loss of her touch in that moment pained him. He wanted to take her hand in his again, to draw her to him. He was confused. Was it Callum he wanted contact with… or was it Becky? Could he separate one from the other?

"Davey is his father," Becky said. "For good or ill, that is how it is. I'm not going to throw his life up in the air – mine and Eilidh's as well for that matter – just to appease your conscience."

"You think that's what this is about; my conscience?"

"Well… isn't it?" Becky asked him. Duncan frowned, irritated. "Isn't that what this homecoming is all about for you, appeasing your conscience?"

"Where on earth are you getting all this from?"

"You!" she said, apparently surprised by his defensive stance. "You were forced to come back to the island, you admitted as much to me, and then you stuck around having seen the state of your mum's health… likely put on a guilt trip by your sister too, I might add—"

"Hey, leave Roslyn out of this… she's done nothing—"

"Oh aye, hasn't she just!"

"What's that supposed to mean?"

"Aye… well, maybe you should ask her about that."

"Ask her about *what*?" Duncan asked, completely having lost the train of this conversation.

"About Callum… and me… you…"

Duncan stared at her. Becky looked exasperated, shaking her head and stalking off to rejoin the search party leaving Duncan alone, confused.

"Women," Duncan muttered under his breath, not that there was anyone within earshot.

"Over here!"

Duncan looked across to his left. Some of the group was

already at the boundary of the small cemetery and at hearing the shout, several were moving to see what had been found. Caitlyn marshalled them quickly, keeping them back whilst Duncan hurried to make up the ground.

Easing people aside to make room for him to pass, Duncan came alongside Caitlyn, down on her haunches alongside a woman kitted out in full walking gear, poles included. A woollen beanie lay in the long grass at the edge of the cemetery. It was burgundy, knitted in a wide-ribbed pattern, and perfect to withstand a Hebridean chill.

Caitlyn angled her head and using a pen, she pointed to the inner lining of the beanie. Duncan lowered himself to her level and inspected it. There was a discolouration in the burgundy, something having soaked into it. It was a slightly darker shade of the same colour. Duncan and the detective constable exchanged a look but neither confirmed what they both guessed it to be: blood.

Marsali MacGregor arrived, panting, having run across to see what they found, pushing onlookers unceremoniously aside. She fell to her knees and Caitlyn had to put her hands out to stop her from getting too close.

"That's Finn's!" she said, between taking lungfuls of air.

"Are you sure?" Duncan asked.

"Of course, I'm sure! I made it for him," Marsali said, tearing up. She looked around, rising to her feet, studying the surrounding landscape. All that could be seen was the wild grass on the surrounding hills, sporadic vegetation of trees and bushes, all beneath a thick cloud of grey which, along with the cold breeze blowing in off the Minch, gave the area a deep, foreboding atmosphere.

"Finn!" Marsali shouted, the carrying of the sound dampened by the moisture in the air. "Finn!" she screamed again. Everyone present must have felt for her, looking around forlornly, but there was no sign of Marsali's son. She turned back to the rest of the group as Duncan stood up. She stared at him, imploring him with her eyes. "Where is my son?" she asked, choking back the deep sobs that threatened to over-whelm her.

Duncan glanced at Caitlyn. He had no answer for her.

CHAPTER TEN

DUNCAN'S MOBILE rang and he nodded to Caitlyn, letting her know she had to secure the scene for the forensics specialists, while he stepped away from the group. It was Alistair.

"Alistair, what's going on?"

"Had quite an interesting morning, in your absence," Alistair said. Duncan glanced back at where they'd found Finn's hat and frowned.

"Aye, I can say the same."

"Oh, did yer? Any news on the wean?"

"Nothing good," Duncan said.

"Damn. Anyway, we've had a number of insights come through to us today on the phones."

"Go on. I could do with some good news."

"First off, we've had several sightings of our mystery woman across the island," Alistair said. "And a few of them are possibly accurate, and not just Mairearad phoning in to make conversation, you know."

"Do we have a name for her yet?"

"No, let's no' get carried away," Alistair said. "However,

one sighting has her coming onto the island by way of the Mallaig to Armadale ferry."

Duncan was surprised. Although it was a viable route on and off the island, most people came across the bridge at Kyle of Lochalsh. "Driving?"

"On foot."

"Now that is surprising," Duncan said. That particular crossing was often used by those living on the Sleat peninsula for the convenience of reaching the mainland without having to go up through Broadford to cross to Kyle. Using that crossing as a foot passenger was unusual.

"Aye, thought you'd like that."

"When was this?"

"A fortnight ago."

"Where's she been since then," Duncan asked, "assuming it is her?"

"The caller had her described to a tee, the hair, hiking kit and even the bright yellow coat. None of that was released to the press, was it?"

"No, it wasn't," Duncan said, thinking hard. "What else?"

"One of the locals who lives in Eynort... Paddy McPherson... you know his lad, Barry?"

"No. Should I?"

"I suppose not. Anyway, his wean Barry has a drone. He's been up taking footage of the headland, the length of Talisker Bay to the north and south; taking an interest since we found the body, you know. He reckons he's got footage of a campsite north of Talisker Waterfall. No sign of anyone actually present though."

"Do you think it could be hers?"

"Aye, could be. I've asked him to email the footage over but it's such a large file that it keeps getting blocked by the server. Bloody technology, it's great when it works and it's pish when it doesn't."

"Do we know where it is? I mean... coordinates or something to narrow it down?"

"Oh, aye," Alistair said. "I've got a grid reference... but it's not guaranteed to be accurate, and so I wanted to see the footage before we trekked all the way out there."

"Let's do it," Duncan said, checking his watch. The sun set early at this time of the year, and they wouldn't want to be caught out there in the open once they lost the daylight, but if they set off soon then there was no reason why they couldn't make it, provided they knew, more or less, where they were going. "Where am I going?"

DUNCAN PULLED up in front of the metal five-bar gate at the end of the track. From here on, only the local crofter had access to the track heading south across the moorland towards Talisker Bay. He got out of the car and looked around. The road from Fiscavaig made its way steadily upwards until he'd turned off at the access track where the road then doubled back on itself and continued on until it likely reached the coast, looking west across to Oronsay.

The weather had closed in around him and the cloud level was dropping, no doubt shrouding the summits of the Cuillins to the east and making the landscape around him more enclosed. The sheep grazing on the hillside were close together, and some had nestled in against the hillside, likely seeking shelter from what was coming.

"Aye, you know something I don't," he said to them. There was a small assortment of agricultural buildings along the track from the gate, alongside a substantial sheep enclosure, but there didn't appear to be anyone working out of them this day. Duncan climbed over the gate and drew his coat about him, turning his collar up against the wind and thrusting his hands into his pockets as he set off down the track.

Talisker Bay was a good mile or so from where he was, but if Alistair's coordinates were correct, then Duncan would have to hike less than half that distance to find the campsite. Although, Alistair had warned him that he'd need to leave the track and cross the wilds to reach it, just inland from the coast. Having borrowed a GPS navigator from one of the mountain rescue team – offered to him to limit the risk of their needing to come and find him, Duncan guessed – he was confident of finding the location within an hour.

The track was well used by the crofters but when he did leave the well-worn route, progress did slow as he had to pick his way across frozen ground, rocks and pitfalls masked by snowfall that had subsequently frozen. It was tricky, and more than once he cursed to the heavens as he lost his footing and slipped, landing on his backside in a snowdrift.

Fortunately for Duncan, the tent he was looking for was bright red and stood out from some distance in the surrounding white landscape. The backdrop off the coast on a clear day would be the sight of South Uist in the Western Isles, but with the weather as it was, the horizon was lost in a bank of dark grey cloud looking ominous as it made its way towards Skye.

"Hello the camp!" Duncan shouted, keen not to startle anyone by sticking his head through the flap into the interior. He needn't have worried. The entrance to the tent was open to the elements, the outer flaps not tied back, fluttering in the intensifying wind. The tent billowed outwards, straining at the hooks pegging it to the frozen landscape around it. One side of the tent, facing the sea, had snow banked up against it. The campsite must have been established before the latest weather front made landfall.

Coming under the outer covering, Duncan peered into the tent, seeing a single sleeping bag stretched out on the ground sheet along with a rucksack leaning against the canvas at the far end. To his right, just inside the tent was a portable stove with a connected gas canister. Next to this was a small skillet and a coffee pot.

"A camper after my own heart," he said quietly. Tentatively moving inside, Duncan found some reading material, magazines and a paperback lying next to the sleeping bag. He was loath to touch anything, just in case, and tilted his head to try and see what they were. The magazines were nature and wildlife based whereas the book was an old romance novel. It was tatty, the cover dog-eared. Was it a favourite or had it been purchased in a charity shop? A bookmark protruded from roughly the halfway point and its position on top of the other literature suggested it was the last thing read.

Using the end of a pen to lift the flap of the rucksack, Duncan looked inside. There were clothes neatly rolled and stored to make practical use of the available storage space. All in all though, the camper was travelling fairly light. He found another bag in the corner which contained food. All of it was still in date and some of it was locally branded. If this was their mystery woman's site and she had indeed crossed as a foot passenger by way of Mallaig, Duncan figured she'd likely purchased these items at the Armadale Stores. It was the only outlet in that area if this was the way she'd been heading. With luck, the shop would have her on CCTV. Duncan made a mental note to have Angus chase up that lead.

Beside the bag containing the foodstuffs Duncan noticed

an Ordnance Survey map, open and folded to reveal this area – the Talisker Stack was visible – along with a set of pocket binoculars. Moving the binoculars aside, he squinted to see the details of the map. There were parts just off the coast that had been circled with red pen but as far as Duncan could tell, they were merely encompassing open water. He found that odd.

Backing out of the tent, he was hit by the force of the intensifying wind and a cold intake of breath made him worry for what was coming. Looking out over the water, something caught his eye but he couldn't make out the detail, as sea mist was rolling in towards the island. He went back into the tent and came back with the binoculars, figuring it didn't appear that this was a crime scene, and he had the urge to check something out.

It didn't take much to bring the view into focus and Duncan looked down at what had piqued his interest. There were six circular pens lying just off the coast in the distance. It was one of the many salmon farms that now made up such a large sector of the island's economy. Thinking on it, they could be what the red circles had denoted. At least, they were in the right area. But why would someone be studying them?

Duncan felt eyes upon him. It was something of a sixth sense that he'd always had, often catching people casually checking him out, or just having the sense that he was being watched. However, as he scanned the nearby ground, he couldn't see any signs of movement. Using the binoculars, he looked further afield and then caught sight of a figure in the distance. It was a man, and he was large, heavyset with a thick waxed overcoat. He turned away as Duncan trained the binoculars on him, drawing him into focus. As the figure turned away, Duncan saw his face in side profile. He looked familiar. As the man walked away from him, Duncan took note of his slouching frame and unusual gait, positive now that he knew who it was.

"What are you doing all the way out here," he said to himself, lowering the binoculars as the figure dropped below the crest of the far hillside and disappeared from view.

CHAPTER ELEVEN

DUNCAN GROANED, grasping the door handle to brace himself, as Alistair's pick-up lurched from one side of the track to the other. Alistair attempted to avoid the worst of the potholes, troughs and tears in the ground before them, as they made their way to the coastal site. McKinley's Marine Foods had a small processing yard just inland from the salmon pens, barely a mile or so beyond Fiscavaig.

The tarmac road ended and they'd followed the directions the office had given them, taking the meandering track to the location. Rounding a bend, they came upon a yard, separated from the land by way of an old chain-link fence and a five-bar gate. At one end of the yard were two buildings, one timber clad and the other wrapped and roofed with corrugated metal sheeting. This was rusting in many places and clearly in need of some care.

The smaller building had a sign mounted on the exterior denoting it as the office. The gate was open and Alistair drew the pick-up alongside a silver Mercedes. It was five or six years old, judging from the registration plate, but immaculate apart from the mud and slush thrown up by driving it along the track to the compound. Next to that were two liveried utility vehicles, emblazoned with the company logo and stating the family heritage of the business.

Duncan glanced at the Mercedes as he got out of Alistair's pick-up. "I wouldn't fancy driving that track on a daily basis in that, would you?"

"Nope," Alistair said, patting the bonnet of his vehicle proudly. "I'd much rather be using old Dave, here."

Duncan frowned. "You named your truck Dave?"

"Aye. The bairns said I had to name it… so I called it Dave. What of it?"

Duncan shook his head. "Nothing, I guess." He nodded towards the office and the two of them set off across the yard, avoiding pools of frozen water as they walked. "What do we know of this place?"

"One of the oldest businesses in the finfish industry on the island," Alistair said. "Started up back in the 1960s, around the same time the big firms turned their eyes this way too. Been going ever since."

Duncan read the advertising on the vehicles as they walked past. "Still family owned, is it?"

"Aye, Graeme took it on along with his brother Liam after their father passed away about twenty-odd years ago. Liam sold his shares to Graeme a couple of years back and went off to live somewhere down south, in search of sunnier climes."

"What, like the south of France or something?"

"Dumfries, I think," Alistair said.

"Very sunny are the lowlands," Duncan said with a wry smile.

Their approach was noted and the door to the office opened. A man stepped out to greet them. He was in his fifties, a shock of almost white hair swept up and away from his forehead, neatly kept in place with some sort of hair product. He wore a padded gilet over a fleece-lined check shirt, neither of which was able to hide his belly which hung over the top of his navy flannel trousers. He grinned as he approached, offering Alistair his hand.

"Al MacEachran!" he said, shaking hands firmly. "It's been a while."

"Aye, it has Graeme," Alistair said, releasing the handshake and gesturing to Duncan. "This is DI McAdam."

Graeme offered his hand to Duncan who smiled politely as they shook. Graeme McKinley looked momentarily surprised, glancing at the two of them in turn.

"I didn't expect to have a DS and an inspector investigating this."

"Investigating what?" Duncan asked.

"The break-in, of course."

Duncan looked at Alistair who nodded. "Ah... right, yes." Alistair shook his head. "No, we're here about another matter."

"Oh... I see," Graeme said, deflated. "You'd better come inside then." He turned and beckoned them to follow. "It's not a lot warmer in there but at least we have an oil-filled radiator to take the edge off."

The interior of the structure was basic, windows to both side elevations and enough space for two desks and a row of filing cabinets. Beyond that, there was a small storeroom in which Duncan noted a tiny sink and a kettle beside a microwave. Graeme noticed Duncan looking around.

"I know it's not much, but this is only the site office. We only work out of here when we're harvesting. The main office is back at the house where the wife and I run things."

"Where's the house?" Duncan asked, out of polite curiosity.

"Sconser," Graeme said. "A little way out of the village, overlooking Loch Sligachan."

"Great spot," Duncan said.

"Forgive me, but when you phoned and asked to meet me to talk about the business, I thought you meant the break-in. I only said to come out this way because I thought that's what you were on about, Alistair."

"Oh, did yer, aye?" Alistair said. "Sorry about the confusion."

"You had a break-in here then?" Duncan asked, looking around and wondering what the point of such an action would be.

"Aye," Graeme said. "They came in through the back window of the storeroom there," he said, gesturing through the open door at the far end of the building, "and then wrought havoc in here."

"What did they take?"

Graeme shrugged. "Nothing as far as we could tell. We just found the cabinets forced open... the contents strewn about. Idle kids, I reckon."

"It's some way to come to carry out some vandalism," Duncan said. "I can think of any number of other places that are far more accessible."

"Aye, but that'll be it, won't it? They're not going to be disturbed out this way. Must have been local weans... from Fiscavaig or Portnalong... not far anyway." He looked at Alistair, his eyes narrowing. "You'd think they'd be easy to find all the way out here."

Alistair tilted his head. "The investigation is still ongoing—"

"Aye, we could do with an update."

"I'll have the assigned DC get in touch," Alistair said flatly.

"I'd appreciate that, thank you," Graeme said. Alistair

nodded. "So... if it's not the break-in, what does bring you out this way?"

They all sat down, Graeme behind a desk that was overflowing with so many bits of paper it would make Russell McLean's desk look tidy. Duncan wanted to play his cards close to his chest, unsure as he was of the interest that the fish farm held for him.

"Can we talk a bit about your business?" Duncan asked.

Graeme spread his hands wide. "Aye, of course we can. What would you like to know?"

"This is a salmon farm, right?" Duncan asked, simply stating the obvious in order to get the conversation going. "I gather the industry is thriving in our waters."

"Correct. In Scotland, as an industry, we produce some one hundred and fifty thousand tonnes of salmon each year... it's worth over a billion pounds per year and makes up the UK's largest food export market."

Duncan was impressed. "I didn't realise it was so... big," he said, struggling to think of a better word. Graeme laughed.

"Aye, you'd be surprised. It's one of the largest employers on the island now, much as it is in the Western Isles, off the coast of Argyll, as well as around Orkney and Shetland."

"What is it about those areas specifically; the water?"

"In a way, aye," Graeme said, sitting back in his chair. "Here in Scotland, our hatcheries use imported fertilised eggs to produce larval and juvenile fish. Once these hatch, the fry can be grown in tanks either using freshwater flow-through or land-based RAS—"

"RAS?" Duncan asked.

"Sorry, Recirculating Aquaculture Systems," Graeme explained. Duncan had no idea what that meant but nodded politely. "Then we transfer them to lake-based cage systems through the parr stages to smolt and then from there, they are transferred into open net pens to continue their growth until they reach harvest age."

"And that's what we see off the coast; these pens?" Duncan asked. Graeme nodded. "How large are they? They don't look very big when viewed from land."

"They're deceptive. A forty-metre-wide cage can hold approximately seventy thousand fish."

Duncan's eyes widened. "That's a lot of fish."

Graeme smiled. "It's big business."

"And how long does it take for them to mature?"

"Wild salmon take anywhere from twenty-four to thirty-six months to reach maturity, whereas with farmed salmon it is more like six to twelve."

"That's quite a saving."

"Time is money," Graeme said.

"Speaking of which, how is business?" Duncan asked.

Graeme appeared to shift in his seat, his smile fading a little as he looked away at some far-off point on the wall opposite. He rocked his head gently from side to side. "I'd be lying if I said it'd never been better."

"Problems?" Alistair asked.

"Not unlike any other business operating in a competitive market," Graeme said. He sighed. "Just as you find in any industry, if there's money to be made then there's competition... and when there's big money to be made, then that competition is often found in the form of the big guns." He shook his head. "We do okay... but these large overseas operations are targeting the competition."

Duncan sat forward. "Targeting? In what way?"

Graeme shook his head. "Like I said, this industry is a large employer, one of the biggest in the area. Politicians like job creation... and that puts the pressure on to grant new licences for more farms. Larger farms… create more demand… and on we go."

"Are the larger firms undercutting you?"

Graeme laughed. "They undercut our prices, offer higher wages to the staff, who have their own bills to pay, and the cost of living keeps going up. We either match the pay they are being offered or run the risk of losing our staff… and that's when they come calling to buy us out."

"They want your business?" Duncan asked.

"If they can buy it lock, stock and barrel, then they'll happily do that… at a hefty discount, of course. If you hold out…"

"What happens then?" Duncan asked.

Graeme shrugged. "I guess we're soon going to find out."

"You don't want to sell?"

Graeme smiled but it was a sad expression. "My father started this business back in the days before there even was salmon farming on any scale of note. Then a big firm came here to the Highlands and really got it off the ground. My father's business got swept along with it, which was wonderful for business, for the family… great times." His expression turned melancholy. "We promised him on his deathbed that we'd keep it going, make the McKinley name synonymous with high-quality, healthy produce." He fixed his eye on Duncan. "We made a commitment."

"Was this you and your brother, Liam?"

"Aye…" Graeme looked away at mention of his brother, "but some of us only paid lip service to that commitment."

"You bought him out, didn't you?" Duncan asked.

He nodded. "A few years back. To be fair, Liam's heart was never in it. He was always into cars; owns a dealership down in Glasgow now."

"Mercedes?" Alistair asked.

Graeme smiled. "No, BMW. Which is why I drive—"

"A Mercedes," Alistair said with a smile. "Nice."

Graeme nodded. "I do enjoy pulling up at his house when we do get together, which isn't often these days." Graeme frowned. "As interesting as this trip down memory lane is what has it got to do with yous lot?"

Duncan took a breath. "Well... you've heard about the body we found on Talisker Beach?" Graeme nodded, looking stern. "We think she was camping out on the headland—"

"In this weather?" Graeme asked. "Madness."

"True," Duncan said, "and in her tent, at least we believe it is her tent, we found a map. On it, areas of the sea were circled... and we think they are noting where your open net pens are located."

Graeme stared at Duncan. "Why would she do that?"

"We were hoping you could tell us that."

Graeme McKinley thought about it for a moment, his lips pursed.

"Any idea?" Duncan asked.

"I know some people are not happy with the increase in the number of farms about the island... or the increase in the size of the industry as a whole."

"Why might that be?" Duncan asked. "I would have thought that farming would preserve the wild stocks from overfishing?"

"You would think so, wouldn't you," Graeme said, "but some of these people are never happy, no matter what you do."

"What people?"

"Activists... environmentalists... you know the sort," Graeme said. "The ones who think we should knit our own sandals and make our clothes out of grass."

"They object to your business?"

Graeme shook his head. "They object to *everything!* I can't make a business move without having to counter accusation after accusation… one block after another."

"In what way?" Duncan asked, sensing Graeme was a frustrated man.

"They object to us operating too close to the rivers… saying we stop the wild salmon from travelling up them to spawn, and so we relocate… away from the lochs," Graeme said, throwing his hands in the air, "and then they object to how much waste the fish produce, saying it is polluting the water. So, we move again out into deeper water. That way, the waste is distributed over a wider area and lessens the problem. Guess what?"

"Still no' happy," Alistair said.

Graeme pointed at Alistair. "Spot on, Alistair. They are still not happy, and they won't ever be. It's becoming impossible to do business… unless…"

"You're one of the big players?" Duncan asked.

Graeme nodded forlornly. "Aye… the system is picking off the little guys one by one. If it's not increased regulations… competition or rising feed stocks… the margins are narrowing so much that it's just becoming impossible."

Duncan took everything in. "Tell me, have you had any direct contact with any activists or protesters? I'm thinking about your break-in."

Graeme was dismissive. "No… that was just kids, I'm certain. Why would anyone target us? There are far bigger fish to fry than us, if you'll pardon the pun."

Duncan glanced at Alistair who shrugged. Duncan turned back to the businessman. "Can you think of any reason why someone would be paying such close attention to your business?"

Graeme shrugged and then shook his head, splaying his hands wide. "Why on earth would they?"

"Okay, Mr McKinley, I think we'll leave it there for now. Thank you for your time today."

They all rose, and Duncan shook hands with Graeme. Alistair winked at him before heading for the door. He looked back as Duncan passed him, stepping outside.

"I'll have my DC get in touch, Graeme," Alistair said. "Even if he hasn't made any headway, he should at least give you a courtesy call to let you know what has been done."

"Thanks very much, Alistair," Graeme said, coming to the door and standing there as the two detectives walked back to the pick-up. By the time they were both in the cabin, Graeme had gone back inside.

Alistair exchanged a look with Duncan as he started the engine. "What do you make of that then?"

Duncan arched his eyebrows. "Whoever was watching those pens was doing so for a reason."

"And that reason being?"

Duncan shrugged. "Damned if I know."

CHAPTER TWELVE

THEY WERE DRIVING SLOWLY through Merkadale, stuck in a line of vehicles behind an ancient tractor, which Duncan thought incredible that it was still functioning, when his mobile rang. It was Angus Ross, back in Portree.

"Hello, sir."

"Angus, how are you getting on?"

"A couple of things for you, sir," he said. "We've had confirmation from the forensic lab that the substance found on the hat Caitlyn found in the cemetery at Portnalong is definitely blood—"

"Thought as much," Duncan said, glancing sideways at Alistair who was grumbling.

"It wouldn't hurt to just pull over for a second to let us all past," he muttered.

"Have they been able to compare the sample with that supplied by Marsali MacGregor to confirm a match?" Duncan asked.

"Erm... no."

"No, they haven't managed to match it, or they haven't done the comparison?"

"They haven't matched it," Angus said, matter-of-factly. "It's no' Finn's blood."

Duncan was surprised. "And they are sure? I mean, they haven't cocked up or anything?"

"Not as far as I know," Angus said. "Although... how would I know?"

"Fair point. Have you told his parents?"

"I spoke to Mrs MacGregor earlier, aye. She seemed..."

"Seemed?"

"Like... a bit off about it, you know?"

Duncan frowned. "No, not really. Is she still saying the hat is Finn's?"

"Absolutely, she's adamant it is his."

"Interesting," Duncan said. "Can you have them run the sample through the database against anything we do have on record. You never know, it might yield a match."

"I can do that, sir."

"Anything else?" Duncan asked.

"Yes, as it happens. I spoke with the ferry staff, you know, the ones working out of Mallaig on the Armadale crossing. One of them is absolutely certain he saw our victim crossing with them. He was the one who phoned in—"

"Aye. You followed up and got confirmation. Good work. Did he have anything else useful to say?"

"She definitely left on foot, walking up from the ferry towards the stores. The ferry didn't have a fast turnaround, so he was one of a couple who went up to the stores to buy some food for lunch... anyway, that doesn't matter. They saw her outside the stores in the car park, hitching a lift."

"Hitching or being picked up?" Duncan clarified.

"He said hitching. She got into a lorry. It was a Co-op one that had been on the same crossing as her. Maybe she got chatting with the driver or something."

"Okay, see if you can trace the driver. He might have some knowledge of where she was heading."

"Will do. There's one more thing though…"

"Go on."

"I've just had a really odd phone call come through into the incident room… and I don't know what to make of it."

"Try me," Duncan said.

"It was from a guy who claims to have seen the victim…"

"And… that's a good thing. Where?"

"That's just it… it's not only where but who she was seen with," Angus said, hesitant. "It was in Bracadale."

"Bracadale?" Duncan repeated, reaching out and tapping Alistair's forearm and pointing towards the left. Alistair was signalling to turn right at the junction, onto the A863 towards Sligachan.

"What do we want to go that way for?" Alistair protested.

"Head for Bracadale," Duncan told him, insistent.

"That'll add twenty minutes at least—"

Duncan took the phone away from his mouth and offered Alistair a withering look.

"Okay," Alistair said, "Bracadale." He switched the indicator to the other direction and pulled away. Two cars were to his left now, heading that way and they had to stop to let him past. The first in the line sounded their horn in anger. "Wrong time of the month for him, obviously," Alistair said as he politely waved an apology and smiled at the man driving the car.

Duncan turned his focus back to Angus. "Who was she talking to?"

"Anthony MacGregor," Angus said.

"Are you serious?"

"Aye, I know, right. That's what I thought, and he is pretty sure he saw the two of them talking... Anthony and this woman... or maybe arguing."

"Arguing?"

"He wasn't sure, but that's what he said at first, aye. Back peddled a bit when I pressed him on it, but that was his first thought."

"Give me the address for him, would you, Angus?"

THEY DROVE past the MacGregor house, sitting above the road on the hillside, and crossed the causeway before taking a right turn off the A863 and then immediately turning off towards Lower Totarder. The road looped back upon itself and they crossed a cattle grid before continuing on with the loch to their right. The road bore left, narrowing as it followed the course of the loch which also narrowed before becoming the mouth of the River Amar.

Heading inland now, the hills to either side of the valley grew steeper and soon they came upon the scattered crofting township of Lower Totarder. Little white buildings dotted across the landscape, nestling into the hillside with a hundred feet or perhaps a little more between them. There were ancillary agricultural structures here and there, along with unladen flatbed trailers, livestock cages and assorted farmyard paraphernalia. This was still very much a working community. Whereas others were given over to holiday lets and second homes, people in this community still worked the land much as their families had done before them for generations.

"It should be this one on the left," Duncan said, pointing out a house further up the hillside.

"It should be, because we're running out of road," Alistair said. They were almost at the end of the single track now. The tarmac had ended a hundred metres or so behind them and they were on frozen mud now. The house was looking tired, the white paint was now stained with a brown tinge to it. The windows were modern, double glazed and plastic framed. A lean-to conservatory was attached on the western elevation of the property, likely to make the most of the setting sun later in the day.

Beyond the property was a large arrangement of barns, large by Skye crofting standards anyway. A lone figure was sweeping out the concrete slab and he paused, leaning on the broom as they got out of Alistair's pick-up.

"Well, you were fast," he said as they approached him.

Duncan looked at him quizzically.

"Which one of you two was I speaking with on the phone earlier?"

Duncan smiled. "Neither. That would have been Detective Constable Ross."

"Aye, that was him."

Duncan produced his identification, showing him his warrant card. "I'm DI McAdam and this is DS MacEachran. We'd like to follow up on what you discussed with DC Ross earlier."

The man shrugged. "If you like. I didnae think it was all that interesting, but whatever..."

"Mr McPhee, isn't it?" Duncan asked.

"Aye, Laurie is the name I prefer."

"Laurie," Duncan said. "Can you tell us what you told DC Ross, please?"

"Sure. I was out on the old McLeod place... I took on their ten acres when old Tommy couldn't manage anymore. Anyway, I was coming back on the quad," he said, thumbing towards an all-terrain quad bike in the barn behind him, "with ma dog and I saw them."

"The woman from the artist's impression—"

"Aye... speaking with Anthony, from across the way," he pointed in the general direction of the MacGregor house on the far side of the causeway. "I said to your lad, that was him, definitely."

Duncan looked back along the track. "Where were they?"

"Oh... as you turn off the main road and head down this way, there's a cutting into the hillside. It's used as a pen when we gather the sheep in... they were there, going at it."

Alistair raised an eyebrow. "Can you define *going at it?* Do you mean in a biblical sense—"

"Och no! Nothing like that," Laurie said. "But it looked heated to me. I mean, I know Anthony can be like a bear with a sore head at times... but he shoulda learned by now, that you dinnae mess with a redheaded lassie; all fire and passion they are."

"What were they arguing about?"

He shrugged. "How should I know. I'm not one to stick ma nose into things. What goes on with folks is none of ma business."

"How well do you know him, Anthony?"

Laurie shrugged. "Well enough I guess. Have a drink with him at new year or have a chat if we're passing, but he's a funny old sod at the best of times. Him and his wee wifey."

"Marsali?"

"Aye. Quiet one, she is. You're never quite sure what's going on inside her head."

"How sure are you that the woman you saw talking to Anthony was the woman in the impression?"

Laurie's brow furrowed and smacked his lips. "I'd say ninety-five percent."

"That's pretty high."

He nodded. "I know... but I've a memory for faces. No' so

much for names… but faces are ma thing. It was her. Unless you're looking for another flame-haired woman in walking gear and a bright yellow coat."

Duncan and Alistair exchanged glances. Duncan shook his head. "No, just the one for now."

"Aye, well then," Laurie said, nodding, "it was her."

"When was this?"

"Ah… now that I'm not so sure. I'm good with faces—"

"But no' names or dates," Alistair said drily.

"Aye, we cannae be perfect with everything."

"Speak for yourself," Alistair said. Duncan looked at him and Alistair smiled.

"I think… it would be two weeks ago… this coming Thursday."

"That makes it eleven days ago," Duncan said.

Laurie nodded. "Aye, sounds about right. We hadn't had the snow at that point. It was Baltic, but I hadn't looked to bring the flock down from the high ground by that point."

"And you said they were having a heated conversation," Duncan said, "and was it physical?"

"No, they were standing apart, but they were both flushed red in the face, you know?"

"Did they see you?"

He shrugged. "They might have heard me passing. It's not like the quad is quiet and I was towing a trailer as well," he said, pointing to a small trailer off to his right. "It was midday-ish though. There were a few cars about… but neither of them had eyes for anyone but each other."

"It stuck in your mind though."

"I thought maybe it was some kind of road rage incident or something."

"Were there two cars then?"

He thought about it and then shook his head. "Come to

think about it, no. There was just Anthony's pick-up. Maybe she was crossing, and he nearly ran her over or something. You never know with him, he's prone to a few too many bevvies of an evening, you know. Might have been hung over."

Duncan nodded. "And you never saw this woman again?"

He shook his head. "No, I cannae say I have seen her... either before or since. I'd mind if I did. I have a memory—"

"For faces, aye," Alistair said, "you told us."

"That's right; faces, but no' names or... erm..."

"Dates," Alistair said.

"Aye, right."

"Okay, thanks for the information. It's very helpful," Duncan told him. "Thanks for coming forward as well. We appreciate it."

"You dinnae think Anthony did her in, do you?"

Duncan was surprised. "What makes you ask that?"

Laurie McPhee shrugged. "Well... you're looking for news on this lassie, who's dead, and Anthony was with her... arguing. What am I supposed to think?"

"I'd advise not jumping to any wild conclusions, Mr McPhee," Duncan said calmly.

"It's not a wild theory if you see them having a slanging match and then she turns up dead."

"Almost two weeks later," Duncan said. "There's a lot that can happen in between. We're simply trying to find out more about the lady who has passed away."

"Well, start with Anthony MacGregor." Laurie angled his head and offered them a knowing look. "Oh, what about his wee lad. Has he turned up yet?"

"Finn?" Duncan asked.

"Aye, Finn. Nice lad."

Duncan shook his head. "We're still looking for him."

Laurie frowned. "Shame. Nice lad."

They left Laurie to his work, walking back to the pick-up. Alistair put his tongue firmly against the inside of his cheek, looking hard at Duncan across the bonnet of his pick-up.

"Out with it," Duncan said.

Alistair smiled wryly. "While we're here, shall we call in on Anthony and ask him what the hell he's playing at?"

Duncan looked back down the track in the direction of Bracadale, however, his instinct told him it was too soon. He shook his head. "No, not yet."

"Not yet! Seriously?"

"We don't have anything to talk to him about, not really."

"What?" Alistair asked, raising his eyebrows and pointing a finger towards Laurie McPhee. "After what he's just—"

"The eyewitness testimony of a man who drove past on a quad bike eleven days – maybe eleven days – ago, who has a memory for faces. That's it."

"It puts him talking to our victim," Alistair said, "who, I'll remind you, was stabbed."

"I'm not saying we won't speak to him," Duncan countered, "but I'd like us to have more than this to put to him. Say we call in now, ask him who he was talking to and he says it wasn't him. What then?"

Alistair's forehead furrowed momentarily. "Aye... I see your point."

"We find out who she is... then we might find a link he can't deny," Duncan said. "That's when we speak to him; forearmed is forewarned."

Alistair shook his head. "Sheesh! I've said it before, and I'll say it again; you take all the fun out of this job sometimes, you really do."

"I tell you what we should do though."

"What's that then?" Alistair asked.

"The blood sample on Finn MacGregor's hat…"

"Run it against our victim?"

Duncan nodded and opened the passenger door. "Run it against our victim," he repeated as he got in, hoping he was way off the mark with that thought. However, thanks to their eyewitness, the two cases were coming together.

Looking back towards the barn, Laurie McPhee waved them off absently. Duncan returned the wave as Alistair set the pick-up in motion.

CHAPTER THIRTEEN

Alistair dropped Duncan off in Somerled Square before heading for the rear entrance to the police station where he'd park. Space was always limited in that car park but Alistair had a space and no one ever used it, even when he took his annual leave. Duncan felt his energy lacking and went in search of caffeine. There was no way he could stomach one of the freeze-dried instant cups they had available in CID. A decent cup of coffee was about the only thing he ever craved; once he set aside physical company and a single malt anyway.

Across the square, past the bus station, Duncan entered The Granary, his coffee shop of choice. In such a central location it was a popular hangout for locals and tourists alike, although he was pleased to find the queue nowhere near what it was in spring through to autumn. He didn't need to place his order, simply acknowledging the staff with a smile was enough for them to get it ready.

"Can you throw in one of these ham and cheese toasties as well, please?" Duncan said. The barista nodded.

"Do you want it warmed through?"

"Aye, please."

"I can get that."

Duncan turned to see a bright-eyed young woman rise from her seat at a table by the window, coming to stand beside him. She smiled and Duncan nodded.

"Afternoon, Katie," Duncan said. "You know there are rules about bribing the polis for information, don't you?"

"But I haven't asked you any questions?" she said, smiling innocently.

Duncan shook his head, smiling ruefully. "Yet."

"Sorry?"

He turned to her. "You haven't asked me any questions... yet. I sense you're about to though, and I'll tell you now, I can't give you anything more than I gave you at the press conference."

Katie pouted, tilting her head to one side.

"But you can at least sit with me over a cup of coffee, couldn't you?"

He'd been clear, however, something in her demeanour piqued his curiosity. He'd always been straight with the young journalist who wrote for the island's most widely distributed newspaper, with a growing digital footprint, or so the editor told him when they bumped into one another at a pre-Christmas bash.

Duncan cast a searching eye over her expression, and she remained steadfast, unwavering. "All right," he said. "Do you want me to buy you a coffee or something?"

"No, thank you. I'm fine."

Duncan nodded and, looking to the barista, he caught her attention. "Can you make that to have in?"

She nodded and Duncan tapped his debit card against the terminal and the payment went through. He then accompanied a satisfied Katie back to her table. Pulling out a chair opposite her, he sat down as she picked up her half-empty cappuccino, sipping at the contents and then wiping the chocolate powder and foam from her lip with a napkin. Duncan noted a second cup, empty, along with a plate bearing a few crumbs and another with sticky, sugary residue on it.

"It looks like you've been here for much of the day," he said. "A big story brewing in the catering industry, is there?"

Katie shook her head. "No such thing, as far as I know. Unless you've heard something?" She asked the question with a mischievous grin.

Duncan laughed. "No. And if I had, I—"

"Wouldn't tell me anyway," she said, smiling. "You have such a bad view of people in my profession, DI McAdam. Where does that come from?"

"Working in Glasgow," he said. His coffee and toastie were brought across and set down in front of him. He thanked the barista.

"You're welcome, Duncan," she said, leaving them and moving back behind the counter to serve the next customer.

"Well, we're not all sharks like those you got used to in the big smoke, you know."

"Aye, some of you are even worse," he said, lifting his toastie and immediately putting it down as the melted cheese burned his fingers. Katie Matheson feigned offence.

"Now, if I didn't know you better, I'd be insulted by that comment, Duncan."

"DI McAdam… when I'm on the clock, young lady."

"Miss Matheson," she said firmly, "if we're keeping the boundaries."

Duncan smiled. "Okay, what are we talking about? Because," he said, glancing around, "I almost have the feeling you've been hanging out in here waiting to catch me… by chance, obviously."

"Obviously," she said. "I mean, it's not like you don't

come in here almost every day at more or less the same time… and always on your way into the office first thing, is it?"

"I am a creature of habit… that is true."

"How's Grace?" Katie asked.

Duncan fixed her with a focussed gaze, blowing the steam off his coffee before sipping it. "Grace?"

"Och… you know, Grace! She's a pal of mine from school. She told me the two of you have been… out together, on occasion recently."

"Aye… that's true. I've not seen her for a bit though."

"Something you ought to rectify," Katie said, arching her eyebrows knowingly. "If you know what's good for you anyway."

Duncan wasn't comfortable discussing his semi-casual relationship with a local journalist, however close she might be to Grace. Perhaps, particularly because she was so close to Grace.

"Aye, I'll call in." He sat forward, resting his elbows on the table. "Now, I'm sure you didn't try to ambush me over a macchiato and a ham and cheese toastie, to discuss my relationship with Grace…"

"No, I didn't, that's true," Katie said. "How is it going with the investigation into the woman found out at Talisker?"

"I told you, I'm not at liberty to say any more than I did at the press conference."

"So you're not getting anywhere then," Katie said, nodding.

Duncan laughed, risking a bite of his toastie. His stomach growled. He hadn't eaten since breakfast and that had been nothing more than a bowl of cereal eaten on the fly.

"Working on it," he said, covering his mouth with the back of his hand as he chewed.

"And Finn MacGregor?" Katie asked. "Any developments there?"

Duncan's eyes narrowed as he detected a shift in her tone.

"Not found him yet, no, but we will."

She nodded, absently toying with the handle on her cup, rotating it on the saucer. "Are they connected; the two cases?"

Duncan eyed her as he chewed, swallowing before answering. "What makes you ask?"

"Ah… answering a question with a question," she said, tilting her head to one side. "That's evasive behaviour, DI McAdam. Policing one-o-one."

"Aye… but I am the policeman, remember. Who's connecting the two cases?"

"I am," Katie said flatly.

Duncan's eyes narrowed and he picked up a napkin, wiping the grease from his fingers. "What makes you say that?"

"Are you telling me they're not connected then?"

"No… I'm telling you… the investigations are ongoing, but I sense there's something you're not telling me… and maybe you should."

"Finn MacGregor is good pals with Callum Mcinnes, isn't he?"

"Aye, but what's that got to do with anything?"

"They are inseparable, so I hear… and where one goes, the other is usually not too far behind. And Callum is no stranger to trouble recently."

Duncan nodded. "So I'm told. But you didn't answer the question, why are you linking the cases?"

Katie picked up her cup and finished drinking what remained. Duncan thought she was considering her next words carefully. She still didn't answer the question, altering tack completely.

"Have you spoken to Graeme McKinley at all?" she asked, casually. Too casually in Duncan's mind.

"Have you been stalking me or something? There are laws to restrict that, you know?"

"Ah, so you have spoken to him."

Duncan wasn't going to confirm it. He sat back, lifting his coffee cup. "You tell me why I should."

Katie looked around them briefly, possibly checking they wouldn't be overheard. The Granary was quiet now though, this late in the day and the staff were making ready to close up, cleaning down the empty tables and packing the food stuffs away for the next day. There was no one else sitting in the shop.

"The word is that Graeme McKinley's firm is in trouble," she said, lowering her voice anyway.

"And when you say trouble, you mean…"

"I mean big trouble. He could go under within the next couple of months at this rate."

Duncan's brow furrowed. Graeme had described the industry as operating under tough conditions, but he didn't get the sense from their conversation that the business was in trouble. "And why should this interest me?"

"McKinley has been playing the system."

"Explain," Duncan said, lifting his cup to his lips.

"There's been a lot of push back against the farming of salmon in particular," Katie said. "There have been numerous studies highlighting the ecological impact the industry has on wild species, the eco systems of both the fresh and sea water locations along with the health concerns surrounding the fish."

"I thought salmon was considered healthy," Duncan said. "I mean, it's fish… and farming reduces the impact on wild stocks, right?"

Katie nodded with a half-smile on her face. "You have spoken to Graeme, haven't you?"

"I might have," Duncan said, returning to his toastie.

"And did he lay it on about how hard done by he's been by the environmental concerns?"

"He might have," Duncan said, smiling briefly as he took another bite.

"I'll bet," she said, shaking her head. "Did he mention how he's been exploiting loopholes in the regulations to bypass the controls on animal welfare concerns?"

Duncan arched an eyebrow but didn't comment. Katie nodded.

"Aye, didn't think so."

"What's he been up to then?" Duncan asked.

"The sea farms suffer from parasitic infestations… sea lice which harm the fish, spread throughout the farm population and is then transferred to the wild species, risking harm to the wild Atlantic salmon population and sea trout as well."

"Sounds bad."

"It is. Which is why there are regulations to mitigate the problem. It is estimated that anything from twenty percent of the farm population dies in the cages prior to harvesting, which is appalling. Farms are responsible for submitting sea lice data to Marine Scotland on a weekly basis and that data is used to monitor the businesses in relation to its environmental responsibilities."

"Aye, sounds… like it's in hand."

"Apart from the businesses can suspend the reporting of that data if they are *harvesting*. The withdrawal period, the one leading up to the slaughter for market process, gives them the opt out of the mandatory process."

"And you're saying McKinley has been… what… extending these periods to avoid reporting the infestations?"

"McKinley has handed over no counts for almost thirty weeks now," Katie said, looking around again and adopting a conspiratorial tone. "That translates to zero reported figures for over six months of the last eighteen months of the marine production cycle."

Duncan frowned. "I'm sure this – if it's true – puts Graeme McKinley on dodgy ground morally, if not legally… but what does he have to gain—"

"Money! A lot of money," Katie said. "Harvesting of diseased stocks that should rightly face culling to minimise the ecological impact on the ecosystems, maintains his profit levels, if not increases them, and avoids sanctions for animal welfare and the knock-on impacts to costs if he has to maintain proper standards."

Katie sat back in her seat, looking like a weight had been lifted from her shoulders. Duncan sipped at his drink.

"It sounds like you've been looking into this for a while."

"I have," she said quietly, looking down at her hands, cradling them in her lap. "Graeme McKinley has been flouting the rules, the same rules that everyone else operates under, repeatedly and been getting away with it for almost two years."

"That'd make quite a story," Duncan said without any hint of irony. He set his cup down. "Why hasn't anyone run it?"

Katie shook her head. "It's big business… and it's worth a lot to the island. Ever since the fishing industry declined… farming has really boosted the island economy. It's not in anyone's interest to see that damaged."

"But shady practices will damage the wider industry if it comes to light further down the line," Duncan said.

"That was my argument too," she replied forlornly. "And it didn't cut any ice with my editor either."

Duncan sighed. "No one wants to hear the bad side of

something good, do they?"

She shook her head. "At least not from me. Some of the national papers have run similar stories on other companies around the country. I mean, there are two hundred fish farms in Scotland... and even if we're talking about a small percentage who are playing the system to their advantage..."

"It's still a lot of money," Duncan said. Katie agreed. He fixed her with a stern look. "So... where did you get your information from?"

She shot him a coy look. "A good journalist never reveals her sources, Duncan. You know that."

"I'm told that too," he said.

Katie gathered her mobile phone along with her purse, placing them both into her handbag before getting up. She took her coat from where it was draped over an adjacent chair, put it on, freeing her long blonde hair from inside it and pushing it to one side over her shoulder. Looping the straps of her handbag through her right arm and over her shoulder, she looked down at Duncan. Bending down, she picked up a pen, scribbling something on an unused paper napkin and pushed it across the table towards Duncan.

Curious as to what she'd written, Duncan turned the paper to face him. It was a name, Ava Caldwell. It didn't strike him as one he recognised. Glancing up as Katie left the coffee shop, Duncan exhaled. The manager of The Granary looked over at him, tapping an imaginary watch on her wrist. He glanced at the clock on the wall. It was approaching half past five. They usually closed at five. Downing what was left of his macchiato, Duncan scooped up the remainder of his toasted sandwich and headed for the door, waving to the two remaining staff members as he left.

"See you in the morning, Duncan!" they both said in unison.

CHAPTER FOURTEEN

SLEET WAS STEADILY FALLING as Duncan drove over the cattle grid and onto the driveway leading up to the croft. The lights were on inside the house, and he could hear the excited barking of a dog who soon appeared at the window, leaning on the top of a sofa cushion in order to see out of the window.

Duncan got out and made his way around the building to the rear door, seeing the dog leap down from the sofa and knew it was coming to meet him. Despite the cold weather, the door to the kitchen was open and the dog came out, leaping up at Duncan and bouncing on its hind legs as Duncan made a fuss of him, scratching behind the ears.

Pushing the dog aside, he went indoors, the claws of the animal scraping on the lino as it tried to gain traction to get ahead of him. Duncan followed the sound of a loud television and walked into the living room.

"I thought it was you."

Duncan glanced down at his old friend, Archie Mackinnon, sitting in an armchair eating his supper from a bowl. If you could call a bowl of porridge and some fresh fruit supper, at any rate.

"Hey, Archie," Duncan said, nodding towards his food. "Interesting choice for your evening meal."

"I was up late… then away to ma bed early. This is breakfast," Archie said staring straight ahead at the television. It was the evening news.

"What's happening in the world?"

Archie sniffed in between mouthfuls. "No idea. I was just waiting for the weather forecast at the end."

"You still put faith in the BBC forecast of lies?"

Archie chuckled. "I like to see how wrong they get it."

"Well, I can save you the trouble," Duncan said, shaking his coat and watching the melted ice water fall away. "The sleet is coming down. If it gets colder, it'll turn to snow and if it gets warmer, it'll turn to rain. Either way—"

"It's gonna be cold and wet," Archie said. "Aye. I know that sure enough. It's January on Skye. If it was any different, the world will be slipping into the fires of hell."

Duncan laughed, coming around to the sofa and sitting down. The dog leapt up beside him and dropped its head onto his leg, looking up at Duncan with sad eyes.

"When did you last feed your hound?" Duncan asked.

Archie glanced over, smacking his lips, and frowned. "Earlier."

"This morning, afternoon or evening?"

Archie's frown deepened. "Earlier," he repeated.

"Ah, good. Not vague at all."

All the discussion of food appeared to intrigue the dog who raised his head, ears pricked, eyes tracking both men in turn and probably waiting to see which, if any, moved first. When it became clear neither man was going to feed it, the head lowered back to Duncan's leg. Duncan scratched behind his ear and the dog stretched out, getting more comfortable and settling in.

"Dinnae worry, man," Archie said. "I tend to leave the bag open and he helps himself whenever he gets hungry."

"Aye, my mum used to do the same thing."

Archie grinned. "Speaking of whom… how is Mrs McAdam getting on?"

Duncan pictured his mother, sitting beside the window with her thick woollen blanket and knitted throw across her knees, staring out across the water towards Raasay, the best view from her care home window.

"No change," he said. "She still has her good and bad days. Mainly… bad I have to say but there are fleeting glimpses of the person she once was. Ros and I hold onto those as much as we can."

"Precious," Archie said. Duncan nodded. Discussion of his mum and her deterioration amid the onset of her Alzheimer's made him feel melancholy, so Duncan pushed the thoughts aside.

"What have you been up to recently then, Arch?"

Archie shook his head. "Nothing. Same old, same old, you know?"

"Aye. I know." Duncan didn't say anything else for a minute, allowing the silence to grow. Archie didn't appear to mind though. He was comfortable in his own skin and was always himself regardless of who he was talking to.

"I had a letter from Fiona," Archie said, casually.

Usually, the mention of his estranged wife who'd left him for a postmaster down Broadford way, would pitch Archie into a period of self-destruction the likes of which would make an Alcoholics Anonymous meeting group blush. Not this time though.

"How… erm… is she?" Duncan asked, fearful of poking the bear.

"Aye, braw," Archie said, spooning another mouthful of

porridge into his mouth. He pointed at the television. "Here it is!"

They both turned to watch the weather forecaster standing before the map of Scotland. At least the Scottish forecast wasn't as wide of the mark for Skye as the British forecast which would describe the weather in the Highlands and Islands in almost one breath, as if multiple areas didn't have their very own microclimate, even at different elevations of the same town.

Archie gesticulated at the map. "There you have it, Dunc! I'll bet they're at least eight degrees wide of the mark overnight, tonight. Muppets."

It was as if this passed for sport in Archie's mind. The forecast was always wrong. The only time they got it right was when they forecast twenty-four hours of solid rain, and even then, it was due to the fact it was already raining.

"What did Fiona want?" Duncan asked as soon as Archie picked up the remote and turned the television off having set his empty bowl down on the floor beside his chair. The dog hopped off the sofa and scampered over to lick the bowl clean.

"Fiona?" Archie asked, looking confused. "Oh, right... my Fiona." He frowned. "I don't know. The letter was from her solicitor."

"Not from her then?"

Archie shook his head. "No. Did I say it was?"

Duncan nodded.

"Ah, no. I should have said. It was from the solicitor, who speaks for her now. That bast—" Archie raised a flat palm, then pointed his forefinger in the air. "The man she's taken up with," he said softly, "you see, I'm learning to maintain my composure," he said, smiling. Duncan returned the smile. "He won't let her speak to me directly, so all communication has to come through the solicitor. Weedy little man, he is. I could hammer him into the ground like a tent peg, you know."

Duncan sighed. Archie raised a flat palm once again.

"I won't, obviously. I'm not daft."

"What did he say?" Duncan asked. "In the letter."

"Oh, she wants to move the official separation onto the next stage."

"Which is?"

Archie frowned, looking to the ceiling and searching for the right word. "Divorce, I think."

"Oh, that's bad."

Archie shook his head. "To be expected, sooner or later."

"Anything else in the letter?"

"She wants half the assets of the marriage."

Duncan arched his eyebrows, looking around. Archie followed his view.

"I know what you're thinking, Duncan. There isn't much, is there?"

"I wasn't thinking that at all."

"No?"

Duncan angled his head to one side. "Okay... the thought crossed my mind. Does she want half the croft?"

"She cannae have that. It's all tied to ma family... the crofting commission would have something to say... all very messy."

"So... nothing to worry about then?"

"Erm... well... there is the inheritance."

Duncan looked at him quizzically. He hadn't known of a family bereavement. "What inheritance?"

"You remember my old dad... worked himself to death on this place? Always struggling?"

"Aye."

"Well, he had a niece, daughter of my uncle who I didn't

know, seeing as they fell out before I was born – I never knew her either – but seemingly she was worth a bob or two… and she died quite suddenly. Cancer. Very sad."

"Sorry to hear that, Archie. How old was she?"

"Early twenties, I think."

"That's awful."

"Aye, isn't it. Anyway. She has no living heirs… and she never made a will, so it all went through… what's that thing they do when someone dies?"

"Probate?"

"Aye, that's it. Anyway, some firm comes knocking on my door in search of relatives for… erm…" he snapped his fingers in the air. "Whatever her name was."

Duncan shook his head.

Archie pointed at him. "I didn't know her, what can I say. Anyway, long story short—"

"It's proving pretty long as it is, Arch, I've got to tell you."

"I'm the sole heir!" he said, triumphantly. Then, his expression changed and he switched to a more suitably reverent look. "Not that I wish to profit from someone else's untimely death, you understand?"

"Of course not," Duncan said. "But you are."

"Aye."

"And… Fiona has got wind of this?"

He nodded. "Aye, she did. And so did that bloke of hers. He wants to get his grubby little hands on ma money as well as ma wife."

"So, what does your solicitor have to say?"

"Ma solicitor?" Archie asked, his forehead creasing.

"Aye. Does she have a claim if you received the money after the separation?"

Archie pondered the question. "Good point. I don't know."

"Your solicitor will, surely."

"I don't have one."

"What?"

"A solicitor," Archie said. "Why would I want one of those vampires bleeding me dry?"

"Because otherwise your ex-wifey will bleed you dry," Duncan said, sitting forward and shaking his head. "Seriously, get some professional advice."

Archie winced. "All right. I'll think about it."

"How did Fiona find out about it anyway?"

"Oh, I told her."

Duncan was stunned. "Why would you do that?"

"Well…" Archie looked glum, frowning. "I thought if she knew money was coming in, then… well… you know?"

"You thought she might come back?"

"Aye," Archie said, sheepishly. He met Duncan's eye. "Daft, eh?"

Duncan took a deep breath. "They say love is blind."

"Love is daft," Archie said. Exhaling a deep sigh, he smiled. "Ah, well. Onwards." He looked at Duncan. "What are you doing here anyway? I didn't think I was seeing you until the weekend?"

"Where were you this morning, Archie?"

His friend remained straight faced, staring at Duncan. "Out and about for a bit. Why do you ask?"

"Were you out Minginish way?"

"If you're asking then presumably you already know that I was, right?"

Duncan nodded. "Aye."

"Then why the cryptic question trying to catch me out? You dinnae have to be a polisman all the time you know?"

Duncan grimaced. "All right, fair point. Old habits and all that. What were you doing out there?"

"I was minding my own business, that's what I was

doing." Eyes widening, Archie stared at Duncan. "Just like you should be doing."

Duncan held his hands up. "I was only asking."

"And I was *only* telling," Archie said.

"Then consider me telt!"

Archie smiled. "I was doing a bit of walking, all right? If exercise is still allowed by the polis?"

"Absolutely," Duncan said.

"Good. Do you want a drink?"

"You've only just had breakfast."

"Relax. I was only talking about a cup of tea or coffee," Archie said. Duncan's mobile phone rang and he reached for it in his pocket. "Hold that thought."

Archie got up, picked his bowl up off the floor and went through into the kitchen. The dog followed, hopeful of more food no doubt. Duncan answered the call.

"Angus, how are we?"

"Ava Caldwell, sir."

"Yes, what can you tell me about her?"

"Well… she's definitely dead," Angus said. Duncan sighed, another dead end. "And we have her body lying in our mortuary."

CHAPTER FIFTEEN

"Ava Caldwell arrived in Glasgow three weeks ago," Angus said as Duncan, Alistair and the rest of the team either gathered around his desk or turned in their chairs to listen, keen to hear what the detective constable had found out. Angus glanced around and, happy he had their attention, he continued, "She came in on an overnight flight from Bangkok."

"Thailand?" Russell asked. For once he wasn't eating whilst sitting at his desk.

"Do you know of another Bangkok?" Alistair asked him drily. "Aside from the one in Thailand?"

"Could be one someplace," Russell said, almost as if the put down hadn't been made at all. "Could be one in Africa or something."

Alistair shook his head. "Africa… honestly."

Angus carried on.

"She was travelling on a one-way ticket," Angus said, "with no onward flights booked out of Glasgow or any other airport as far as I can see."

"Where is she from?" Duncan asked.

"She's from here," Angus said, glancing at Duncan. "From Skye. At least, originally."

Alistair looked at Duncan, raising an eyebrow. "Are you sure you don't—"

"Don't finish that question, Alistair," Duncan said. "I beg you."

"All right," Alistair said. Turning to Angus, he patted him on the shoulder. "You said originally. When did she leave?"

"As a teenager," Angus said. "As far as I can tell anyway. I've still got some digging to do because records are a bit sketchy from back then. Now, everything is digital and we can get most things within a few clicks but electoral roll information, council tax records and all of that type of thing are a bit harder to find when they were paper based."

"Didn't Highland Council start a big process of transferring their archives onto a computer database?" Caitlyn asked.

"Didn't go entirely to plan though, did it?" Angus said.

Alistair smiled. "Aye, paying someone minimum wage to scan all that into a computer… a recipe for disaster."

"Okay," Duncan said. "What do we know about her?"

"She lived on the island with her parents but after they split, she went with her mother to live on the mainland. Social Services documented her movements for a while—"

"Why were they involved?" Duncan asked.

Angus shrugged. "It's on my *to find out* list. Anyway, I lose her for a while and then she pops up again when she comes back to Skye and attends school, here in Portree."

Alistair looked at Duncan. "You are nearly the same age. You must have been at school with her." He held up a hand apologetically. "And I know, it doesnae mean you know her."

"I don't recall a Caldwell at the school, but if she was in a different year then…" He shook his head. "I don't know. She's a British national then I take it?"

Angus nodded. "Dual citizenship with Canada, through her mother, I believe."

"Add a phone call to the Canadians to your list, Angus. They might know something about her that we don't." Duncan frowned. "I doubt we'll get a great deal of help from the Thailand authorities. The volume of people passing through their country who are foreigners will be huge, but maybe it's worth a call."

Angus nodded. "I also trawled social media to see if I could learn anything about her from that."

"And?" Duncan asked.

"It's minimal, but she seems to be a bit of a hippy... going from place to place, living a... what do they call it, these days? A *natural lifestyle?*"

"You mean," Alistair said, "she's one of the great unwashed?"

Angus grinned. "She tries to minimise her impact on the environment around her, if that's what you mean, sarge?"

"I mean exactly what I said, young man. What does she do for money?"

Angus shook his head. "I can't find anything against her name with the HMRC which isn't surprising if she spends most of her time abroad. No employment records at all though... no former employment check-ins on her social media accounts." He shrugged. "I've no idea what she does to support herself."

"The mystery deepens," Duncan said. He put a supportive hand on Angus's shoulder. "Good work, young man. Keep at it. See what else you can find out. Everyone leaves a footprint somewhere." Duncan stepped away, taking out his mobile phone. He dialled Katie Matheson's number. It was her work mobile that the police used if they wanted to notify her of a press conference. The call cut straight to voicemail. Duncan sighed.

"Problem?" Alistair asked, coming to stand with him. Duncan shook his head.

"No, I don't think so. I'm just trying to find out how Ava Caldwell came onto Katie Matheson's radar, and then why she put her onto ours?"

"She no' answering?" Alistair asked.

"No, but she must have known I'd be calling. For some reason, she doesn't want to get involved."

"What's going on?"

Duncan was at a loss. "Perhaps she was warned off something. Katie pretty much told me her story on Graeme McKinley was binned because it would rock the boat, but whose boat might be the question we should be asking. Now it looks like the woman who may have been feeding Katie the information turns up dead. Maybe she's dropped out of sight for self-preservation."

"That's not looking good at all," Alistair said. "Self-preservation or arse-protection?"

"Could be either. They're not necessarily mutually exclusive." Duncan lowered his voice. "Do me a favour, would you. Have a sniff around Graeme McKinley. See if he's been up to anything recently that we ought to know about."

"Aye, I can do that."

"Quietly though. I don't want it to look like he's a suspect."

"Don't worry, tactful is my middle name," Alistair said with a wink.

Duncan scoffed. "Pull the other leg, Alistair, it has bells on it."

"Isn't he?" Alistair asked, ignoring the jibe.

"Isn't he, what?"

"Graeme McKinley; a suspect?"

Duncan blew out his cheeks. "We'll know soon enough. Has the comparison been done between the sample of blood on Finn's beanie and Ava Caldwell yet?"

Alistair shook his head. "Underway, but we've not heard back yet."

"Chase it up, will you?"

DUNCAN TRIED the handle on the double doors, two massive barriers – painted bright red – that barred entrance to McNab's. They were locked. Duncan looked around for a bell or an intercom but there was nothing to be seen, so he reverted to old school hammering on the door with a closed fist. He waited patiently, but no one came to answer. Stepping back from beneath the overhang, he looked along the length of the building. There were small windows, mounted high on the walls, but nowhere where he could peer inside.

He was about to head around the side of the building and try his luck at the delivery entrance when he heard a bolt sliding aside, shrieking in protest, one of the doors opened. A heavily tattooed man looked out at him from the gloomy interior of the bar's lobby, no lights were on behind him.

"We're not open yet."

"Aye, I know that," Duncan said. "I'm not after a bevvie. Is Grace about?"

The man's eyes narrowed, and he cast a wary eye over Duncan.

"Grace?"

"Aye, McFadyen."

"Who's asking?"

Duncan shook his head and took out his warrant card, flashing it at him. "Polis. Is she here, or isn't she?"

"Aye, come on in," he said, stepping aside and allowing Duncan to pass. He looked beyond Duncan and then closed the door, dropping the bolt into the floor and locking the door again. They were in near darkness. "Follow me," his guide said, setting off through another set of double doors which Duncan knew led into the lounge which bordered the hall where you'd find a larger bar running almost the width of the building alongside the dance floor. It would be wall to wall with patrons on the weekend, or at a midweek event if they had one on, but right now their footsteps on the polished wooden floor echoed as they passed through the empty rooms.

The sound of glass being stacked, and crates moved about carried to them as they approached the larger bar which had access to the rear delivery entrance.

"Gracey!" Duncan's guide called out and the noise from the back room stopped. "There's someone here to see you!"

Grace McFadyen appeared from the storeroom, wiping her hands on a bar towel, and upon seeing Duncan she launched it at him. He deftly caught it with one hand before it struck him.

"What the hell was that fer?" Duncan asked, placing the towel on the bar.

"For not showing up," Grace said. She looked at her colleague. "Thanks, Barry. I'll take it from here."

"Not showing up where?" Duncan protested. Barry looked sideways at him, raising his eyebrows.

"Good luck, buddy. You're gonna need it!"

With that, Barry left them, and Duncan turned to Grace who had her hands balled into fists, resting on her hips.

"Seriously… are you annoyed with me or something?" Duncan asked, worried.

Grace's expression softened and her face split into a smile.

"No, of course not," she said. "I just wanted to see your reaction is all." She winked at him. "It's quite a picture, I can tell you."

Duncan went to grab the same bar towel in order to return the favour and throw it at her, but she deftly intercepted his reach, scooping it up and waving it in the air by way of a victory.

"So, what can I do for the *very Detective Inspector Duncan McAdam*?"

Duncan smiled. "How have you been? I'm sorry I've no' been in touch lately—"

"Relax, Duncan," she said. "It's not like we're exclusive or anything, is it?"

Duncan pondered that comment for a moment. It was true, they were never officially an item, but they were seeing a fair bit of one another, and he wasn't aware of any competition for her attention.

"Are you… erm…"

"Seeing anyone else?" she asked.

"Well… aye," Duncan said, both embarrassed by his anxiety and, worse still, surprised by it.

"Not really any of your business, is it?"

"Ah… no, I suppose it's not…"

He met Grace's eye and tried to shrug off the cloud of social awkwardness that had descended on him. She smiled again, cracking the facade of seriousness. He sighed, relieved. "Och… bloody hell, lass! Will you give me a break?"

"You deserved it," she said, her smile broadening. "Coming in here making all manner of assertions about the type of girl I am."

"No… I wasn't doing any such—" he paused, cocking his head and taking her measure. "You're winding me up again, aren't you?"

She shook her head. "It's way too easy, Duncan. How have you been keeping?"

"Aye, busy, you know?"

"What's the craic with this wifey over Talisker way then?"

Duncan shook his head. "Still working on it."

"Then what are you doing in here at this time of the day?" she asked, leaning on the bar. "Out with it."

"Katie."

"Matheson?" Grace asked. Duncan nodded. "What about her? She's not interested in you. You're not her type."

"Pleased to hear it," Duncan said.

"Me too."

Duncan shut his eyes, his mind drifting off topic. "Have you spoken to her recently?"

"Define recently?"

"Since last night."

"Er… no, I was working last night," Grace said. "We don't live in each other's pockets. Why do you ask? What's she done?"

"She hasn't *done* anything, but I'm trying to get hold of her and she's not answering her phone."

"Maybe she doesnae like you," Grace said playfully.

"I'm sure that's not the case," Duncan replied. Reading Grace's sceptical expression, he went on the defensive. "She doesn't know me well enough to know whether she likes me or not. Can you call her for me… see if she's okay?"

"Why wouldn't she be okay?" Grace asked, fear edging into her voice. "What have you done to her?"

Duncan, exasperated, sighed. "Can you just give her a phone, please?"

"Aye, I can do that," Grace said, reaching into the back pocket of her jeans and producing her mobile. She dialled Katie's number, keeping half an eye on Duncan as she held the phone out in front of her in that annoying way that people tend to do these days, so everyone can hear a call rather than keeping it private and pressing it to your ear. They listened to the ringing... and then the call went to voicemail just as Duncan's had earlier.

"Damn," Duncan said quietly. Grace tapped out a quick text message and then put her phone back in her pocket, fixing Duncan with a stern look.

"What have you got my pal into?"

Duncan spread his hands wide. "Not me... I swear."

Grace stared at him, her eyes narrowing as she gauged his sincerity. "All right... but if you have put her in the shite, you'll have me to answer to. Got it?"

"I completely understand," Duncan said, raising his hands aloft. "Like you said, maybe she's just avoiding me and taking some time out."

"It's not like her to avoid me though," Grace said. "She's always taken my calls before, even when she's working. What has she been talking to you about anyway?"

Duncan winced. "Cannae say, sorry."

Grace accepted that without further questioning. "While you're here, do you want a drink? I'm due a break anyway."

Duncan checked his watch. "Aye, I could stick around for ten minutes."

"A whole ten minutes, Duncan? You know how to make a girl feel special, don't you."

"I can probably stretch it to twenty, if you behave yourself," he said, smiling.

"I think we can agree that's not going to happen," she said, turning around and checking the coffee machine was on and at working temperature. "I'm not serving you alcohol because you're on the clock," she said over her shoulder. "As am I. Black coffee?"

"Aye, please," Duncan said. His mobile beeped. It was a text from Angus. He immediately hit the call button, stepping away from the bar.

CHAPTER SIXTEEN

"Angus... tell me what you found," Duncan said.

"Now we have a name against our victim, I was able to start piecing together her digital footprint," Angus said. "The Keck said I should just tell you myself, rather than relaying it through him."

"Which means you lost him whilst explaining it, right?"

Angus chuckled and then Alistair's voice came down the line. Angus was on speaker.

"No, I'll have you know I understand perfectly well... it's just ISPs, protocols and widgets are a young man's business... and I am—"

"Not a young man," Duncan said.

"A seasoned professional," Alistair said, "and I'm giving wee Angus here a chance to shine."

"Thanks, sarge," Angus said.

"And by God does he need it," Alistair said drily.

Duncan smiled. "What have you got for me, Angus?"

"I've been working my way through the forums searching out Finn MacGregor's contacts and interactions, haven't I?"

"Finn's?" Duncan asked, confused. He saw Grace set down

two cups of coffee on the closest table to the bar, keeping a watchful eye on him. "I thought you were looking at—"

"Ava Caldwell, aye, I know. That's what I was getting to. They crossover."

"Finn knows Ava?"

"Aye," Angus said excitedly. "And what's more, Callum Mcinnes has been in the loop as well. Although, not as much as Finn, but there's been a couple of three-way conversations going on."

"What has Ava Caldwell got in common... ah... the environment. Yeah?"

"That's it. We think," Angus said, "the sarge and me, that Ava is some kind of environmental campaigner or activist."

"And is that why she's back on the island?" Duncan asked.

"We don't know that yet," Alistair said, "not for certain. It's just a theory, but it would stand to reason, and if what that wee lassie from the paper told you yesterday pans out... then it would make sense that she's out there keeping a watchful eye on the farming operation."

"I'll swing by the school and have another word with young Callum," Duncan said. "See if I can get a straight answer out of him for once too."

"One more thing," Alistair said as Duncan was about to hang up. "Craig Dunbar has left a message for you to call him."

"Aye, okay. Did he say what about?"

"No, he only wanted to speak to you."

Duncan found that odd, but it was the doctor's prerogative. "I'll give him a phone. Anything else comes up, you'll know where I'll be."

"Oh, did you find Katie?" Alistair asked.

"No, not yet, but I'm working on it," Duncan said before hanging up. He crossed the short distance between himself and Grace, pulling out a chair and sitting down. She had her coffee cup cradled in both hands, sipping from it as she peered over the rim at Duncan.

"It's going to be less than five minutes before you have to leave, isn't it?" she asked.

He inclined his head apologetically. "Sorry, but…"

"Aye, work," she said, sitting back and lifting one foot to rest it on the adjacent chair. "I'm up against it myself today anyway. No missing people, dead wifeys or runaway teenagers to deal with though."

"Runaway?" Duncan asked. "Do you mean, Finn MacGregor?"

"Aye. that's what people are saying."

"Are they also saying why he might choose to run away?"

Grace shrugged. "Anthony, his father, can be a bit weird."

"Weird?"

"Aye… well, a bit of an arse."

Duncan smiled but said nothing.

"You no closer to finding him then?"

Duncan shook his head. "But that doesn't mean we've stopped looking. What do you know about the family, seeing as you have your ear to the ground."

"I don't know much, just what people say when they come in here, you know?" Grace wrinkled her nose. "And once they've had a few drinks, then they start talking a bit more, perhaps more than they should, but…"

"But?"

She shrugged. "Once they've had a few drinks then perceptions tend to get a bit… wonky. You cannae really trust what anyone has to say once they're propping up the bar. Most people are full of it at the best of times."

Duncan laughed. "Aye, welcome to my world!"

"You see, we're not too different, after all," Grace said,

finishing her coffee. She rose from her seat. "Right, sod off, McAdam. I've got work to do."

Duncan looked at his own cup. He'd barely touched it. Grace followed his eye and shrugged.

"Well, you shouldn't spend so long doing your secret squirrel act on the phone, should you." She headed back behind the bar, putting her empty cup and saucer down on the counter above the dishwasher. "You can see yourself out," Grace said, disappearing into the storeroom.

"When will I get to see you next?" Duncan called after her.

"I don't know," she said, poking her head around the corner. "But you know where to find me."

"If you hear from Katie, tell her to call me, all right?"

"Will do, but she won't. Not unless she wants to."

"Then you call me and let me know she's all right," Duncan said. Grace was gone and he waited to see if she'd heard him. After a moment she looked out at him again.

"All right, I will." She pointed towards the exit. "Go on. Out!"

"Okay, I'm going."

DUNCAN STOOD in the office while the admin assistant called through to speak with Rona MacAllister, Callum's head of year. Something about how the young lady's eyes flicked up at him and away suggested she was uncomfortable with his presence, but he couldn't think why.

"Miss MacAllister will be with you shortly, Detective Inspector," she said having hung up the phone.

"Thank you," Duncan said, smiling. She returned to her work but he couldn't help but notice she was still glancing up at him on occasion while he slowly paced the room taking in the school photographs mounted on the wall. The photos went back for years and Duncan could see the change in fashions through hairstyles. The school uniform remained consistent, but short hair, to collar length and everything in between were on show. If he looked hard enough, he figured he'd find his own photo here somewhere.

He didn't want to see that again. What a torrid time he'd had at high school, although much of it was down to his life beyond the school gates as opposed to within them.

He didn't have long to wait before Rona walked into the office, acknowledging her colleague behind the desk and then smiling at Duncan and shaking his hand again.

"Back so soon, Detective Inspector?"

"Duncan will be fine," he said, smiling back at her. "I was hoping to have another word with Callum Mcinnes, if you wouldn't mind. I hate to interrupt the school day, but it is quite important."

Rona glanced at her colleague and then sheepishly to Duncan. "I'm afraid you've had a wasted journey, Duncan."

"Why? Is he on a field trip or something?" Duncan asked, surprised that they'd be journeying out in the current weather.

"No, Callum hasn't been at school for the last two days."

Duncan was surprised to hear that. "Is he… ill?"

"Apparently so, yes." Rona took Duncan by the arm and guided him out of the office and into the corridor. Once they were alone, she glanced both ways to make sure she couldn't be overheard. "Something doesn't feel right though."

"What is it?"

"Callum didn't come into school yesterday, which isn't unusual, children are often ill. You know how easily things spread through classrooms."

"Did his parents call in?" Duncan asked.

"We have an automated system for reporting absences…

and yes, the school was notified about Callum's absence."
Rona frowned. "Only…"

Duncan was a little lost. He inclined his head, smiling.
"Only what?"

"I saw Callum's father, David, in the car park yesterday
afternoon." She glanced around nervously. "I spoke to him,
asked him how Callum was and he… didn't seem to know he
was off sick. I think he was at the school to pick him up, you
know, to save him from catching the bus."

"Does he often collect him from school?"

"Occasionally, yes. I see him from time to time."

"Perhaps there was just a moment of miscommunication at
home," Duncan said. "It happens."

"Yes, I suppose so. It's probably nothing," Rona said.

"What do you think is going on?" Duncan asked.

She shrugged. "I don't know. It's just… the way he looked
at me. It made me… I don't know… uncomfortable."

"Have you said anything about this to the school?"

Rona glanced over her shoulder towards the office. "I
have… it's a common enough conversation amongst the staff
that… Mr Mcinnes is a little… intense, but nothing official has
been made of it." Rona looked nervous that she'd said
anything and perhaps she was regretting it, Duncan didn't
know. "No one wants to cause a problem, and I wouldn't have
said anything if… not for everything that's going on with Finn
MacGregor. Callum seems to be deeply affected by it all."

"In what way?"

"He has been withdrawn… particularly after your visit to
the school. His concentration levels have dipped even further.
I'm worried about the boy."

Duncan smiled. "Thank you for speaking so candidly. I
need to have a word with him, and so I'll also speak to his
parents—"

"You won't say—"

"No, don't worry," Duncan said, trying to put her mind at ease. "I'll not mention anything you've said to me."

Duncan excused himself and went outside, walking back to his car. It was raining again and with the strength of the wind it was almost horizontal. With a bit of luck it was simply a passing cloudburst and things would settle soon enough. He hurried back to his car and got in, relieved to be out of the rain. Shaking his head free of loose water, he took out his phone and called Becky.

"Duncan?" she said, answering quickly. "A bit of a surprise. What can I do for you?"

"Are you working today?"

"No… no, I'm at home. I have to work this coming Saturday, so this is my day off. Why?"

"How's Callum?"

"Fine… as far as I know. Why do you ask?"

"He's not feeling unwell?"

"No, he's at school."

"He bloody isn't," Duncan said.

"What?"

"I'm at the school now. I came to speak to him and they said he's been off sick since yesterday."

There was silence between them, but Duncan could hear Becky's breathing.

"Bex?"

"Yes, I'm here… well, he's not at home…"

"Did you call him in sick yesterday?"

"No! He left for school at the usual time… I handed him his lunch as he went out of the door with his backpack on. I… I thought he was going to school."

"Did he come home at the usual time?"

"No, he was staying over at his pal's house last night. He'd arranged a study session with Cammy."

"With Cammy? Don't tell me he's in the same work group as that boy?"

"Och… Cammy's okay. And Callum is helping him with his work. No one gets him like Callum… and Finn do.

"So he was staying at Cammy's last night?"

"Aye, that's right." He could sense her frustration. "Duncan, what's going on?"

"Did Davey know?"

"That he was staying at Cammy's… I… might have mentioned it. I don't remember. *Why?*"

"When did you last hear from Callum?" Duncan asked.

"Last night. He called me from his mobile. He was all right," she said. "They'd had pizza for their supper. Duncan, what's the matter?"

"Callum hasn't been at school for two days… and he's been lying to me about what he knows about Finn MacGregor's disappearance—"

"Oh, Duncan. For heaven's sake, can't you just give him a break? He's upset enough as it is—"

"Becky. You don't get it, do you?" Duncan said, shaking his head. "Finn is likely involved in one way or another in the murder of that woman out at Talisker… maybe as a witness or something else, I don't know. Callum knows… he knows something, and now he's pulled a fast one."

"You don't think he's… involved—"

"No, but he's in and around those who are… and that might mean he's in danger. I need to find him, and I need to find him now!"

"I'll call him—"

"No, don't do that," Duncan said. "Give me his mobile number and I'll have it traced… if you call him he's going to know you've rumbled the fact he's not at school and it might make matters worse."

Silence. She was thinking it over, contemplating the rational, reasoned approach versus the mother's instinct to find her son, get him home and protect him.

"Bex… promise me you'll not phone."

"All right, I promise."

"Good, can you give—"

"On one condition."

Duncan felt a sense of dread. "Which is?"

"I'm coming with you to get him."

"No!"

"You dinnae get to say no to me anymore, Duncan. You lost that privilege a long time ago," Becky told him. "If you want my help, that's the condition. Take it or leave it."

Duncan sighed. "All right."

"You promise?"

"I said all right, and I meant it," Duncan said, staring out of the windscreen at some random point in the distance. "Can I have the number."

"Aye. Where do I meet you?"

CHAPTER SEVENTEEN

DUNCAN'S EYES flicked towards Becky, sitting at the small dining table he had in the part-finished kitchen diner of his family croft house, her face lit by the blue glow from the camping lantern Duncan used for lighting just now. Unconnected cables hung from holes in the ceiling or protruded from walls waiting to have the fixtures connected. Duncan still had to choose those, but at least the cabinetry was in place. The majority of the appliances were also sitting in the next room, still shrink-wrapped, waiting for him to put them in place.

"Have you got anywhere with the driver?" Duncan asked.

"Aye, traced him and just now got off the phone with him," Russell said, from his desk back in Portree Station. "He remembers Callum getting on the bus at a stop in Bracadale and getting off again on the south side of Drynoch."

"Drynoch?" Duncan repeated. Becky's eyes darted across at him and Duncan raised his eyebrows to her in an unasked question. She shook her head glumly. "No, I've no idea why he'd be going there."

"Aye, well we're still waiting for his phone to switch on

and then the service provider will tell us where he's at," Russell said, upbeat. "It's only a matter of time."

"Thanks, Russell. Keep me posted, all right."

"Of course. Give Mrs Mcinnes my best, would you?"

"I will," Duncan said, and then hung up. He crossed the freshly painted kitchen to take a seat opposite Becky, setting his mobile down on the table.

She looked around the room. "All white," she said. Duncan followed her gaze and nodded. "Very modern."

"Well, I'm a modern figure of a man, aren't I?" Duncan said, with a half-smile. Becky smiled too. It was the first positive expression he'd seen from her since meeting up earlier to go in search of Callum.

"When do you think you'll be moving in?"

Duncan looked at her, tightly wrapped up in her outdoor coat and still the tip of her nose was red due to the cold.

"I'll need to get the heating connected before I can do that," he said. "I'm waiting on the plumber."

"You going for an oil-fired boiler or pellets?" she asked, making small talk.

"Air source," he said. She raised an inquisitive eyebrow. "I know, but the insulation is good," he looked around with a wry grin, "although it doesn't feel like it just now. Air source and underfloor piping. It's all alchemy to me, but it's supposed to work pretty well."

"Very contemporary," Becky said. "You could rent it out to the tourists... a spot like this... you could retire from the force."

"And stay living in the caravan? No, thank you. I can't believe I've stuck as long as I have."

"At least you have Grace to keep you warm at night."

At the mention of Grace McFadyen, conversation died and they sat in an uncomfortable silence for a couple of minutes.

"Does she make you happy?" Becky asked, lifting her eyes to meet his and then averting them from his gaze almost immediately.

"Grace… she's good fun, you know."

Becky cocked her head. "If you say so."

"You disapprove?"

"It's not for me to approve or not," Becky said, shifting her feet and gently stamping them on the floor. "You need to chase your plumber. It's freezing in here."

"I would light the wood burner," Duncan said. Becky seemed ready to chastise him for not having already done so. "But it's not connected. I'm waiting on—"

"The plumber?"

Duncan tilted his head to one side. "The fitter, aye. Different guy though."

"Does anyone do anything on this island any more?" she asked.

Duncan laughed. "Hogmanay hangovers… last for the entire month."

Conversation tailed off again and they sat in silence. Duncan's thoughts drifted to Callum and he was certain Becky was thinking about her son as well.

"He'll be all right, you know?" Duncan said, lightening his tone.

"Where is he, Duncan? Where's he got to?" she asked, pensively watching his response. "And what has he got himself into?"

Duncan shook his head. "He's a bright lad. He's probably…"

"Probably what?"

Duncan chose his words carefully, "It's probably a misguided attempt at helping someone."

"And by *someone* you mean Finn MacGregor, right?"

"Stands to reason." Duncan looked out of the sliding doors that would open onto his decking, once it was installed. The timber lengths were all stacked up under sheets of heavy tarpaulin out front, waiting for the joiners to come by. "I mean, what would you do for your best pals? I'd do a lot."

"How is Archie? I've not seen him in a while," Becky said.

"Moving from one mess to another," Duncan said. "He made a play to get Fiona back—"

"Oh, did he now?" Becky asked, rolling her eyes. "He really needs to move on from that woman. She wasn't good for him."

"Aye… well, he needs someone to take care of him."

"Oh, and that's a woman's lot in life, is it? To take care of her man?"

"No, that's not what I meant at all," Duncan said, fixing her with a defensive stare.

"What did you mean then, because this modern man schtick you've got going on is taking a bit of a hammering in my mind?"

"I meant…" Duncan said, looking to the ceiling and choosing his words, "that people in relationships tend to live longer, happier and more well-rounded lives than those who live alone. It's about connection." He caught her studying him and he spread his hands wide. "That's all I meant."

"And does that go for you too?" she asked.

"A relationship?"

"Aye, with you and Grace."

Duncan exhaled sharply. "Let's not get ahead of ourselves. Grace and I have seen a bit of one another—"

"A *lot* of one another," Becky said.

"Aye… but it's early days."

"So, I shouldn't buy a hat then?"

Duncan looked at her quizzically.

"For the wedding," she said, and Duncan shook his head. "I was just checking. I could do with a day out. Something to look forward to."

"That'd be a bit weird, wouldn't it?" Duncan asked. "You… coming to our wedding. Not that there's going to be one, mind you."

"Weird for whom? Me or you?" she asked.

Duncan felt discomfort in this subject and chose not to answer. Looking outside, he saw the weather had really turned. Whereas for the last few days they'd seen snow and then a mixture of sleet and rain, it was now purely raining, driving hard against the windows of the house. Becky glanced up at the skylights, set into the pitched roof of the rear extension. The water cascading down the glass.

"Our boy is out in this somewhere, Duncan," she said quietly. "What if someone's taken him?"

"No one's taking him," Duncan said. "He made his own choice to skip school – two days running – and has his reasons for doing so. He'll be fine. The important thing is to bring him home. Everything else can be sorted out later."

Becky looked nonplussed, possibly due to Duncan's casualness but didn't argue with him. He was concerned, but experience told him that whatever Callum was up to, it was on his own terms.

"Will you line up a search for him?" Becky asked. "Like you did for Finn?"

Duncan hesitated and she noticed.

"Oh right, so it's good enough to get the island out looking for Finn MacGregor but not when it comes to your own son?"

Duncan scoffed. "Right, he's my son when you need him to be but when it comes to any other aspect of his life then I've got no say. Is that how it is?"

"Och what are you talking about?"

"School," Duncan said. "For starters anyway. He should be staying on in his education… maybe looking at university, not going to work in a nothing job—"

"A nothing job?" Becky countered. "It's part of what's kept this island going for centuries. Crofting is a way of life. Your father did it, and so did Davey's… your sister lives on a working croft for crying out loud. Now it's for Callum to take it on."

"And have you actually asked him if he even wants to?"

Becky looked away.

"No, I didn't think so. Maybe he should get a say rather than have it forced upon him."

"He likes being outdoors," Becky said, "and it will be good for him."

"Davey has years of work left in him. If he ever wants to retire or quit, that's when Callum should take it on," Duncan said. "There's plenty of time for that. Let him spread his wings… live a little."

"Like you did?"

"Aye…" Duncan said before sensing a hidden meaning behind her question. He had made a bit of a mess of his life up until this point. "Aye… like I did… only, maybe he could do it better."

"Let's face it, he couldn't have done it much worse, could he, Duncan?"

Duncan shrugged. "Maybe he could learn from my mistakes?"

She shook her head. "Why do you want to be a part of his life all of a sudden?"

"*All of a sudden?*" Duncan asked. "This is the only chance I've had, remember?"

Becky looked away from him, down at her hands cradled in her lap. "I just want my boy home, Duncan."

He leaned across the table and took her hands in his. She allowed him to. He squeezed them gently, shooting her an encouraging smile at the same time.

"I've seen weans do this kind of stuff so many times. Whatever he's up to, he'll be back. They almost always come home… and he'll probably pretend he's been at school all day as well."

Becky met his eye. "Almost always," she said quietly. Duncan regretted his choice of words and was about to say something reassuring when they heard the front door opening.

"Hello!" Roslyn shouted. Duncan stood up and went to meet his sister as she came inside, shaking her coat off in the hall. "I saw you weren't in the caravan and figured you must be in the house. Working late?"

She stopped at the threshold, seeing Becky sitting at the table. They exchanged a pleasant smile, but Duncan realised his sister's was just as artificial as the one Becky returned.

"Sorry," Ros said, "I didn't know you had company."

"Callum is missing," Duncan said, and Ros looked between the two of them, eyes wide.

"What's happened?" she asked.

Duncan shrugged. "We don't know yet, but he's taken himself off somewhere. We've been out looking… and we have people asking questions…"

"I'm so sorry," Ros said to Becky, and it was clearly heartfelt. Duncan knew that his sister wasn't the biggest fan of Becky's, and by the coldness of her instinctive reaction, it would appear the feeling was somewhat mutual.

"Thank you," Becky said with a slight nod.

Ros turned to Duncan. "I was stopping by to see if you wanted to come to ours for your supper, but… I suppose you have other things on." She looked between them. "I can't stop, Ronnie is waiting for me in the car."

The front door opened again, and Ronnie Macdougall came in. He didn't offer a greeting, simply walked in and probably followed the sound of voices and joined them. He looked at Duncan and upon seeing Becky, arched his eyebrows.

"I didnae realise you were having a party of your own in here tonight, Dunc."

"Hardly," Duncan replied, detecting a hint of venom in his brother-in-law's tone.

Ronnie cast an eye around the interior; he didn't seem to approve. "When are you going to have it painted?"

"It is painted," Duncan said.

"Oh… right," Ronnie replied, nodding. "I see. Like that is it." He shrugged and looked at his wife. "Come on, lass, let's get ourselves off home…" He glanced between Duncan and Becky. "Leave these two… to it."

Duncan was about to protest at Ronnie's barely concealed insult, but Ros placed a hand on her husband's forearm. "Wee Callum has gone missing."

Ronnie looked at her, his expression unchanged. "Ah, has he now. I wonder what that's all about then?" He looked at Becky. "Trouble at home is there?"

Ros took a swipe at his arm and Ronnie flinched. "I was only asking… you know what with—"

"Let's go home," Ros said firmly, grasping her husband's arm and steering him back into the hall. Duncan looked apologetically at Becky who stared straight ahead. Duncan followed the pair back through the house to the front door where Ros practically pushed Ronnie out into the rain. She turned to Duncan and winced. "I'm so sorry. You know what he's like?"

"Aye, I do when he's anywhere around me. What did he mean?"

"Mean?" Ros asked.

"Just now, when he said *what with*? He was looking at me and Bex."

Ros looked flustered, waving away the comment and reaching out to Duncan's arm with a fleeting touch. "Nothing. Forget about it."

Something about her haste to dismiss it piqued his interest. In and of itself, it was an innocuous comment, but taken in a wider context it would mean a lot. That wider context being the dynamic between Duncan, Becky and Davey off the back of Callum's parentage. Then it clicked. He grasped her arm as she turned to leave.

"He knows, doesn't he?" Duncan asked. Ros bit her bottom lip. "Which means... you know too, don't you?" Ros flushed and looked at Duncan's hand. He let go of her arm. The lack of a denial, even a cursory one, spoke volumes. At least she respected him enough not to lie. "How long?"

"Have I known?" Ros asked. Duncan nodded. She sighed. "From pretty much the time she came back to the island."

"What?"

"Well..." Ros lowered her voice, peering past Duncan towards the kitchen. He looked over his shoulder but neither of them could see Becky. "I was always quite good at maths at school, Duncan, and I have had a child of my own and so I know how these things work."

Duncan glared at her, lowering his voice. "Why didn't you tell me?"

She shook her head. "I didn't think it was my place to."

"Not your place... are you kidding me?" Duncan said, his voice rising. Roslyn urged him to quieten down, fearing they'd be overheard. "Tell me, does everyone know my business on this bloody island?"

"Oh, behave yourself, Duncan. You're acting like a petulant child."

"Am I? You knew I had a son and you didnae tell me. What the hell is going on?"

"How was I to know you didn't know... and it's not like you and I have really been on close speaking terms in the last few years, is it? Maybe you weren't interested in the boy... and..." she shrugged "he has a father who was around for him."

"Unlike me, you mean?"

"Well... you weren't here, were you?"

"I didn't know, Ros! It's a bit hard to be there for someone you dinnae know exists, isn't it?"

"Look... I did what I thought was right," Ros said and before Duncan could reply she raised a hand, "for all parties. Let's be honest, you've not exactly been father material, have you?"

That comment cut him deeply. "Thanks very much."

She smiled apologetically. "Come on, Duncan. You know you've not been on top of your own emotions – possibly ever – and so how can you expect to shape a wean's?"

"I'd have done a better job than ours did, I'll tell you that."

She inclined her head. "That, at least, is true."

"I never got the chance, Ros," he said. "I never got the chance."

She touched his hand affectionately, smiling weakly at him. "I know you didn't." A car horn sounded. "That'll be Ronnie. I'd better go."

"Hang on," Duncan said, and Ros hesitated as she made to leave, glancing at him. "Ronnie... why does he hate me?"

"Och... he doesn't hate you... as such."

"Bloody does," Duncan said. "His father... ran out on his mum when he was a bairn, didn't he?"

Ros looked at him nervously and nodded.

"Is that it?"

She nodded. "I should imagine so, aye. He detests absent fathers."

"He hates me for abandoning a wean I didn't even know I had?"

Ros screwed up her nose. "Well, he didn't know that you didn't know... so you cannae blame him really."

"Oh, so that's my fault too, is it?"

"I didn't say that," Ros said, shaking her head. "Look, I have to go." She leaned over and kissed his cheek, and then patted the back of his hand. "Can you keep me posted on Callum?"

"Aye, of course I will," Duncan said, almost lost for words. Roslyn closed the door behind her as she left. Duncan wondered if Ronnie's attitude would change once he found out Duncan wasn't what he thought he was. Somehow, he doubted it. Attitudes formed over long periods of time seldom changed, even when presented with evidence to the contrary. He made his way back into the kitchen.

Becky was standing by the sliding doors on the far side of the kitchen. He thought she was staring out at the sea, but then he saw the mobile phone in her hands. She spun to face him, excitedly.

"Callum is with Davey!" she said, almost squeaking with joy and relief.

"He is? Where?"

Duncan's mobile rang and he swiftly answered it. It was Russell.

"Sir, Callum's mobile network operator has been in touch. His phone pinged off a cell tower twenty minutes ago—"

"Where?"

"Satran… do you want me to get a couple of cars out there to look—"

"No," Duncan said, seeing Becky's smiling face, staring at her mobile phone screen. "That's not necessary. We know he's already safe."

"Ah… right you are, sir. Do you need me to… erm… do anything?"

"No, you can crack on with what you were doing, Russell, thanks."

"I was going to head home for ma supper… if that's okay?"

"Yes, we can pick everything up in the morning, don't worry," Duncan said, feeling his own relief at the news Callum was fine. He hung up.

Becky rushed over to him and hugged him fiercely. The years fell away from her face. "He's okay, Duncan."

"That's great. Where's he been?"

She shook her head. "I don't know, and I don't care but he's with Davey and that's the main thing. I've texted back… Davey will swing by here on his way back to pick me up."

They'd left Becky's car in town, and both gone in Duncan's to search for Callum. They hadn't given any thought to collecting her car when they'd come back to Duncan's whilst waiting for news from either Russell or anyone else about Callum's whereabouts.

CHAPTER EIGHTEEN

BECKY WAS like a ball of nervous energy, pacing the room in anticipation of Davey's arrival. When she heard his car pull up at the front of the house she ran to the door and was outside in the rain before he'd even switched the car off, hauling Callum out of the passenger seat and throwing her arms around him. They embraced, Callum looking embarrassed.

"He's perfectly okay," Davey said, getting out of the driver's side and looking over at his wife and son. "Let the poor lad breathe woman."

Becky ignored him, leaning away from Callum so she could see his face, but she kept her palms resting on his cheeks. She had tears welling in her eyes. Callum put his hands on her forearms, smiling at her. Davey saw Duncan standing at the front door, pulling his coat on before coming out to join them.

"Come on, Becky, let's be away home."

"Oh," she said, glancing at Duncan. "I've left my phone inside. I'll just get it." Reluctantly, she let go of Callum and hurried past Duncan and back inside the house. Duncan nodded to Davey.

"Davey," he said. "Good to see you got him back. Where has he been?"

"Just decided to skip a day of school," Davey said, his eyes flicking momentarily towards Callum and then back at Duncan. Callum didn't meet Duncan's eye. Davey spoke to him. "Get yourself back in the car, son. We'll be away home in a minute."

Callum went to do as he was told but Duncan wanted to speak to him first.

"Callum, where did you get to today?" Callum looked at him and then glanced towards his father, Davey. He shrugged. "And yesterday for that matter?"

"Just around, you know?" Callum said.

"It's just that—"

"Give the lad a break, Detective Inspector!" Davey said. "He's skipped a bit of school. It's hardly a CID matter, is it?"

"It is if he was with Finn MacGregor, or knows where the boy is," Duncan said. "Then it's very much a CID matter."

Davey waved the comment away. "He was nowhere near him." He looked at Callum. "Were you, lad?"

Callum shook his head. "No."

"Then where did you go?" Duncan asked.

"I just wanted away from school for a bit. Everyone keeps asking me stuff… and I dinnae like it."

"About Finn?" Duncan asked.

Callum nodded. "Aye."

"You know, it's really important that we speak to your pal," Duncan said. "His parents are really worried about him."

"I know," Callum said, his eyes drifting to his father.

"Leave the boy alone, Duncan," Becky said, coming past him. She ushered Callum towards the car and Davey made to get back in himself.

"Becky, it's important—"

"And so is getting this boy home and into some dry clothes," she said, patting Callum's coat and trousers, shaking her head. "He's wet through."

"I need to—"

"You heard her," Davey said, cutting Duncan off. "The boy needs to get home, warm and dry. He's probably hungry too. You can speak to him another time." He stared at Duncan. "Unless you're saying he's committed some kind of a crime."

Callum looked horrified, and Becky, anxious. Duncan shook his head.

"Not as far as I know, he hasn't."

"Then anything else can wait, can't it?" Davey said. "After all, he's just a bairn. If you want to speak to him again, you can go through me or his mother."

Duncan registered the apparent united front between the two. He looked at Becky and she agreed with a curt nod. He wasn't going to get a chance to speak to Callum tonight. He stood in the rain as they all got into Davey's car, and not another word was spoken. Watching them driving out along the access track until they disappeared from view over a small rise, Duncan shook his head and returned inside. Closing the door, his mobile rang, and he hurried into the kitchen to answer it. It was Alistair MacEachran.

"Alistair?"

"You'd better get yourself over to Fiscavaig."

"Why, what's going on?"

"Graeme McKinley's yard is on fire."

DUNCAN ARRIVED ONLY a few moments after Graeme McKinley at the yard where he had his site office. The timber-clad structure was ablaze, and the crew of the fire brigade appliance based at Dunvegan were already on site trying to get the blaze under control. The flames had already spread to the nearby barn, and this was the concentration of the crew's focus, trying to halt the fire's progression and thereby save something of the premises. Of the office however, there was precious little that could be done.

"Absolute bastards!" Graeme McKinley shouted, flinging his arms in the air as he practically danced on the spot. He was desperate to do something but was also just as aware of being powerless to do anything. He hopped from one foot to the other, raging.

Alistair stood off to one side, his hands thrust deep into the pockets of his long coat, an impassive expression on his face. He was so calm and unflustered. Duncan never saw him react any differently. He was like the Talisker Stack, standing firm while the sea roared about him. He inclined his head as Duncan approached.

"We got the call three quarters of an hour ago. A local couple saw a glow above the hill, and came to check it out," Alistair said. "By the time the crew got here… well, as you can see, there's no' much that can be done for the office but they reckon they can save half of the barn."

"Half? That'll be scant consolation."

Graeme made for the two of them, his face a picture of barely controlled fury. "Can you see what they've done? Right there!" He yelled, pointing at the raging fire behind him. "Do you see?"

"Who?" Duncan asked.

"*Who?*" Graeme asked. "Those eco-mentalists, that's who."

"Care to name anyone specific that you have in mind?" Alistair asked, drily. His particular tone of scepticism could very easily send Graeme over into the deep end, if Alistair wasn't careful. Not that he was far removed from the deep end already by the expression he currently bore.

Graeme waved a pointed finger at Alistair. "You can start with that weirdo Archie Mackinnon!"

"Archie?" Duncan asked, surprised.

"Aye… that oddball from over in Kensaleyre. He's been hanging about with those activists who are desperate to bring me to my knees. They can smell blood in the water… and they're coming for me!" His face was flushed, the veins in his forehead pronounced. "They'll no' go after the big boys, but they'll come for me. Bastards!"

"Do you have any evidence to link Archie Mackinnon to any of this?" Duncan asked. "Besides… seeing him about this way?"

"Mark my words… he's involved."

Alistair glanced sideways at Duncan. "Well, you've seen him hereabouts… best get him into a cell, seeing as that's all the evidence we need."

Graeme turned on him. "You're a funny man, Alistair. Just do your job, that's all I ask."

"We will, you dinnae have to worry about that. Some people say you're in a spot of financial bother at present, though, Graeme," Alistair said.

"Is that right?"

"Aye. It'd be a decent result for you… if this place is properly insured, wouldn't it?" Alistair asked.

"What are you insinuating?"

Alistair replied, dead pan. "Simply that you are insured, am I wrong?"

"Of course, I'm insured. I'm no' daft!"

"That's good to hear," Alistair said. Graeme shot daggers at him, but Alistair was unfazed by it. Then Graeme glared at Duncan.

"You'll no' hear the last of this if you don't find out who's to blame for this," he said, looking around at his burning business. The fire brigade crew seemed to be getting on top of the situation, but it still looked touch and go for their efforts to save the rest of the barn at this point. They were powerless to do anything but watch the crew at work.

THE WEATHER FRONT having passed on was a double-edged blade for the burning site at Fiscavaig. On the one hand, the lack of rain was unfortunate for it would have helped douse the blaze but on the other, the wind had also eased and that had undoubtedly assisted the fire brigade by not fanning the flames. Although, the breeze had still assisted in the passing from the site office to the barn. Mother Nature hadn't seen fit to be overly kind.

As it was now, with Duncan and Alistair watching Graeme McKinley standing at the edge of the cordon, established by the station officer, they could see little left of what was an established operation. It was dark and all that illuminated the scene were the lights from the two appliances, a second having arrived from Portree to assist the first, bathing the charred and smoking ruins in artificial light.

Graeme hadn't said much after his outbursts, making accusations about who was responsible. Seemingly resigned to his fate, he stood alone, surveying his livelihood. Alistair lowered his voice to ensure he wasn't overheard but with all the apparatus, pumps and hoses along with continued communication between the two fire brigade crews, their words wouldn't carry far.

"Does he look like a man who has lost everything to you?"

Duncan was pensive. The value in his business was in the

livestock, and that was all still in place, within the sea pens off the coast. The processing site was destroyed, but it could be rebuilt in time. Graeme McKinley looked a little lost, shocked and overwhelmed, possibly. Everyone processed extreme events in their own way.

Duncan came to stand beside Graeme who didn't acknowledge his arrival, staring straight ahead at the remnants of his facility.

"My father started this business back in the early sixties," he said quietly. Glancing sideways at Duncan, he pursed his lips. "Did I tell you that?"

"Aye, you did. You've been going a long time."

Graeme sniffed. For Duncan, too, the acrid smell of burnt timber mixed with who knows what that was stored in the barn made Duncan's eyes water and left a strange smell in his nostrils. It was unpleasant.

"Not for much longer," Graeme said, and Duncan detected an edge to his tone, was it regret? It certainly struck of finality.

"You can rebuild."

Graeme shook his head, his gaze fixed on the smouldering structure, now only recognisable from the steel frame, all that was left standing. The roof had collapsed, and the walls destroyed. "It's over."

"I know it looks that way now, but once you get the insurance payout—"

"There will be no payout, DI McAdam." Graeme looked sideways at him. "Mark my words."

Duncan was astounded. "Why not?"

"Because... when your business is drowning... the first thing you cut back on to stay afloat are the things you never use, and hope you'll never need." He smiled, still staring straight ahead. There was no humour in it though. It was a smile of resignation.

"You told Alistair that you were insured, just now."

Graeme shook his head. "Aye, well… the last thing I need is a smug look from Alistair MacEachran to make me feel even more like a bloody clown."

"So… you're not covered?"

"Do you know how much it costs to insure these facilities?"

Duncan had no clue. "I can't say I do, no."

"The headline number doesn't matter. It was more than I could afford… and when the renewal came in, it was up forty percent on the same cover last year."

"How is that justifiable?"

Graeme laughed. "They're all working off the same spreadsheets, DI McAdam. And if they all move the goalposts, then it doesn't matter which field you go to play on, does it? I cut back on my cover… and now I'm going to pay the price for it."

Duncan felt for him in that moment, having watched his family business burn to the ground, knowing it was likely the final act of his stewardship.

"What will you do?"

Graeme shrugged. "If I cannae find a way to make it work… I'll take an offer from one of the other operators, I suspect. Although, in light of this," he gestured towards the ruins, "I shall expect the size of the offer to decline somewhat."

"Will it be enough?" Duncan asked.

Graeme looked at him quizzically. "To start again?"

Duncan nodded.

"Aye… a fresh start of sorts. Doing what though?" He shook his head. "This is all I've ever known. It's all I ever thought I would do." He looked at Duncan and he could see Graeme was welling up. "What am I supposed to do?"

Duncan didn't have any words of comfort for him. Starting again at any point in life was hard enough, but to do so at his age, when he'd been the managing director of his own family business for his entire working life, must be incredibly daunting.

"Something will turn up," he said. The words sounded hollow. They were hollow and no doubt offered scant comfort.

"Aye, let's hope so, eh?"

"Listen, I know this is a bad time, but I have to ask you about what you said before… the suggestion that someone—"

"Burned my livelihood to the ground?" Graeme asked. "Go ahead."

"What makes you think so? That this is what happened here tonight?"

Graeme took a deep breath. He was remarkably calm now, a far cry from his earlier demeanour. Reality had sunk in perhaps, or he was simply in shock.

"I had a visit…" he glanced at Duncan. "Some woman… telling me – no, warning me – that what I was doing was wrong and that if I didn't make changes, she would see to it that I was held accountable."

"What did you think she meant by that?"

Graeme laughed and pointed ahead of them. "I didn't think she meant this! People have made allegations before… and I've pushed back. I'm not someone who gives in lightly, DI McAdam. I'll fight my corner."

"Who was this woman?"

He shrugged. "I don't know. I'd never clapped eyes on her before."

"When was this?"

"A couple of weeks back, maybe more." Graeme sighed. "I've been *so, so busy* just trying to stay afloat… working all the hours I could, trying to find investors… extend credit lines at the banks and push my clients to cut me a break and pay me faster. Not that they did, mind you. Wasted my time, didn't I?"

Duncan inclined his head. "Have you been keeping up with the news recently?"

Graeme looked at him, his brow furrowing. "No, I cannae say I have. Why?"

"You know we found a woman's body down at Talisker?"

"Aye, of course I heard. I've been really busy but I've no' been under a rock."

Duncan took out his mobile. He had an image saved on it. He sought it out, opening it to full screen and passed it to Graeme who took the device and looked at it.

"Aye... that's her all right," he said, surprised. "What's she done?" he asked, handing Duncan his phone back.

"She's dead," Duncan said flatly. Graeme stood open mouthed, confused.

"Seriously?"

Duncan nodded gravely. "Stabbed to death."

Graeme exhaled heavily. "Shite."

"Any idea who might want to do that?"

Graeme McKinley straightened his back, eyes widening as it dawned on him where Duncan was going with this line of questioning. "Now... just you hold on a minute. I had nothing to do—"

"I never said you did," Duncan countered. "Although, it is a remarkable coincidence."

"Coincidence, my backside. As if I dinnae have enough to worry about as it is, you think I'd want to add a murder charge to everything else?"

"Things happen in the heat of the moment," Duncan said, "when you're under intense stress for a prolonged period of time."

Graeme scoffed. "Do I need to get myself a solicitor to have this conversation?"

Duncan cocked his head. "Do you have anything to hide?"

"No, I don't!"

"Then you have nothing to fear."

"Aye, if only history didn't prove you very wrong on that score."

"I'll need to know your movements and whereabouts for the last few days," Duncan said.

"I keep a busy diary," Graeme countered. "Like I said, I've been all over trying to rob Peter to pay Paul… not literally, you understand? There are scores of people who'll vouch for my whereabouts in the past week. I've been nowhere near Talisker, I can assure you."

"Good. The sooner I can eliminate you from the investigation, the better it will be for all of us."

"Too right," Graeme said, a veil of indignation descending across his face.

"What did she have on you?" Duncan asked. Graeme looked at him, his eyes narrowing. "When she threatened you. What did she have to use as leverage?"

"Nothing."

"She must have had something," Duncan argued. "People can't threaten to harm your business without something."

Graeme stood in silence for a minute, Duncan allowing the air to thicken between them.

"It couldn't be something to do with your evasion of welfare protocols, could it? She'd been watching your operation for some time as far as I can tell."

Graeme turned to face Duncan. Their eyes met. "If you want to bury me alongside my business, that's your prerogative, Detective Inspector, but don't ask me to supply you with the nails for my coffin too, all right?"

Duncan held his gaze and said nothing. Graeme saw the approach of Alistair, who sported a curious expression, clearly keen to hear the content of their discussion. Graeme McKinley shook his head, grinning sarcastically.

"You lot," Graeme said. "I don't know who's worse, the scumbags stealing from me, the corporations bleeding me dry… or you lot, circling above me like vultures; all of you waiting to take your pound of flesh."

Duncan didn't care for the hyperbole. "You mentioned Archie Mackinnon before."

"Aye, he was with her… that woman."

"When she threatened you?"

"Not beside her, no," Graeme said, "but he was waiting on the hill outside. I saw him."

"You know Archie?" Duncan asked.

"Everyone knows Archie," Graeme said, "and one of these days I'd catch him stealing from me and I was going to…"

"Going to what?"

Graeme smiled at Duncan. "Report him to the police, of course."

Duncan also smiled. "Of course."

Graeme turned to look at both of them in turn. His expression was cold, his jaw set. "If you'll excuse me, detectives. I have to go home and explain all of this to my wife. She deserves to hear it from me before the press get their grubby hands on it."

"I'll need those details of your movements first thing tomorrow morning," Duncan said calmly. Graeme paused as he walked past him, glanced sideways at him and nodded. Alistair watched him walk out of the yard and get into his Mercedes parked to the side of the access road, up on the verge.

"He's not looking good, is he?"

Duncan followed Alistair's gaze. "No. I think it safe to say, he's a broken man."

"You don't think all of this is an inside job, then?"

Duncan took a breath. "Well, if you're going to go to the effort of torching your own business, you'd think you'd be savvy enough to make sure you had adequate insurance cover, wouldn't you?"

"He never…" Alistair said.

"In his own words, he's finished."

"Poor bastard."

CHAPTER NINETEEN

DUNCAN PULLED up at the front of the house. He was barely out of the car before Archie's terrier appeared by his side, leaping up at him, his stumpy tail twitching with excitement.

"Hello wee fella," Duncan said, reaching down and scratching the dog's head behind the ears. "Is your master home?"

The dog dropped back onto four legs and took off around the house. Duncan followed. He found Archie in his kitchen, standing at the sink washing up. Duncan entered and smiled at his old friend.

"How's it going, Archie?"

"Braw, Dunc. How's yourself?"

Duncan nodded, glancing around the kitchen. He'd never seen it so clean and tidy. Where there had always been accumulations of what Duncan could only describe as *stuff*, now there were clear surfaces, spotlessly clean and everything had been put away or disposed of entirely.

"Aye… all good." Duncan frowned. "What's going on?"

Archie paused what he was doing and looked at him. "Going on?"

"With this place," Duncan said. "Have you hired a cleaner or something?"

"No. I've no need of a servant. I can do it myself."

"You… did all of this?"

"I did."

Duncan was surprised. "Don't take this the wrong way, but are you feeling, okay?"

"I'm perfectly fine."

Archie did seem bright eyed, which in and of itself was quite a shift away from normality. Usually at this time of night, if he wasn't out on one of his nocturnal sorties, Archie would have had a skinful and would be fast asleep on the sofa by now. Something strange was going on here.

"I'm sure you have your reasons, Archie," Duncan said, "and I'd like nothing more than to tease them out of you because you'll never offer it willingly… but I need to speak to you about something more pressing."

"Aye, aye," Archie said, pulling off his rubber gloves with a snap having tipped the washing up bowl upside down in the basin. He tossed them aside and folded his arms across his chest. "You've got that… polis expression all over your face, I know it well. What's up?"

Duncan exhaled. "What were you doing up on the hills when I saw you the other day?"

"Och… not that again. Away with you, man—"

"Archie, this is serious, I need to know."

"Why? What's so interesting about me being out walking. I wasn't doing anything."

"Then there should be no harm in telling me, right?"

Archie fixed Duncan with a stern look. He was displeased, his body language defensive. "I was out for a—"

"Walk, aye," Duncan said. "So, you keep saying. What were you doing at Graeme McKinley's site a while back?"

Archie looked away. "Who says I was—"

"Archie, come on… this is me you're talking to."

"Aye, a professional busybody… with a uniform."

"My uniform wouldn't fit me anymore," Duncan said absently.

"That's because you spend too much time sitting behind a desk," Archie said, looking back at him, "or driving about the island annoying honest folk."

Duncan laughed. "Honest… you? Do me a favour."

Archie shrugged, flushing. "I only take what I need… or can sell." He held up a hand. "Not that I'm justifying anything, it's just a man needs to get by somehow."

"And with your inheritance, I presume you'll be able to go legit now, yes?"

Archie wrinkled his nose. "It seems I… maybe overestimated my share of what was coming to me."

"You did?"

"Aye, it turns out my niece has another uncle on the other side of the family… and he has bairns…"

"I'm… sorry to hear that," Duncan said. "I think."

"Well, it'll still be a bit of a windfall, so you cannae complain, can you?"

"Great use of deflection, Archie, but what were you doing at McKinley's place?"

"It's a free country."

"With Ava Caldwell," Duncan said, staring at him, almost daring him to offer another denial.

"Ava…" Archie bit his bottom lip, his eyelids fluttering in an involuntary movement which Duncan recognised as something that'd always struck his friend in moments of stress. Particularly so when he was unprepared. That'd befallen him once at school when Archie had been asked to dance by one of their classmates.

"Ava," Duncan repeated. "You know her, don't you?"

Archie nodded. "Aye, I do. Known her for a long time."

Duncan pulled out a chair at the small dining table nestled into the corner of the kitchen. "Tell me about her."

Archie frowned. "I'll need something with a kick if I'm going to do that." He left Duncan and went through into the adjoining living room, returning with a bottle of scotch. He found a glass in a wall-mounted cabinet, holding it up to Duncan who shook his head. "Just me then," Archie said, setting the glass down on the table and pouring himself a generous two-finger measure. Duncan noticed he didn't put the cap back on the bottle as he sat down, glass in hand.

"You said you go back a way, you and Ava?"

"Aye… known her since we were weans."

Duncan was confused. "How come I don't remember this girl?"

Archie laughed. "You only had eyes for a blonde, if I remember rightly."

Duncan flushed and nodded. "Even so." He thought hard. "If you knew her, then I should—"

"Mind, I only came up to Kensaleyre when I was nine, though."

Duncan had forgotten that. It was so easy to remember Archie as a constant fixture in his entire childhood, but he was right, they'd only met at that point.

"Where were you before that?" Duncan asked, searching the depths of his memory.

"We were on the south of the island, living near Tarskavaig," Archie said.

"Aye, that's right. Sleat," Duncan said, nodding. "I'd forgotten that."

"My father used to work for several people down that way, and then he tenanted a croft for a few years before he had the opportunity to take on this place," Archie said, looking around and lifting his glass to his lips. "I knew Ava from back then."

"Who was she to you?"

"Oh, her mum and mine were pals," Archie said, "so we used to spend a lot of time together, you know? Not that I liked hanging out with a wee girl... I mean, who would at that age, right? I didnae have much of a choice about it though, at the time. If only I'd known back then what I know now... maybe I'd have felt different. Anyway, my father was always out working until all times of the day and night, doing what he had to do. Ava's father was the same."

"And her father, what did he do?"

"Oh, he was on the trawlers... captain of his own boat, too, as I recall," Archie said. "It wasnae a big boat and had a small-ish crew, but he was a grafter." He took on a thoughtful expression. "You know, I cannae mind what he looked like which just goes to show you how little I saw of him back in the day."

"Did she go to our high school too?"

"Oh aye, she did," Archie said, finishing his drink and pouring another. Duncan felt bad. Clearly his insistence on having this conversation had pushed Archie back into his usual habit of an evening. "For a time, anyway."

Duncan frowned. "I really can't recall her."

Archie laughed. "Well, she was one to keep to herself. She was at the school a while before I realised too, and I'd known her for years." Archie waved away Duncan's concern. "She left again soon after too. Her mother took her onto the mainland."

"What happened, a divorce?"

Archie's expression shifted to one of melancholy and he

sipped at his drink. "No, her father passed away… it was sudden."

"And the boat?"

Archie shifted in his seat. "He'd already lost it, I think. It was a tough time for the industry back then."

"I don't think much has changed in that regard when it comes to the smaller crews."

"Aye, well… her mum took her onto the mainland, Glasgow, I think. She had relatives down that way."

"Wasn't she Canadian?" Duncan asked.

Archie was thoughtful. "You know, I think you're right. She was, aye. She'd been in the UK for years, though. I don't mind Ava ever talking about anyone or anything Canadian, so she cannae have visited much."

"How often did you see or hear from her?"

Archie shook his head. "That's just it. I hadn't seen hide nor hair of her for years. I'd forgotten all about her, to be honest."

"Until?"

"A few weeks back. She just turned up here at the croft. I barely recognised her, but as soon as she started talking, then I knew who she was. It was a hell of a surprise." Archie necked his second glass of scotch and went to pour another.

"Go easy," Duncan said, indicating the bottle in Archie's hand. He nodded and set it back down, leaving his glass empty. "What was she doing back here?"

Archie shrugged. "Visiting, or so she said. Planning to do a bit of walking… taking in the old haunts. She hadn't been back to Skye for years and missed it a lot."

"It doesn't sound like a place holding happy memories for her," Duncan said.

Archie agreed. "Aye, thought it strange myself, I have to say."

"How did she get out here?" Duncan asked. "Was she driving?"

"No, bus and hitching I think." Archie's forehead furrowed as he thought. "She had no plans as to where she was heading either. She crashed here with me for a couple of days, ended up borrowing some of my kit."

"Camping?"

"Aye." Archie nodded and then looked sideways at Duncan with a trace of a smile. "I dinnae suppose there's a chance of getting my stuff back anytime soon, is there?"

Duncan sighed. "No, there isn't. And you went with her to Graeme McKinley's place?"

"I went with her... but not to Graeme's." He shook his head. "The man doesn't care for me at all, and I thought it best not to poke the bear, you know?"

"Aye, he reckons you've been poaching from him."

Archie feigned offence. "As if I would! He should be so lucky, growing all that diseased stock."

"Ah, now that sounds like Ava talking," Duncan said. "Did you know she was an environmental activist?"

Archie wrinkled his nose. "I did get that impression, aye. She was very passionate... made a good case for change too. Not that she needed to convince me."

"I didn't have you down as a disrupter," Duncan said. "Someone keen to evoke radical shifts in policy."

Archie laughed. "Radical... me..." He shook his head. "Nah... but it doesnae mean I'm no' of the same opinion. I just think... who wants to hear what I have to say on anything."

"I would," Duncan said.

"Aye, but you're not exactly someone who matters, are you?"

"Thanks very much."

"No, that's not how I mean it and you know it. I'm just

saying the people who can change things, they don't care what I think. I'm just one voice... all the way out here. I count for nothing."

"That's why there are activists," Duncan said. "People like Ava."

"Aye... people like her." Archie poured himself another drink, tilting the bottle towards Duncan. "Are you sure I cannae tempt you to a wee dram?"

"Ah, go on then. Just make sure it is a wee one though, aye?"

Archie smiled and got up, returning to the table with another glass and poured Duncan a drink, keeping it small as requested.

"Why didn't you tell me you knew her?" Duncan asked.

Archie shrugged. "I didn't know it was her until... until I saw you at her campsite. By then... I figured you'd have it all worked out soon enough."

"You should have come forward, Archie—"

"Why?"

"Because your friend has been murdered, that's why? Your information could help find out who did it."

Archie frowned. "I keep myself to myself, Duncan, you know that. I'm no' one for sticking my nose into other people's affairs. And I dinnae want to have the polis all around me. Cramps ma style." He spread his hands wide. "No offence, you're different."

"You make an exception for me, aye?"

Archie nodded. "Besides, what good have I done for your investigation in this conversation, eh? I don't know who might have killed her, or why, any more than you do."

"You know she went to see Graeme, though."

"Aye... but she didnae say anything to me about why... and I didn't ask."

"Oh, come on, Archie! You expect me to believe that?"

"Believe what you want, Duncan, but she didn't say. As far as I know, they could have been old pals." He winked at him. "Maybe lovers."

"She threatened him... and his business."

Archie frowned, then shook his head having considered it. "Nah, I don't believe it. Ava wasn't the type."

Duncan cocked his head. "Graeme was insistent."

"Then he is full of it!" Archie said, raising his glass. "To Ava."

Duncan lifted his own and sipped at it, while Archie drank half of his in a single swallow.

"She must have spoken to you about Graeme's practices... or her suspicions he was getting around the regulations."

"Oh aye, she did talk about that," Archie agreed. "And she wasnae pleased about it. She was scathing about the whole finfish farming industry... I cannae say I agree with her on that. People need to eat... and the world has a lot of people in it."

"Could that be what brought her to the island then?" Duncan asked. "Perhaps to investigate the fish farming industry?"

Archie shrugged, staring at his scotch. "Maybe."

"You suggested Ava and Graeme might be past lovers—"

"God man! I was only joking, although... she may well have had someone on the island she cares for but whether it was an old flame that still smouldered, or not, I doubt it."

"Who else was she planning on seeing while she was here, did she say?"

Archie turned the corners of his mouth down, but he wouldn't meet Duncan's eye.

"It's important, Archie. Someone killed her, you know?"

He lifted his head and glanced at Duncan, looking despondent. "I know… and that's very sad. Ava was a nice lassie. She didnae deserve to go out that way."

"Does she have family locally? We haven't been able to locate anyone."

Archie shook his head. "She didnae mention anyone to me. Her mother died years back, and she was an only child. I gathered she was a bit of a rolling stone, you know?"

"Aye, gathers no moss," Duncan said. He sat forward, locking eyes with his friend. "I have to ask you something."

"Oh… sounds… bad, if you're looking at me that way. I didnae do it, Duncan."

"Do what?"

"Whatever it is you're about to ask me…"

Duncan shook his head. "Graeme McKinley's site out at Fiscavaig burned down earlier today."

"Did it now?" Archie said, eyes wide. His expression then changed. Duncan found it peculiar and a little hard to read. "Maybe that's an example of karma for you, happening in real time."

Duncan took a deep breath, not amused. Archie noticed and held his hands up in supplication.

"Tell me you had nothing to do with it, Archie, please."

Archie looked genuinely offended. "That's not ma style, is it, Duncan? Come on. I like a quiet life, you know that. Arson is… not me."

Duncan nodded. He hadn't thought there was anything in Graeme's accusations anyway. Poaching, on the other hand? Archie was certainly capable and would be caught bang to rights one of these days, but he wasn't the type to get involved in anything on this scale. What would he have to gain from doing such a thing anyway?

"I know… but I had to ask, sorry."

"Aye, nae bother, Dunc."

"Do you know if Ava came here alone, to the island, I mean?"

Archie thought hard. "As far as I know, aye. She didn't mention anyone else to me."

"And she didn't talk about visiting anyone else?"

Archie shrugged, picking up his glass and draining it. Curiously, he didn't directly answer the question. When he put the glass back down, Duncan looked at him sternly.

"Did she?"

"No," Archie said, holding Duncan's gaze. "She didn't."

CHAPTER TWENTY

DUNCAN HUNG up on the call as it cut to voicemail, cursing softly. This was the third time he'd made the call and, on this occasion, there were several rings before the transfer occurred. The phone had been off, but now it was on, however she still wasn't picking up. At least, not to him.

Alistair rapped his knuckles on the door, poking his head around to get Duncan's attention. Distracted, Duncan nodded at him and called Becky again. It went straight to voicemail. Irritated, Duncan put his phone down on the desk and looked at Alistair, still waiting patiently.

"Yes, Al. What is it?"

"A couple of things actually."

Duncan sighed. "Give me the most positive one first, if you don't mind." He pinched the bridge of his nose, closing his eyes. He'd woken with a headache, and nothing seemed able to shift it.

"The big man upstairs is after an update on the search for Finn MacGregor," Alistair said. "Apparently, the MacGregors have dispensed with the advice of our liaison officer and gone public. They'll be on the telly at lunchtime."

"Shit," Duncan said. "That's all we need."

"Aye, and big trousers," Alistair said, referring to their detective chief superintendent in his own respectful way, "doesn't like negative press. Bad for the pension."

"His career, you mean?"

"One and the same thing, in my mind," Alistair said. "Anyway, excrement flows downhill, and so he's kicking off; wants something positive to say to the media who are laying siege to his office. I know he has a secretary to field the calls for him, but he's no' a happy bunny."

Duncan sighed. "I did ask for the positive one first, Alistair."

"Aye, and that was the positive."

"Great. What else?"

"Ava Caldwell's murder is already being linked to the fire at McKinley's place."

"By whom?"

"You know what these things are like, people talk, and nothing gets people talking more than a suspicious death and the hint of a bit of corruption."

"The idea of a bit of scandal around the farming, you mean?" Duncan asked.

"Aye, that's it. Usually, I would say it was the norm, expected… but it's about to get a massive injection of steroids."

Duncan looked at him quizzically. "What are you talking about?"

"Anything surrounding the fishing industry is fairly emotive among the general public, and there will always be those looking to tap into that base," Alistair said, arching his eyebrows, "to make capital for themselves."

"You're talking about politicians, aren't you?"

"Aye. The leader of the opposition is going to raise a

question today and, we believe, is going to specifically link it to our investigation. A whole... *look at the consternation this is bringing to our communities,* type of thing. You can imagine how big trousers feels about the prospect of that happening."

"I'm surprised he's not summoned me upstairs and set about me with that letter opener he keeps on his desk for opening his personal mail."

"Nah," Alistair said. "He's no' a letter opener kinda guy, it'd be more a blunt spooning he'd subject you to..."

Duncan smiled. "Any progress on linking Finn MacGregor to Ava Caldwell?"

"No, not yet. Angus is still working on it but boy, those teenagers can talk. I mean, they will jabber on about nothing for ages. Sifting through it would drive me insane."

"Has anyone in the media made the link yet?"

"No, not yet. Your wee pal, Katie Matheson hasn't reappeared yet. I should imagine if it was going to come from anywhere, it would likely be her. She's been on the money so far."

Duncan was thoughtful. "Aye, her story was shelved and so I doubt they'll be listening to her anytime soon, unless it suits her editor anyway." Duncan sat forward in his chair, resting his elbows on his desk. "You know, we assumed Ava was Katie's source..."

"And that her death has scared Katie into silence, aye," Alistair said. "Stands to reason. Why do you mention it?"

"What if... it's someone else entirely, but that person was close to Ava?"

Alistair shrugged. "Aye, interesting thought but unless you know who that someone is, then it's purely academic."

"True."

"You'd better get a move on," Alistair said. Duncan looked

at him, confused. "I told big trousers you were on your way to see Craig."

"Oh damn, Craig." Duncan had completely forgotten to return his call, so distracted was he with Callum's disappearance. "What is it he wanted to speak about?"

"I think it was something about blood test results, but he didn't want to speak to me, just the organ grinder." Alistair frowned. "Today though, he's got some word back from the specialists he reached out to regarding the abnormalities we discussed after the postmortem."

"Right," Duncan said, rising and picking up his mobile and glancing at the screen in hope of a notification. There were no messages from Becky. "If you need me, I'll be with Craig."

"It's about time you came back to me, Detective Inspector McAdam," Dr Dunbar said, as Duncan walked into his office. "I was beginning to think I was persona non grata with you or something."

"Person of what now?" Duncan asked. Craig Dunbar waved the question away. "You've had the blood tests back, Alistair tells me."

"Er... yes, and no."

Duncan was perplexed. "Is it yes or is it no, it cannae be both."

"Funny you should say that," Craig said, smiling. "But I'll come to that later, and I assure you it will be worth the wait."

"Okay, what's first then?" Duncan asked, scanning the little office. It was incredibly neat and tidy. Dr Dunbar was clearly a fastidious man when it came to staying on top of things. This place was like one of the hot desks they kept clear at the station for visitors to use, with no personal effects left to clutter the space.

"You recall," Craig said, "I came across some anomalies with the deceased, specifically surrounding the concentration of proteins in the cerebrospinal fluid." Duncan nodded. "And I'm quite certain you had no idea what I was talking about."

Duncan inclined his head, a trace of a smile crossing his lips. "I doubt much has changed, to be honest."

"Well… quite," Craig said, tapping away on his keyboard and accessing a folder of documents. "I must admit I was surprised when my colleagues came back to me. It was fascinating."

Duncan pulled out a chair and sat down opposite him. "What is?"

"Your victim, of course." Craig peered at Duncan over the rim of his glasses. "How familiar are you with mitochondria?"

"Basics, please Craig."

Dr Dunbar grinned. There was never any hint of him expressing his intellectual superiority at any time in their interactions, but Craig was genuinely fascinated by the human body.

"Mitochondria, are cellular organelles within eukaryotic cells that convert food into chemical energy that cells can then use to power their biochemical reactions."

Duncan listened carefully. This was important, it had to be, although the sciences were his worst subjects at school.

"Now, mitochondrial DNA is the circular chromosome found inside the cellular organelles called mitochondria—"

"Head's spinning already, Craig."

"Bear with me," Craig said. "The mitochondria are small rod-like structures found in every cell within the body – converting chemical energy into food, as I just said – and this enables the cells to function in whatever purpose they have.

Now, should there be anything that interferes or interrupts this process, then you can imagine what could happen."

"Cells won't function properly…"

"Correct. On a base level, the cells won't be able to function and that can have knock-on effects to the body. There are diseases which can have these negative effects but, in this case, what I've been directed to is a particular syndrome, a rare syndrome that results in abnormalities within the mitochondrial DNA."

"Ava Caldwell suffered from this… syndrome?"

"Yes, she did. It is abbreviated as KSS, or Kearns-Sayre Syndrome; a neuromuscular disorder; a mitochondrial DNA deletion syndrome that has multi-system effects." Craig brought up a page on a website, angling the monitor so that Duncan could better see the screen. The images depicted the make-up of a cell. Duncan gave it a cursory look. "The majority of the research into this particular syndrome has been carried out in the USA, unsurprisingly with their budgetary levels for research, where it is estimated fewer than fifty thousand people across the population suffer from it. I haven't got any numbers for the UK, but I didn't think that was necessarily relevant."

"What are the effects?" Duncan asked.

"Let me ensure I have this correct," Craig said, switching tabs on the screen and reading from another page on the same website. "Chronic… progressive external ophthalmoplegia is most notable," he said, looking over at Duncan and lifting his glasses from his nose. "That is to say, weakened or paralysed muscles around the eye area; so, the eyelids may droop or eye movement may well be impaired. The salt-and-pepper effect on the retina that caught my eye," he tilted his head to one side, with a sideways smile, "no pun intended, is another common effect."

"Very good," Duncan said, half-heartedly praising the pun.

Craig's smile dissipated and he cleared his throat, putting his glasses back on. "The technical name for that symptom is pigmentary retinopathy, which is where the light-sensing retina is permanently damaged. There are, however, far more noticeable effects visible to the naked eye, and not just in a postmortem. Sufferers can struggle with coordination of their limbs; their gait and posture can be disturbed as can their balance. They can have weakened muscles in both their arms and legs, kidney function complications, and suffer from deafness or have cognitive issues. The high protein concentration I found exists in the spinal fluid and also around the brain."

Duncan ran a hand through his hair, considering the information. "To a layman, that sounds fairly debilitating."

Craig nodded sombrely. "These are a very wide range of effects, and there is no guarantee that every person with KSS will suffer in the same manner, which makes it a tricky condition to diagnose. Not least because of how rare it is."

"Is it a progressive illness?"

"Aye, and again, it affects different people in different ways, and so there is no rule of thumb, so to speak."

"Treatments?" Duncan asked, although he knew it was purely academic in Ava's case.

Craig shook his head. "This is a genetic syndrome, passed from the female to the child because it is the egg cells, rather than sperm cells, that contribute to mitochondria in the forming of an embryo. There is no cure... until we manage to reconstruct mitochondrial DNA at any rate... but that is well into the realms of science fiction rather than factual reality, at this point. There are various treatments for the conditions that arise though, so there is some help for the afflicted there."

"If it is diagnosed, presumably," Duncan said. Craig acknowledged that with a brief nod. "Was it a life-threatening condition?" Duncan asked, curious to know because if it was then Ava may well have made her life choices based on that information.

"I'm afraid it is a progressive disorder... and as is the case with these things, the degenerative effect gets worse over time." Craig was momentarily thoughtful. "Statistically, it is usually in a patient's fourth decade of life that they pass away. The sufferer can begin exhibiting symptoms from a variety of ages, from infant or preadolescence through to adulthood. The nature of such a disorder does make it likely, in my mind at least, to be more noticeable at childhood. We see clumsy children, for example, but this would be more regular and therefore more visible, more pronounced shall we say, one would think. Although, I'm only hypothesising. It could be easily missed, one might imagine. Children trip over their own feet frequently, so I'm led to believe."

"You don't have children?"

Craig shook his head. "Far too needy and demanding of one's time for me, I'm afraid. I'm far too selfish. You?"

Duncan didn't answer the question. "What was it you were going to tell me about blood tests that was so interesting?"

"Oh... yes, that's right," Craig said, looking to both left and right before reaching down and opening the bottom drawer of his pedestal. He produced a brown manilla folder and put it in front of him on his desk, opening it up and casting an eye over the summary. "Yes, here it is. Your forensic people asked for a blood sample from Mrs MacGregor... Finn's mother... for comparison?" He looked at Duncan for confirmation.

"Aye, that's right. We were going to compare it to the sample of blood taken from the beanie that Marsali, Mrs MacGregor, identified as her son's."

"Ah… that's right," Craig said, sitting back and taking off his glasses which he held in the air before him, his forehead creased in concentration. "Hmm…"

Duncan shrugged. "So, what's up?"

"It's not his blood," Craig said, jabbing his glasses towards him, which piqued Duncan's curiosity. He sat forward.

"There's more though, isn't there?"

"Aye, and that's where the yes and no, I mentioned comes from," Craig said, his demeanour lightening as he raised his eyebrows. "I should say, it's either not Finn's blood or Marsali isn't his mother."

"What?"

Craig Dunbar exhaled slowly. "I say this without trying to cause a sensation, far be it from me to cast aspersions on someone's honesty and integrity," he said, "but the lab ran the sample taken from the beanie against the records we have for comparison, for elimination purposes as much for confirmation. They checked their results with me for fear that samples, at best, had been mixed up somewhere along the line, or at worst, there had been some cross contamination in the forensic process."

"You're confident there hasn't been though?" Duncan asked.

"Positive. Everything is correctly logged, and the chain of evidence has not been broken." Craig pursed his lips.

"So… what are you telling me?"

"I'm telling you that the sample taken from the beanie does not share any biological markers with the sample provided by his mother, Marsali."

"So, it's not Finn's."

Craig spread his hands wide. "Which is why we asked for his father, Anthony, to pop by for us to take a sample of his blood to help with the comparison. He has failed to do so, despite several calls in which he assured us he would attend. Failed to show, twice."

"He has a lot on his mind, to be fair," Duncan said.

"And finding out if his child has an injury would be high on that list, wouldn't it?"

"You would think so," Duncan agreed. It certainly struck him as odd. "Was the sample run against known cases in the database?"

"I believe so, and there were no hits." Craig put his hands together in front of him, interlocking his fingers. "The mystery deepens further, Detective Inspector."

Duncan smiled. Dr Dunbar was correct; however, the pieces were starting to come together rather like a massive jigsaw puzzle. He just needed that connection, and everything would fit into place. Despite outward appearances to the contrary, this new information made him feel more confident and not less.

CHAPTER TWENTY-ONE

ANTHONY MACGREGOR'S car was parked outside the house. Duncan couldn't see Marsali's vehicle, and he wondered where she might be. Hopefully, the couple were not taking part in a live press conference where the actions, or perceived failure, of the police in finding their son were the topic of conversation. Duncan, mobile phone pressed to his ear, turned and looked down over the inlet of Loch Beag below. Houses on the far bank of Struan and Bracadale already had their lights on and despite it only being the middle of the day, it was dark enough to pass for evening in most parts of the country.

"Have you got all of that?" Duncan asked.

"Erm… I think so," Angus said.

"Are you sure?"

"Aye… I'm just a bit confused as to why… but I get it, aye."

"Don't worry, young man," Duncan said, "there's method to my madness. Get back to me as soon as you can."

"I will. I'll get right onto it."

Duncan hung up, standing with his back to the house. He

felt the breeze against him. The wind, having switched direction and now coming from the north once more, was bitterly cold. The recent rain of the past day had been due to warmer fronts pushing up from the southwest leading to snow falling on the higher ground of the peaks and giving the rest of the island some respite.

That would all come to an end now. Duncan was experienced enough to know that whatever would come down later that night, it would be snow. The often-said phrase, *it's too cold to snow* came to mind. Utter nonsense.

"I hope you're coming with news," Anthony MacGregor said from behind him. Duncan turned and nodded a greeting.

"I'm pleased you're home."

"Where else would I be? I've been sitting here waiting for the phone to ring, just as you said I should."

Duncan approached. Anthony was reserved, not hostile but the interview the couple gave to the press heralded their lack of belief in the police efforts to find their son.

"You sent your liaison officer away?" Duncan asked without judgement.

"She made us nervous," Anthony said. "She was a constant reminder of the situation and not helping."

"She was the bridge between the investigation and the family," Duncan said. "But we respect your wishes." Anthony stood across the doorway, arms folded. "May I come in?"

"If you want," Anthony said, turning and going inside. Duncan followed. Inside, Duncan found the house in disarray. Anthony led him through to the rear and the kitchen. The work surfaces were stacked with dirty cups and plates, odd bits of paper and clothing also lay on surfaces or across chairs.

Anthony's initial demeanour was replaced now by embarrassment as Duncan looked around them.

"Things have… got on top of us a bit this past week. I'd

offer you a cup of tea or something, but we haven't made it to the shops."

Duncan nodded. "It's understandable." He felt for the man. His son was missing, and life was on hold until that was resolved. For Duncan's part, hopefully that resolution would be positive. "I know you and Marsali aren't... happy with what steps we've taken—"

Anthony held up his hand. "I know you're doing your best, Detective Inspector. I do. Marsali... well," Anthony said, looking away. He looked exhausted, every line on his face seemed deeper now than it had done when they met a few days ago. "She'll come to understand, much as I have, that... Finn will come home when he's ready."

Duncan studied him. "You've never truly believed he'd been abducted or had an accident, have you?"

Anthony inclined his head but didn't answer.

"Why is that?"

Anthony sniffed, wiped the end of his nose with the back of his hand and pulled out a chair from beneath the dining table. He sank wearily down onto it. "Takes after me, that one."

"In what way?"

"If he has a problem, he can't deal with... first off, you ignore it and hope it goes away."

Duncan arched an eyebrow. "And if it doesn't? Go away, I mean."

"Hide from it until it does," Anthony said flatly, leaning forward and resting his elbows onto his knees and drawing his hands down across his cheeks, turning his face to the ceiling.

"You think your son is hiding?" Duncan asked. "From what?"

Anthony shrugged. "Me... his mum... life," he said,

shaking his head. "All of the above. How the hell would I know, I'm just his father."

Duncan leaned against the counter, thinking about his approach. He'd expected hostility, a belligerent attitude perhaps, but this wasn't what he was facing. This was something else entirely, resignation.

"Where's Marsali?" Duncan asked.

Anthony shrugged. "No clue."

Duncan's mobile rang and he saw it was Angus. Anthony didn't flinch and Duncan took the call right there in the kitchen.

"Angus, how did you get on?"

"Aye, it was quite easy to confirm it, but I think there must be something wrong somewhere along the line," Angus said. "There's no registering of the birth here in Portree, but Marsali is known to the children's service team on the island. Finn's birth was registered in Glasgow. That disnae sound right to me."

"No, that pretty much confirms what I was expecting. Thanks, Angus."

"Really? I thought I must have put the wrong name in or something…"

"No, don't worry, lad," Duncan said. "You did well to get that back to me so quickly."

Duncan hung up and slipped his phone back into his pocket, fixing his eye on Anthony. "It's hard when you have to watch your child growing into their own person," Duncan said. "Developing their own thoughts, views… personality."

Anthony glanced up at him and nodded. "Aye. Argumentative little beggars sometimes too."

Duncan smiled. "You've always lived here? In this house, I mean. Obviously, you've always lived on the island."

"Aye, we moved in here when Marsali was pregnant," he said. "And islanders born and bred. Much like yourself."

"You've been asking around, have you?"

"It's good to know who you're entrusting your family's safety to, you know?"

Duncan nodded. "I've spoken with Craig Dunbar, he's our forensic medical examiner and also—"

"I know Craig, aye."

"He tells me you've missed two appointments to provide a blood sample for comparison," Duncan said, moving to the window and looking out over the hillside at the back of the house. "Why is that?"

"I've been… I've had things on my mind."

Duncan turned back to face him. "I don't doubt it. The thing is, we're trying to find out if your son has suffered an injury, and so it's quite important."

"Aye, whatever. I'll do it first thing tomorrow… or later today if you need me to."

"It's just that Marsali has already given her sample. She was reticent to do so, mind you. Any idea why that might be?"

Anthony shrugged. "Always had a fear of needles… and doctors for that matter," he said. Duncan walked over to the far side of the kitchen where a framed photograph of the family was mounted on the wall. Finn was between his parents, Anthony with an arm around Marsali's shoulder and one hand on his son's. He pointed to it.

"A lovely picture. Taken around here?"

"Aye. No better place to be."

"I was tempted by the bright lights of the big city once," Duncan said. "Along with half the country, I thought I'd make it big on the mainland. No idea doing what, mind you, but it was going to be big. Did you ever think about migrating to the central belt, along with the rest of us?"

"Pah! Me? No way," Anthony said. "I wouldn't last five minutes in a city like Glasgow. It'd chew me up and then spit me out."

Duncan nodded. "You know anyone down that way?"

Anthony fixed his eye on Duncan. "What's with all the questions? I thought you were here to talk about the search for Finn?"

"Oh, I am. I'm just wondering..."

"About what?" Anthony asked.

"About how you and Ava Caldwell crossed paths, that's all." It wasn't a question. Duncan had made a statement. Anthony hesitated. There was a brief flicker of recognition before he looked away, but it was more than enough to confirm Duncan's suspicions. "How do you know her?"

"Who?"

"Ava," Duncan said. "The woman you were arguing with not a quarter of a mile away from where we are just now."

Anthony swallowed hard. His mouth must have run dry. "I... dinnae know what you're talking about."

"No? So, it was someone else, your twin brother perhaps, having a stand-up row with the woman lying in our mortuary over in Portree."

Anthony put his head in his hands, shaking it side to side. "No, no, no."

"Anthony, I'm tired of people lying to me. If you want anything resolved, then sooner or later, you're going to have to start telling me the truth."

His head snapped up and he glared at Duncan. "It's not what you're thinking."

"I don't know what to think just now, I really don't," Duncan said, truthfully. "What I do know is that there's a real question mark around whether Marsali is Finn's mother."

"She is his mother!" Anthony leapt up from the chair

catching Duncan by surprise. He didn't advance on him though, which Duncan was grateful for. He cocked his head.

"The blood sample suggests otherwise."

"It takes more than blood to make a mother," Anthony countered, "and she's got more than enough love for that boy than any biological connection would offer."

Duncan took a breath. Finally, he was getting some honesty.

"What's the betting that if we run your blood sample against it, we'll get a similar result?"

Anthony sat back down, put his head down, rubbing the sides vigorously with his hands. "You dinnae understand," he said, frustration in his tone. "You dinnae understand," he repeated in a whisper.

"Try me."

"She came to me… a few weeks or so back," Anthony said, staring at the floor by his feet. "She must have followed me or something, I don't know. I came out of the wholesalers… and she was there, standing beside my pick-up, waiting for me."

"Ava Caldwell?" Duncan asked. Anthony nodded. "Where do you know her from?"

He shook his head. "I've known her for years… since we were weans. My father worked with hers…"

"On the trawler?"

"Aye, but that was a long time ago. After her father…" he paused, looking up and steeling himself, "after he passed, things were really tough for Ava and her mother. They'd been struggling for a long time, so had we, what with our fathers working together. When they lost the boat… Ava's father, Bruce, couldn't… he couldn't find a way to cope. He tried… I know he tried, but… he couldna take it anymore."

"What happened?"

"He hanged himself. Ava came home from school one

afternoon and found him." Anthony shook his head. "I dinnae know what that does to a young bairn, but it wasnae good."

"That was why she left the island, with her mother?"

He nodded. "Aye, they... they had family on the mainland. They were distant family, but you come together in adversity, don't you?"

You would hope, Duncan thought but didn't say so.

"Did you keep in touch?"

He shook his head. "Maybe now things would be different, but mobile phones weren't even a thing back then. At least not for the likes of us. City types, maybe. Even... social media, wasn't even a dream back then. We had a Christmas card on occasion and my mum tried to keep in touch for a time, but things drifted on."

"So, when did you next see her?"

Anthony pursed his lips. He was considering lying. Duncan could tell.

"It was a while. Years." He sat upright, straightened his back and took in a deep breath. "Are you a spiritual man, Detective Inspector McAdam?"

"No."

Anthony laughed, but it was a sound without genuine humour. "You're direct, I'll give you that."

"It's both a blessing and a curse."

"I hear you," he said, meeting Duncan's eye. "If there's no divine power guiding all that we do, what about fate... destiny?"

"I feel the same about those too," Duncan said. "We have the life we make for ourselves... which, all too often, becomes the life we deserve. For good or for ill."

"Poignant." Anthony got up and walked to the sink. Picking up and inspecting a glass on the counter, he deemed it suitable and filled it with water. Taking a sip, he again struggled to swallow. Setting the glass down, he braced himself against the counter with both hands, avoiding Duncan's eye. "You see, for me… for us – Marsali and me – we do believe in a higher power." He glanced at Duncan. "We're not devout… we're not even very good Christians, but we do believe that there is a plan for all of us. What is sent to try us, will make us stronger. It's the only way to make sense of it all."

Duncan would beg to differ. The world as he saw it was a mass of heaving chaos beneath a thin veneer of control and organisation. A veneer that could easily be stripped away should the right, or indeed the wrong, conditions present themselves.

"You've lost me," Duncan said. Anthony looked at him and slowly nodded. He took a deep breath and gestured for Duncan to come with him.

A rack was mounted beside the rear door to the house, multiple thick winter coats, hats and scarves were hanging from hooks. Anthony took one, slipping his arms through it but he said nothing further. Opening the door, he held it for Duncan and the two men walked out into the back garden which stretched off to the west and up a fairly steep rise. Duncan could make out the fenced boundary above them.

A light flurry of snow was falling now and the hills in the distance Duncan could see when he'd arrived were now lost in cloud. The snow would intensify, and Duncan's thoughts turned to Finn, hoping his father was correct and he was hiding somewhere, shielded from the elements. Duncan drew his coat about him, fastening it up and turning the collar against the wind and snow, hunching his shoulders as he followed Anthony up the steep hillside.

The ground beneath their feet was frozen solid, and despite the rain, the grip they had was sufficient to make the short walk with relative ease. Even so, Duncan found himself breathing hard when the ground levelled off into a natural plateau. Anthony led them to a lone birch tree, towering above them at roughly fifteen foot tall. The branches were bare, but Anthony gazed upon it, his lips pursed. Duncan suddenly felt the cold. The house had been warm and why Anthony had them out here, he couldn't fathom.

"She's a lovely tree, isn't she, Duncan?"

He looked at it, casting an eye up and down it. "Birch, isn't it?" he asked, recognising it as one of the few species he could identify from the silver colouring of the bark.

"Aye, a silver birch," Anthony said softly, still staring at the tree. He took a moment where they stood in silence, before he turned to Duncan. "This species of tree symbolises new beginnings. The tree that will take root, grow... thrive in a landscape where previously no other tree would stand."

"Did you plant it?" Duncan asked.

Anthony nodded. "I did. It has double meaning for us," he said, glancing at the tree and then back at Duncan. Suddenly, he seemed hesitant, reluctant to explain but Duncan waited patiently, his arms clamped against his sides, his hands thrust deep into his pockets. He was already starting to lose the sensation in his toes. "This tree marks our new beginning... our life as a family with Finn," he looked at the base of the trunk, "and also the place where we laid our daughter to rest."

"Your daughter..."

Anthony met his eye and nodded. Even in the failing light, Duncan could see the tears in his eyes and as he bowed his head, they fell with the freshly falling snow.

CHAPTER TWENTY-TWO

THE GROUND WAS ALMOST FROZEN solid. Fortunately, the shift in the direction of the weather front, bringing slightly milder air up from continental Europe, ensured the team were still able to break ground. Duncan stood beyond the cordon, his collar up, both hands clamped around a warm cup of coffee that had just been handed to him. Alistair was alongside him, stamping his feet in the snow in an attempt to get his circulation moving.

"It's a dark omen when you're doing this sort of thing in the dead of night," he said. Duncan looked sideways at him.

"It's only eight o'clock," he said wryly.

Alistair tilted his head. "It may as well be the dead of night," he said, raising his eyes to the heavens. The snow was still falling, illuminating the landscape around them. The portable lights running off the nearby diesel generator lit up the area, casting a white light over the hillside to the back of the MacGregor residence. There was also the flashing blue lights of several patrol cars keeping the adjacent road clear of voyeurs, well-wishers and any passers-by who might fancy investigating the abnormal scene. "A dark omen," Alistair repeated quietly.

"I didn't have you down as the superstitious type, Alistair."

"This job has thrown a lot of weird things my way over the years… but this," he said, nodding towards the forensic team, clad in their coveralls beavering away beneath a makeshift cover attached to the birch tree and then staked out to either side a few metres away, providing them cover in which to work, "this is something else." He shook his head. "I never thought I'd see something like this on the island."

Duncan had to agree. They were still to explore the circumstances of how it came to this, with Anthony MacGregor clamming up almost as soon as Duncan made the call back to Portree.

"We'll have to wait and see if he's telling the truth."

"You think he might be lying?" Alistair asked. "That would be weird."

Duncan arched his eyebrows, an action probably unseen by his detective sergeant.

"Who knows? We come across all sorts of oddballs in this job."

"Aye, maybe down in Glasgow, but not out here. Not like this anyway."

Duncan nodded. Dr Dunbar came out from beneath the covering, beckoning them forward. Duncan threw his coffee away and put the cup down before they both ducked under the cordon, moving to meet Craig.

Usually, a tent would be erected over the site of such a dig, but the close proximity of the established tree made this impossible. The tent would have two main purposes, to ensure the integrity of the dig site by avoiding contamination of foreign objects but also to keep the procedure out of sight, allowing the team to work without fear of intrusion. Fortunately, where they were located was sparsely populated and, with the weather as it was, passers-by were limited. Even so, the heavy uniformed presence would keep prying eyes away.

"You should probably see this," Dr Dunbar said. Leading the two detectives back underneath the canopy, the forensic technicians who were working made way for them, all bar one who stood with a shovel in his hand, standing in the excavated hole. He nodded to both Duncan and Alistair, only his eyes visible from within the hood and face covering.

They had methodically dug down into the hill, reaching a depth of roughly four feet, Duncan guessed, taking layer after layer of earth from the ground, cutting it out in steps. Duncan came to the edge of the hole, dropping to his haunches as he surveyed the base of the excavation. They'd come across a wooden crate. It was a little over a foot wide and perhaps a foot and a half long. To Duncan, it looked like one of those old vegetable or apple crates you would find at a farmer's market but had been lined with more timber to close off the gaps between staves.

Duncan gave the go ahead to the forensic technician who carefully knelt down beside the crate. Another technician passed him a small metal bar, similar to a moulding removal tool Duncan had back at the croft, and the technician put the edge in the narrow crack between the side panel of the crate and the lid. He started gently at first, trying to tease the lid off but it was so securely fastened that he soon had to apply more pressure. Moving around the edge of the lid, he levered it up bit by bit, releasing the nails one at a time, doing so as delicately as he could.

Soon, the lid was free, and he passed the tool back up before lifting the lid to reveal the contents. Inside the crate was a bundle of fabric. It looked like a length of hessian material, the type used to make sacks for transporting grain or coffee beans. One of the technicians began photographing it in situ before the man in the hole determined it was a length of fabric rather than a bag. He carefully unwrapped it and beneath this layer, he found another blanket. This one was much softer, possibly once a pale blue or perhaps cream, it was emblazoned with cartoon puppies. An infant child's blanket, used in a cot or a pram to keep the baby warm.

Duncan held his breath, glancing at Alistair beside him who stood there, stone faced and silent. Duncan nodded and the technician folded back the blanket to reveal a tiny skull, lying on its side, barely larger than a balled fist. There were no words spoken. The only sound carrying in the night air was that of the wind rustling through the canopy and the dull, repetitive humming of the generators powering the lights.

Duncan caught the eye of the technician and nodded, rising and stepping back from the edge of the excavated hole. He turned to Craig Dunbar.

"Once you have the opportunity, I'd like to know what you think the child died from."

Craig nodded soberly. "Unless there's been some dramatic trauma to the bone structure, I won't be able to tell you tonight... if ever."

"Do the best you can, Craig," Duncan said. He turned away, looking down and past the police exclusion zone, denoted by the liveried patrol cars and their flashing lights, he saw the illuminated windows of houses along the shore on the far side of the inlet. A passing car moved slowly in the settling snow, heading north through Struan.

Alistair stood beside him at the edge of the cordon, sharing the view of the vista. "Well... I didn't have this on my bingo card for the week. How about you?" Alistair asked with no hint of humour in his tone. There was no dark humour that could hope to lighten the mood tonight.

Duncan shook his head. "Come on, let's go and speak to Anthony. See what he has to say for himself."

Entering the house from the door into the kitchen, Duncan saw Anthony MacGregor sitting alone at the dining table in the exact same pose as where he'd been when Duncan left him. DC McLean came over to see them, all three men had their eyes on Anthony.

"Has he said anything?" Duncan asked.

Russell shook his head. "No. Not a word."

"Any phone calls, texts or anything I should know about?"

Again, Russell shook his head. "He's just... sat there, like a statue. His expression hasn't changed one bit since I got here."

"In shock, possibly," Duncan said quietly.

"Aye," Alistair said. "The shock of being found out. It was bound to happen sooner or later. He must have been half expecting it one day."

Duncan moved around to stand opposite Anthony. After a moment, he glanced up at him and there was a spark of recognition.

"Anthony MacGregor," Duncan said, "I am arresting you on suspicion of committing an offence by knowingly carrying out a burial in respect of which no approval has been granted, in direct contravention of Section 8, subsection 1 of the *Burial and Cremation Act of 2016*. I believe that keeping you in custody is necessary and proportionate for the purposes of bringing you before a court or otherwise dealing with you in accordance with the law."

Anthony stared at Duncan and simply nodded. "Aye... sounds about right," he said softly. "You found her then."

Duncan nodded. "Are you going to tell me what happened?"

"There's no' much to tell, if I'm honest."

"I doubt that very much," Duncan said, pulling out a chair and sitting down opposite him. "I should advise you that you do not need to say anything—"

"Aye, it's a bit late for all of that, isn't it DI McAdam?" Anthony said, sighing and raising his eyes to the ceiling. "Whatever I have coming my way in this life will be nothing in comparison to what I'll likely face in the next."

"I'd like to focus on the here and now, if that's okay with you, Mr MacGregor?" Duncan asked. "Can you confirm the identity of the remains we've just unearthed on your property?"

Anthony closed his eyes for a moment, took a deep breath and nodded. "It is our daughter, Morven." He exhaled heavily. "February... twenty-first, next month... would have been her sixteenth birthday." He lifted his hands up and probed his eyes with his fingertips before dragging his hands down across his cheeks, stretching his face. He flexed his jaw, blinked away tears and set his hands down on the table in front of him, palms down.

"Care to tell us how she ended up buried out the back?" Duncan asked.

"She was born here... a month prematurely," Anthony said. "Marsali had... been suffering some symptoms of pre-eclampsia and the doctors were concerned about her, but she... and her sisters, had all been born at home and she wanted the same experience." Anthony shook his head. "I should have pushed it more at the time... maybe if she'd been at the hospital then things might have been different."

Duncan glanced at Alistair and Russell; the latter was taking notes of the exchange.

"Anyway," Anthony continued, "we all do what we think is for the best, don't we?" Duncan nodded but said nothing.

"Morven was… she died before she was born. Do you have any idea what that is like, Detective Inspector, to give birth to your child only to find out she had already passed?"

"No, I don't," Duncan said.

"Neither do I," Anthony said, "but for Marsali it must be the most traumatic and dreadful experience a mother can have, I should imagine. It was hard enough for me…"

"Had you called for assistance, for an ambulance perhaps?"

Anthony shook his head. "There was no time. It all happened so quickly. You hear of labours lasting for a couple of days, but this was over in a matter of hours. Before we knew what was happening… it was *all* happening."

"So, let me be clear, you are saying that Morven, your daughter, passed away from natural causes; that she was stillborn?"

"Aye, I am!" Anthony said, staring hard at Duncan. "What do you think I am, some kind of a monster? You think I'd kill my own child?"

"It takes all sorts," Duncan said and before Anthony could speak again, Duncan shut him down, "and the vast majority of people tend to call the authorities when something like this happens."

Anthony nodded vigorously. "I know, I know!" He put his head in his hands. "I should have done that… I know, I should have done that."

"Why didn't you?"

Anthony MacGregor shook his head. "It's just no' as simple as that. Marsali… she couldn't accept the fact that she was gone. She wouldn't give her up. She sat there with the wee thing, all wrapped up, in her arms. She hugged her, kissed her and… wouldn't acknowledge what had happened."

"What did you do next?"

"I called my mother," Anthony said. "She was still with us at the time… she's long passed the noo but… I talked to her. She was very supportive."

"How did you come to the point of burying Morven's body in the garden, Anthony?" Duncan asked. Anthony pursed his lips, avoiding Duncan's gaze. "You may as well tell us, because just now, this isn't going to go well for you, I can assure you."

Anthony sighed. "My mother had been in contact with Ava around that time. Ava's folks… her mother had passed away and she was alone, down in Glasgow. She came to my mother for help. And she was only too willing to help her. Ava was like a surrogate daughter to her. That's how close our families had been, our fathers working together, going through what they did back in the day."

"What has this to do with Morven?" Duncan asked.

Anthony met Duncan's eye. "Because she was pregnant, heavily pregnant at the time."

Duncan's eyes flicked to Alistair, and he nodded almost imperceptibly, his tongue pressed firmly into his cheek.

"Ava had fallen pregnant by some… married man," Anthony said. "She was at her wits' end. She'd been unable to work as the pregnancy had complications – I don't know what they were – and she was thinking she was going to be home-less." Anthony looked at Duncan, his forehead creased in consternation. "The poor lassie didn't know what to do like, you know. Anyway," he said shaking his head, "she was due in late February of that year, as it happened. She'd looked into giving the wee baby away when it was born… and… well, my mother suggested we could…" He took a deep inhalation, steadying himself. "We agreed to take him after he was born.

My mother put me in touch with Ava and we discussed it, what it would look like."

"There are proper channels for that sort of thing," Duncan said.

"I know that!" Anthony bit back aggressively. "But if you'd seen... if you'd seen the state of Marsali," he said, blinking away tears. "The mess she was in with her state of mind. I didnae think she'd even accepted Morven was gone. To this day, I think she's blanked all of that out. The birth... the baby and me... digging the grave."

"How did you make it happen?"

"With Finn?"

Duncan nodded.

"We waited... and Marsali stayed at home," Anthony said, his brow furrowing. "We told people it was due to the late stage of the pregnancy. I mean, she was in no state to see anyone anyway. My mother travelled to Glasgow and rented a place for her and Ava. After the baby was born – in hospital – they took her home, back to the house. Ava went to the registry office, as if she was Marsali, and had Finn's birth recorded... with my name listed as the father."

"And your mother brought Finn back home to Skye," Duncan said, "and you both presented him to the world as your own." Anthony nodded; his head bowed. Duncan sat back, processing the enormity of the situation. "Ava Caldwell came to you, didn't she?"

Anthony averted his eyes from Duncan's gaze. "She did, aye. It was a couple of weeks back. She turned up out of the blue. I–I managed to get her away from the house before the wife came home, you know. I don't know what might have happened if they'd come together."

"Why do you say that?" Duncan asked. "Did they not get on?"

"Oh no, it's nothing like that. It's just… Ava… it was all settled back in the day. Ava agreed that Finn was nothing to do with her any more and that she'd no' interfere in his, or our, lives. It was all agreed. We gave her…"

"You gave her… what, money?"

Anthony hesitated. "Aye, but it wasnae like that. It was… to help her along the way, you know?"

"And is that what Ava wanted when she showed up," Duncan asked, "to be a part of his life again?"

Anthony shrugged. "I dinnae know what she wanted."

"You don't know? You mean you didn't ask?"

"I had to get her away from the house! Finn has a life, a good life… here with us. I couldna have Ava causing confusion in his mind, bringing her destructive life choices to our door. I couldna have it."

"How do you mean?"

Anthony shook his head. "She was not like everyone else. Ava… she lives a madness, going from place to place… taking up causes, wreaking havoc everywhere she went. You know, you must have looked into her life, am I right?" he asked, looking at Duncan and then to Alistair and Russell, both standing silently in the background, listening and observing. "You must see what she was like."

"What I do know, is that Ava Caldwell is dead, Anthony. She was stabbed and fell, or was thrown, from a cliff. What should I, in the light of everything you've just told me, make of that?"

A shadow of emotion crossed Anthony's face. Whether he'd not considered how Ava's death may be related to all of these events or had somehow managed to compartmentalise it, separating it all from his family life, Duncan didn't know, but realisation was coming to him in that moment.

"I… I… don't know what to say about that."

Duncan scratched the side of his head. A new motive for murder had just presented itself to them in this case, and it was arguably the strongest they'd come across.

"Let me be clear," Duncan said, "Finn is not your child. He is Ava Caldwell's, yes?"

"Aye," Anthony said with a curt nod. "Not that he knows. Not that anyone knows besides myself and my late mother… and I suppose, Marsali. To her though, Finn *is* her baby and always has been. She'll never accept it any other way. I think she truly believes it, I do."

Duncan caught Anthony's eye. "Where is she, where is Marsali right now?"

Anthony held Duncan's gaze. "I don't know. I really don't."

CHAPTER TWENTY-THREE

THE SOUND of footsteps in the hall along with the telltale beep of a police radio heralded the arrival of PC Fraser Macdonald, who entered the kitchen, looking around at all of those present. Seeing Duncan, he approached.

"Could I have a word with you, sir?" he asked. Duncan got up and left the table. Anthony MacGregor, perhaps processing the enormity of the situation as well as its potential consequences for the first time, put his hands to his face, head bowed as Duncan walked away.

"What is it, Fraser?"

"We've had a call come in from a member of the public over Ardtreck way. They think they've found a body."

Duncan rolled his eyes. This was all he needed.

"He's alive, mind," Fraser said. "They called for an ambulance, but it sounds like he's been the victim of an assault. He was found with a head injury, unconscious."

"Where is the victim now?"

"Portree, in the hospital. He was found an hour ago, but it's only now the details are filtering back through the control room, you know?"

"Is the victim unconscious now?"

"Aye, he hasn't come around, and the reports suggest it's serious. He's been taken into surgery for a possible bleed on the brain. It was Ronnie who went out there when the call came in," Fraser said, referring to his colleague, PC Ronnie Macdonald.

"Do we have a name for the victim?"

"Aye, we do," Fraser said, hesitantly.

"Who is it?"

"It's your pal, Archie Mackinnon, sir." Fraser winced as he spoke. "I'm sorry to be the bearer of bad tidings and all."

Duncan was stunned. "That's okay, Fraser. Thanks for letting me know." He thought on it momentarily. "Is Ronnie still out that way?"

"Oh aye. He's found Archie's car over there. Not that the body was anywhere near it."

"And he was assaulted?" Duncan asked.

"So, I'm told, but I'll wager Ronnie knows more than me."

"Okay, thanks, Fraser."

PC Macdonald smiled weakly, nodded to Alistair and Russell before returning to his place at the police cordon, down on the main road.

Alistair came over to stand beside Duncan. "If you want to head back to Portree, see Archie at the hospital," he said, looking at Russell, "me and the big man can take care of things here. I'll put the word out for Marsali. She cannae be too far."

Duncan nodded. "Thanks, Alistair. But, if Archie is going into surgery, then there's nothing I can do for him there."

"What do you want to do then?"

Duncan considered the next steps, glancing out of the window above the sink where he could see the forensic team working on processing the scene. "You do as you said, keep things organised here. Have Marsali picked up on sight and taken to the station. In the meantime, I'll head over to Ardtreck and try to figure out what Archie was doing over that way."

"You don't think he was just on one of his usual shopping runs?"

Duncan shook his head. "Not in this weather. He's shifty, I know... but he's not daft. He was out there for something else."

"Such as?"

Duncan shook his head. "I don't know, but I'll try to figure it out."

Alistair looked at Anthony MacGregor, staring straight ahead at the wall in front of him, showing no visible signs of emotion. If anything, he looked utterly drained. "What do I do with him?"

"Take him back to the station as well, but make sure the custody sergeant knows to keep him under observation."

"Suicide watch?" Alistair asked, lowering his voice.

"He's lost everything... and who knows what else is to come. Aye, keep an eye on him."

Dr Dunbar opened the back door, clearing his throat to get their attention. Duncan excused himself and crossed to where Craig waited, casting a nervous look over at Anthony who had his back to them. The two men stepped outside in the falling snow which, thankfully, had eased a little. This was yet another day where a weather forecast on the island counted for absolutely nothing.

"What can you tell me?" Duncan asked.

"Not much, I'm afraid. It is difficult with one so small and," he glanced around them to indicate the conditions, "in this light. The poor thing doesn't show any signs of broken bones, which in the event of a suspicious infant death, is what I would look for, blunt force trauma."

Duncan winced and Craig nodded gravely. "I'm afraid so. It is often a violent reaction that leads to an infant's murder. I see no evidence of it in this case, though. I'll caveat that though. Once we get the poor wee soul under an x-ray machine, we will be more confident."

"Can you suggest a preliminary cause of death?"

Craig shook his head. "I'm afraid the body has completely skeletonised. Without evidence of trauma, there will be little way we can prove anything either way." Craig sighed. "This one will be down to you and your detective skills, I fear."

"Thanks very much," Duncan said.

Craig looked horrified. "No, I only meant that forensic medicine is unlikely to solve this one for you. You'll have to do it the old-fashioned way. I'm sure you're more than capable."

"Thanks for the vote of confidence," Duncan said, allowing the doctor to return to the grave site.

AS THE CROW FLIES, Ardtreck and Bracadale were only a little over two miles apart but without a boat to cross Loch Harport, that journey was closer to fifteen. Inclement weather, a half an hour drive would have got Duncan there but with the freshly laid snow, poor visibility and driving with caution, it took Duncan almost an hour to reach Portnalong where the roads became even more treacherous.

Heading southwest, Duncan came to a crossroads and took the right turn at the bus stop, continuing towards the village of Ardtreck; one of the northernmost, although sparsely, populated locations on the Minginish peninsula. Ronnie Macdonald's patrol car was visible from a distance as Duncan negotiated a narrow bend on a downward slope, feeling the wheels losing grip as he made the turn.

The people living out this way were used to these narrow tracks, and they also had the good sense to stay in their homes in these conditions, waiting out the passing weather front. The lack of tracks in which to line up his car only made Duncan more cautious, fearful of leaving the road. It would only take a momentary lapse in concentration or, more likely, a mistake and he would be in trouble.

The flashing lights on the roof of Ronnie's car were like a beacon of safety, much like the nearby lighthouse, bearing the village's name, must be for passing sailors. The line of lighthouses marking safe passage through the Little Minch, the Atlantic Sea channel separating the Outer Hebridean Western Isles and the Isle of Skye, saved countless vessels from being wrecked on the rugged coastline of the islands.

Ronnie got out of his car as Duncan approached, fastening his high-viz jacket to the collar and sporting a plastic cover over his cap to keep it from getting wet. Duncan slowed his car and parked it behind the patrol car, Ronnie bending down as Duncan lowered his window.

"How're things, Ronnie?"

"I can think of many places I'd rather be on a night like this," he said, peering into the cabin. Duncan looked past the car and could see another vehicle at an angle at the side of the road, his wipers clearing the view, pushing the falling snow away from the glass. The offside rear wheel of the vehicle was raised from the ground. Ronnie followed Duncan's eyeline. "Aye, ditched it."

Duncan raised his window and, wanting to keep the car warm and free of the falling snow, he left the engine ticking over, and got out. Outside of the warm interior, Duncan shivered as he walked with Ronnie towards the stricken vehicle, recognising it as Archie's Defender. Drawing closer, Duncan could see the front end had left the road and pitched into the drainage ditch running along the side of the road. Cut into the rough landscape to aid clearing the road of heavy rain running off the hillside, it was a metre deep.

"Came off in the snow do you think?" Duncan asked.

Ronnie turned on a torch he was carrying and directed the beam up the road in front of them. "At first, I figured he was heading north and lost it," Ronnie said, "but then I checked out the state of the car." He turned the torchlight towards the car, projecting it onto the rear. "You see the brush and shite caught on the nearside rear?" Ronnie asked, indicating with the beam where Duncan could see vegetation caught in the rear bumper and wheel housing.

"Aye."

"I reckon he was coming south, lost it some ways up there," Ronnie turned the beam back towards the road ahead of them, "clipped the bank on the righthand side before losing traction, then snaked down the hill this way..." Ronnie followed the suspected trajectory with the torchlight, "before he spun it and ditched it where we see it the noo."

Duncan considered the theory. It was a fairly straight stretch of road they were on, and it was difficult to see how Archie could have lost control if he'd been heading north. It was a sound hypothesis. They approached the car and Ronnie lit the interior for him. There must have been a bag of groceries in the rear which had spilled its contents across the seat and into both footwells. The almost empty carrier bag was a Co-op branded one. It seemed odd to him that Archie would be out this way if he'd been buying the basics. The nearest Co-op was a far cry from here.

He had Ronnie aim the torch at the headlining of the cabin.

The driver's side window was intact, and he couldn't see any blood visible where Archie may have struck his head.

"Fraser said Archie was found unconscious with a head injury," Duncan said.

"Aye, over this way," Ronnie said. Together, they walked further along the road and Ronnie stopped almost ten metres away from where the car left the road. He angled the torch into the ditch here although there was no sign of where Archie had lain. The snow had settled now, and the area looked virgin. "He was down there. Face down in the base of the ditch." He pointed up the road to a small croft house on the cusp of the next bend. "The owner there heard something and came out to investigate." Ronnie nodded towards the ditch. "He found Archie in there."

Duncan looked at the house. It was at least forty metres away from them, fifty from the crash site. "What did he hear?"

"A loud crunch," he said, "as he was letting his dog out in the back garden for a…" he shrugged. "Well, you know."

"Did he see anyone else about?"

"See anything? No," Ronnie said, shaking his head, "but he heard another car driving away in the distance. No suggestion it was related to this though."

"Didn't see it?"

"No," Ronnie said. "Big engine though. Throaty sound… so he says."

Duncan frowned, looking up the road and then down towards where the Defender lay. "I don't see him being thrown from the vehicle, do you?"

Ronnie shook his head. "I cannae figure out why he was up this way either."

"Head injury, you say?"

"Aye, left side of the head. It looked really nasty too. A lot of blood."

"Anything else?"

"The paramedic reckoned he'd a broken or dislocated ankle too. That could have been a result of the fall into the ditch." Ronnie rocked his head from side to side. "Maybe he got out of the car and was walking up to the house looking for help, slipped and fell into the ditch?"

Duncan nodded. "Possibly." He gestured for them to return to the crash site. Duncan came alongside and then pointed to the rear quarter. "Can you put your light on here for me, Ronnie?"

PC Macdonald did as requested, lighting up the rear quarter panel. The wheel arch and the panel above and behind it showed signs of recent damage. There were other scrapes and dents, as one might expect from an old working vehicle operating in terrain like this, but here, the scrapes were recent showing no signs of any further deterioration of the surrounding paintwork.

"What do you make of that then?" Duncan asked. He could see Ronnie's expression of consternation as he also examined it.

"Recent."

"Tonight, recent?" Duncan asked.

Ronnie shook his head. "I dunno." He looked down the road. "A collision?"

"Might cause him to leave the road," Duncan said.

Ronnie nodded. "Aye, it just might. But who would be daft enough to get this close in conditions like this?"

"If it was an accident, then someone who shouldn't be driving," Duncan said.

"What do you mean *if*?"

"Well, if someone was looking to put him off the road," Duncan said, indicating where the damage was done, "then that's exactly where you strike the vehicle."

"Aye, classic training manoeuvre," Ronnie said. "Bloody daft to do it out here, mind you. Who'd do such a thing?"

"Someone with a grudge," Duncan said.

"You'd have to be proper upset to try that in this," Ronnie said, looking up and blinking fiercely as wet snow struck his face.

"Have the Defender brought in and have forensics cast an eye over it, would you?"

"Who'd have a grudge big enough against Archie Mackinnon to do something like this… and then crack his skull for the hell of it?"

Duncan had one name in mind.

CHAPTER TWENTY-FOUR

DUNCAN PUSHED his fears for the success of Archie's surgery to one side, forcing himself to concentrate on the road ahead. The worst of the storm front was now crossing the island and the swirling snow in the beam of his headlights as he drove through it was mesmerising, as well as distracting. Fortunately, much of the island was hunkering down to wait it out and the roads were devoid of traffic. Even so, Duncan was still relieved to reach the relative safety of the A87, turning right at Sligachan Bridge and driving towards Sconser with the loch on his left.

Approaching the township, he passed the pier where the Calmac ferries depart for the short run across to Raasay and then came across the golf course on the south bank of Loch Sligachan. He didn't slow down though. The road here had been treated and cleared what with it being one of the main arterial routes of the island, the gritters and ploughs had done their job.

Graeme McKinley's house was set back from the main road, at the end of a sweeping driveway that wound its way up the hillside. From the vantage point, the views across the loch, and to Raasay itself, would be stunning on a clear day at any time of the year.

The gardens surrounding the property, all the way down to where the boundary met the road, were landscaped with a mixture of established hedgerow, mature trees and cultivated foliage. Being so far north and living in such a harsh land-scape facing the Atlantic winds, having such a garden must entail a huge investment in both time and money, should you hire someone else to maintain it. Graeme McKinley didn't strike Duncan as the type to be out trimming foliage on a weekend.

Graeme's Mercedes was parked in the triple garage, located to the side of the main house, on the west side of the plot. The door was raised, and Duncan parked his car on the drive and got out. He'd promised Alistair he'd meet him there, and that he'd wait until they were together before he approached Graeme. They hadn't discussed nosing around the property though.

Lights were on inside the house, and Duncan made his way over to the garage. He walked in, casting an eye around the interior but he was mostly interested in the car which was parked inside forward facing. Walking down the nearside, he examined the bodywork, running a flat palm along the paint-work. When he came to the wing, he felt some roughness to the front of the wheel arch.

Using the torch function of his mobile, Duncan dropped to his haunches and inspected the panel. It was scuffed where it met the front bumper and the latter was pushed out a couple of inches, indicative of a coming together with something immovable. It wasn't conclusive. The damage could have been done at any point and Duncan tried to recall if the car had been in this condition when they called at the site the other day or on the night of the fire. He couldn't recall which frustrated him. Leaning in close, he tried to see if there was any telltale paint within the scuffs, the green of Archie's Defender, maybe. There wasn't.

He stood up and checked his watch. Where was Alistair? The house lights flickered briefly and then everywhere went dark. There were no streetlights in this area but stepping out of the garage and into the falling snow, Duncan looked down the hillside and across to the northern bank of the loch. Where there had been pinpoints of light in properties opposite, now there was only the swirling snowstorm to see.

"Well, that'll make everything much easier," Duncan said quietly. The house was in darkness. Duncan could handle Graeme McKinley. He walked to the front door, a contemporary, reinforced aluminium-clad affair, and hammered the satin metal knocker against it. A dull thud resounded. Duncan waited but there was no response from within. Stepping back, he glanced to both left and right before choosing the left side to walk around to the rear.

Grateful for the snow covering to light the way, Duncan walked through several inches of freshly fallen snow. The house was at a significantly higher elevation than the road below and the snow here was much thicker. The rear of the house wasn't fenced off, the route around the building was open. The east facing of the property had a large, decked area with a wall of glass opening onto it. Duncan couldn't see any movement inside.

The wooden deck was slippery, the previous snowfall probably melted with the brief and sudden rise in temperature the previous day, only to refreeze overnight and the fresh snow now sat upon a layer of sheet ice. Duncan reached a sliding glass door, two metres wide. Trying the handle, he found it unlocked and the mechanism must have been a high-quality construction because it opened effortlessly, moving aside with the minimum of effort on his part.

He opened it just enough for him to slip inside. He could smell alcohol and stale smoke in the room. It was an expansive kitchen dining room with a casual seating area beside the glass wall. Even with only the reflective light from the pristine snow outside to aid him, Duncan could see how neat and tidy everything was. The kitchen surfaces were clear, light reflecting off the polished granite of the island and counter tops.

The only mess and clutter he found was on the small table set out in the seating area, between the low-backed sofas arranged in a u-shape. On this table were three wine bottles, two red and one white, and all were empty. One of them was on its side and it slowly rocked back and forth in place as if a slight draught was shifting it from side to side. One wine glass was present with perhaps a sip left inside.

Duncan stood still, attuning his ears to the sound of the interior. Outside, the wind was raging, whistling as it passed through the trees that had all long since lost their foliage with the passing of winter. Wishing he'd closed the sliding door behind him, he tried to work out if he was as alone as it seemed. The windows were triple glazed, and only the sound through the open door and a gentle whirring could be heard. He looked up and saw a vent in the ceiling, assuming there was an air recycling system in operation.

The further he moved into the interior and therefore away from the reflected light from outside, the gloomier the house became. In a few minutes his eyes would adjust to it, but Duncan considered using his mobile to light the way, although he dismissed that idea as it would also give away his location.

Entering the property alone now felt like a daft idea and he silently chided himself for doing so.

He approached a doorway leading out into a wide hall. It was a double height space with a vaulted ceiling where a huge chandelier hung down between the staircase and a galleried landing above. To the right of the front door was the entrance to a home office whose footprint was larger than the entire caravan Duncan had called home for the past few months. It was empty. The desk and surfaces were also clear. Graeme McKinley was fastidiously tidy.

Hearing something, he turned, glancing upstairs to the landing but he was confident the sound had come from the ground floor. A set of double doors were on the other side of the front door, opposite where he was now. That was likely a living room and he moved towards it. Standing beside the closed doors, he listened but when he heard nothing, he grasped one handle and slowly turned it. The latch moved and it sounded like fingernails on a blackboard in the silence.

Easing the door open, Duncan peered into the gloom. He was wrong. It wasn't a living room, but a formal dining space. The table had ten chairs around it and still there were at least two metres of free space all the way around to the surrounding walls. This house was massive. Duncan entered, hearing his shoes squeak on the smooth porcelain tiles. He passed down the length of the table to an open door which led back into the kitchen diner.

Back in a familiar space, he looked to his left. A narrow corridor ran off deeper into the house. It was dark. There were doors off it to both sides, but they were all closed. He took a step and then heard something to his right. He turned his head as something flashed past him in a blur. Glass shattered against the wall beside his head and instinctively, he ducked, just as another bottle was launched at him. It too, missed, smashing behind him. Duncan looked for the attacker only for a shape to hammer into him. Feeling his legs go out from under him, he was moving through the air and as he struck something hard and unforgiving, a great weight upon his chest and air exploded from his lungs.

Duncan screamed but with no air in his lungs, it was a silent scream. He was prostrate across the dining table with someone on top of him. He used his momentum to instinctively shift his body weight and roll his attacker off him. They both fell to the floor, Duncan feeling a sharp pain in his left arm as they hit the tiles. Rolling away, Duncan felt powerful, if uncontrolled, arms scrabbling to get a hold of him and he batted them away as he pushed off with his feet, attempting to put some distance between himself and his attacker. As fast as he scrabbled for traction on the polished stone surface, his assailant did too and they must have made a comical sight, chasing each other across the surface.

The man grunted at the exertion and Duncan managed to turn from on his back to on his front and push off from the floor, trying to get to his feet. Upright now, Duncan turned only to be barged in his stomach and flung against a wall cabinet housing an array of crystal glasses. The cabinet door opened, and they were showered with wine glasses, goblets and tumblers, most intact but some broken by the collision.

Duncan's attacker stank of alcohol and his clumsy assault suggested he was heavily intoxicated. That was both a blessing and a curse. He was acting aggressively and without thought, which was easier to overcome, but he was also fixated, and Duncan knew from his time handling drunks on a Friday and Saturday night in the West End of Glasgow, it could take five grown officers to subdue one violent drunk who was off on one.

Bringing his knee up into the man's stomach, he heard him

groan but his attack didn't falter, and he grasped Duncan by the lapels of his coat, almost lifting him off the ground, spinning him in the air and launching him across the dining table. The glass surface aided Duncan's passing, and he slid headfirst over the edge, landing face first in a heap on the other side. Tasting a salty liquid inside his mouth, Duncan hastened back to his feet and turned just as a shape flew past his head to the left. He raised his right arm just in time to stop the next projectile, a crystal tumbler, from striking his face. It bounced off him, smashing upon the floor.

Duncan bobbed and weaved as he ran from the room, glass smashing all around him, seeking refuge in the open space of the kitchen diner. He would have room to move, to anticipate and indeed to flee if the need arose. Once back through the door, he moved to his right but lost his footing on the smooth surface, coming down hard and sliding briefly before he could steady himself and get back to his feet.

That was enough to allow his assailant time to close the gap and Duncan got to his feet just in time to be clattered by his opponent running at full speed. They pitched backwards, falling over the sofa and coming down on the shallow table before the wall of glass. The bottles scattered around them and Duncan, realising with the benefit of the exterior light, that he was facing Graeme McKinley.

"Graeme, stop!" he bellowed. "Police!"

He didn't stop though, instead gathering an empty wine bottle and grasping it by the neck, clearly intending to use it as a weapon. A broken bottle could cut you deeply, whereas an unbroken one could break your skull if it connected well enough. Duncan didn't fancy either outcome. He leapt back as Graeme swung the bottle at him in a wild arc, well wide of the mark. Thankfully, he was hammered.

"Stop!" Duncan yelled again, stepping to his left and

narrowly avoiding a second swing. The follow through caught the frame of the sliding doors and the bottle smashed. Now, the weapon was a different level of deadly. Duncan held up both hands in front of him, hoping to show he wasn't a threat. Graeme McKinley, eyes wide and gleaming, stared at him. He was unfocussed, and out of control. "Graeme!" Duncan yelled.

A movement from Duncan's right caught his eye and a shadow came from nowhere. Graeme let out a groan as he sank to his knees and then there was silence as a second blow knocked him face down, out for the count.

"I told you not to come inside without me. Didn't I say that? I'm pretty sure I did, because I was standing right there when I said it!"

Duncan exhaled, the rush of adrenaline causing his hands to shake as he stared at Alistair. "I told you, *sir*."

"You're bleeding, sir," Alistair said, moving into the nearby kitchen space and returning with a small hand towel he'd found.

"You took your time," Duncan said, dabbing at his cheek with the towel having first checked it was reasonably clean. The wound to his cheek appeared shallow, likely from a passing fragment of glass hurled at him by a drunken Graeme McKinley.

Alistair grinned. "I think you'll find the word you're looking for is *thank you*."

"That's two words," Duncan said.

"Ah, right it is…"

"And thank you," Duncan said.

Suddenly the lights flickered back into life and both men were left blinking as the overhead spotlights all came on at the same time.

"And He said, let there be light," Alistair said. Duncan looked at him as he rested his extendable baton on his shoulder, looking down at Graeme McKinley. Alistair nodded towards the unconscious figure at their feet. Alistair put his baton against the floor, pushing down and collapsing it. They moved to stand either side of Graeme. Duncan knelt and checked him.

"He's breathing soundly enough. I think you might have cracked his head."

"Ah, he'll be grand. At least he's still alive. Imagine the paperwork if he'd gone and died on us!"

Graeme mumbled something incomprehensible and then began coming round.

"Can you hear me okay, Mr McKinley?" Duncan said, raising his voice. Graeme's eyes flickered and moments later appeared to focus as he stared up at Duncan. "Do you feel okay?"

"Where am I?" Graeme asked.

"You're at home."

"What time is it?" he asked.

"It's late," Alistair said.

Graeme looked up at them, blinking. "My head... hurts," he muttered.

"That'll be all the thinking you're doing," Alistair said. "It's not good for you."

"What happened?" Graeme asked, confused.

"You had a fall," Alistair said. "Very sad."

"Can we help you up?" Duncan asked, sensing Graeme's violent outburst was well and truly over. He appeared calm now, if still intoxicated. Graeme stared at him.

"What am I doing on the floor."

"You slipped," Alistair said. "It's these shiny floor tiles you have here. An accident waiting to happen."

Both of them reached down, looping one arm each under Graeme's and then together, they hoisted him up and onto the sofa. Graeme McKinley looked at the two of them in turn, focussing on the sweaty form of Duncan.

"Have you been out running or something?" It was as if he had forgotten the fight entirely. His gaze then drifted around the room, seeing the broken glass all over the floor, he grimaced. "I've overdone it again, haven't I?"

"What have you been doing?" Duncan asked.

"I've been on another bender, I think?" He frowned. "What happened?"

Duncan and Alistair exchanged looks. They needed to have Graeme assessed before they could speak to him officially. It could be a concussion, thanks to Alistair, or he could be suffering from a blackout brought on by alcohol.

"Graeme," Duncan said, attracting his attention. "Where's your wife?"

He shrugged. "No clue. Probably got her legs open for that fitness instructor she's been shagging behind my back."

"Oh, has she now?" Alistair asked, straight faced.

"Aye. She thought I didn't know… but I have eyes…" Graeme said, looking forlorn. "He can have her. Let's see how long he sticks around now she hasn't got any cash to throw around."

Alistair surveyed the house. "This place will fetch a bob or two."

"Nah," Graeme said, smiling ruefully. "Mortgaged to the hilt… negative equity… leaving me, she's… what's the word I'm looking for?" he asked, frowning.

"Screwed?" Alistair said.

"Aye," Graeme said, grinning maniacally. "That'll do."

"Ambulance?" Alistair asked Duncan, inclining his head towards Graeme.

Duncan shook his head. "In this weather. We'd better take him ourselves. It'll be quicker."

"It's all my fault," Graeme said, lowering his head into his hands. He started crying and Alistair arched his eyebrows at Duncan.

"I think it'll be a while before we get any sense out of this one."

CHAPTER TWENTY-FIVE

THE OPS ROOM was busy as Duncan entered. A couple of heads turned in his direction and acknowledged his arrival. He'd been for a quick shower and to get into a change of clothes having found glass fragments in his clothing. Alistair came across the room to speak to him.

"Feel better?"

Duncan nodded. "Aye. What's the craic?"

"McKinley is settled into a cell for the night. The staff at A and E were keen to get shot of him. They're busy enough as it is and there are no signs of a concussion to speak of. He was just pished."

"By the state of him I imagine that's a regular occurrence," Duncan said.

"His way of coping I guess," Alistair agreed. "Either way, he's no' fit to be interviewed until first thing tomorrow, otherwise anything he tells us will be considered suspect. Have you any news on Archie's condition?"

"No, not yet. He was still in surgery the last time I called the hospital."

"He'll be all right. He's a tough bloke," Alistair said. "What do you think?"

Duncan rubbed at his face. He was feeling tired now that the adrenaline shot he had after scrapping with Graeme McKinley had worn off. "About Graeme being the one who did for Archie?"

"Aye," Alistair said, although to Duncan, he didn't seem enthused about it.

"You're not buying it?"

Alistair frowned. "If he's prone to getting that blootered… I'm sure he has the temper to lash out at Archie, but do you see him being able to drive in that capacity? Well enough to run him off the road and then get the better of him in a physical confrontation." Alistair smiled. "He couldn't even get the better of you."

"Thanks very much," Duncan said. Alistair had a point. Archie could take care of himself, and for Graeme McKinley to have pulled it off, it would have taken some doing. Until he sobered up though, or until Archie came round after surgery, they had no way of putting it to him.

"Sir?" Angus called and both men looked over to where the young DC was sitting at his desk, hanging up his telephone. "I've just had Finn MacGregor's mobile phone service provider get in touch." They both moved to join him. To Duncan, he seemed perplexed.

"What is it?" Duncan asked.

"I thought it must be a mistake," Angus said, "but I had them double check and then check again."

"Triple checked?" Alistair asked, glancing sideways at Duncan. "Must be serious."

"What is it?" Duncan asked.

"They got a GPS hit on Finn's mobile. Someone has switched it on in the last couple of hours."

"That's interesting. Can they tell us where?"

"That's just it, sir," Angus said, frowning. "It connected to a cell tower on the Trotternish Ridge." He hurriedly shifted things around on his desk and unfolded a map of the island, quickly identifying the rough location of the tower. "It's about here, so they tell me."

Duncan pored over the map, drawing breath. The tower offered access to the network on the east coast of the peninsula. "Was it on the move?" Duncan asked.

"No, they said it connected for only five minutes and then dropped off the network again."

"Enough time to make a call," Duncan said, "or exchange some texts. Do we know the content of any action?"

"One phone call," Angus said. "For a duration of three minutes and twenty-two seconds."

"Incoming or outgoing?" Duncan asked.

"Outgoing," Angus said, "but it was to an unregistered number, with an overseas prefix code."

"Which prefix?" Duncan asked, his curiosity piqued.

"0066," Angus said. "I don't know that one." His fingers worked quickly on his keyboard, and he brought up the international country dialling codes list, scanning down it with both Duncan and Alistair doing the same thing.

"There," Duncan said, pointing and stopping Angus from scrolling further. "Thailand."

"Who the hell does Finn MacGregor know in Thailand?" Alistair asked.

Duncan looked down at the map again, closing his eyes. "He doesn't know anyone," he said softly. "Not any more. Come on."

Alistair's brow furrowed. "Er... where are we going exactly?"

Duncan pointed at the map. "Who does Finn know who lives on the eastern side of the Trotternish?"

Alistair looked at the map and Duncan put his forefinger on the crofting settlement of Maligar. "Callum Mcinnes?"

"Callum Mcinnes," Duncan repeated. "Get your coat. I don't know about you, but I've had enough of the runaround from these boys."

THEY PULLED into the driveway of the Mcinnes' croft and Duncan switched the engine off. Both Davey's pick-up and Becky's hatchback were parked in front of the house. There had barely been any conversation on the drive up from Portree. Duncan's mobile rang and he answered it.

"Hey, Dunc, it's Grace."

"Hi, Grace," he said, raising a finger to Alistair to signal he'd just be a moment. Alistair gestured to ask if he should leave to give him privacy, but Duncan shook his head. He was struggling to hear her above the sound of the music in the background. The noise lessened and he heard a door close, her voice becoming muffled. "How are you doing?"

"Just taking a moment to pass on a message."

"Aye, what's that then?"

"I spoke with Katie earlier," Grace said. "I told her you were looking for her and she... doesnae want to speak to you. She was quite insistent on that."

"Really? She came to me first..."

"Aye, well a woman has the right to change her mind, eh, Duncan?"

He laughed. "I suppose. As long as she's all right."

"Ah, she's grand," Grace said, and the background noise increased as she left the confines of wherever she'd been. He could hear loud voices, laughing and shouting. "You'll have to tell me what you've done to upset her though."

"I haven't upset her," Duncan protested. "I swear."

"Aye, well whatever is going on between you two, I think she's said as much as she is going to, so you'd better drop it. Okay?"

Duncan smiled. "If only it was that easy. Thanks for letting me know, Grace."

"Nae bother," she said, succinctly. "Later."

The call ended and Duncan put his mobile away. "Katie Matheson is fine," he said, "but I reckon she's gone as far as she's prepared to go." He glanced at Alistair. "Come on, let's go and see what Callum has to say for himself." Alistair reached across and placed a restraining hand on Duncan's forearm as he made to get out. Duncan glanced at him.

"I don't know what's between you and this lassie, Becky Mcinnes," Alistair said, his eyes darting towards the house, "but take it easy when we get inside."

"What are you talking about?"

Alistair lowered his voice and fixed a stern eye on Duncan. "I've been doing this job a long time and I think I can read people pretty well. Besides, I also have eyes, you know? My advice, whatever it is, leave it at the door when we go in. I'm saying this as a friend."

Duncan looked at Alistair's hand, still resting on his forearm, arching a solitary eyebrow. Alistair withdrew his hand and Duncan got out without saying another word, irritated by the exchange. Neither man spoke as they approached the house which was in darkness. Duncan rang the doorbell and they waited. He checked his watch, and it was almost midnight. He rang the bell again.

A moment later, the interior light of the hallway came on and two figures could be seen inside, coming to the door. A bleary-eyed Davey Mcinnes opened the door, casting an eye over them.

"Duncan?" he asked. "What... why are you here?"

Duncan looked past him to see Becky standing halfway along the hall, tightening the cord around her dressing gown and watching them.

"I need to speak to Callum," Duncan said.

"At this hour? Are you mental?"

"I'm not asking, Davey."

"Can it not wait until the morn—"

"Oh, let them in, Davey," Becky said, coming to stand behind her husband. Feeling her touch on his shoulder, Davey half-turned his head to look at her and relented. "It must be important, or they wouldn't be here."

Davey drew the door open and beckoned them both in, although his expression showed he was none too pleased about doing so. He was wearing joggers and an old, faded blue T-shirt.

"Thanks," Duncan said to Becky as he and Alistair walked into the house. Davey closed the door after them and the four of them stood in close quarters in the cramped hallway. "Where's Callum now?"

"In his bed," Davey said sarcastically. "Where else is he going to be at this time of the night? It's where we should *all be*, just now."

Duncan ignored him, gesturing for Becky to lead them. She turned away from him and they filed down the hallway. "Callum's bedroom is on the ground floor," she said.

Like many of the old crofting houses, they'd been added to over the years as modern living required greater space. Davey and Becky had pushed the property out towards the rear, adding extra bedrooms as well as enlarging the kitchen. The two-up, two-down, traditional properties were becoming rarer to find these days.

Davey was still muttering under his breath as they came to Callum's bedroom door. Becky knocked on it, gently at first but when she realised she'd likely have to wake him, she knocked again only more forcefully. "Callum, love… the police are here to see you." She glanced at Duncan but there was no answer from inside. Davey stepped past Duncan and opened the door.

"Hey, son…" he said, stopping one step inside the room. Duncan was at his shoulder, looking past him into the room. The duvet was thrown across the bed, wrinkled where someone had lain on it, but the bed certainly hadn't been slept in. Duncan pushed past Davey who glanced at his wife, concern and surprise etched in his expression. Duncan checked the small ensuite shower room just off the bedroom on the far side, but it too was empty.

"But… he went to bed…" Becky said, leaving her mouth open.

A cold breeze blew across them, the open door causing the draught and all eyes turned to the window. The handle was up, and it'd been pushed to from the outside, but the draught from the open bedroom door had now cracked it open again. They could all feel the freezing wind as it gusted into the house through the crack. The window knocked gently against the frame, the sound of the wind intermittently pausing as it did so.

"What time did he go to bed?" Duncan asked.

Becky shook her head, thinking hard. "I… I don't know, maybe ten… a quarter past?" she asked, looking at Davey.

"Aye… around then, right enough."

Davey's obvious surprise had dissipated. Now he was angry. "Duncan, you'd better tell us what's going on here?"

Eilidh, The Mcinnes' daughter appeared at the door,

peering at the four of them. She had one arm at her side and the other holding tightly to a crutch which she used to support her weight. Becky hurried over to her, putting a comforting arm around her.

"You shouldn't be up at this time, love," she said warmly.

"What's going on?" Eilidh asked. It was her father who answered.

"The police want to speak to your brother, that's all."

"Is that why he went out?" she asked. Everyone's focus was on her now.

"What do you mean?" Becky asked, turning to face her daughter, both hands holding gently onto her upper arms. "Where did Callum go?"

Eilidh shrugged. "I don't know. I just heard something and when I looked down from my window," she said, her eyes furtively moving around those in the room, "I saw Callum climbing out of his window."

Becky looked at Duncan and then at Davey. "Why would he... go out?"

"When was this, Eilidh?" Duncan asked.

"About an hour ago... maybe a bit more."

"But that would have been when he went to bed," Davey said, his eyebrows knitting together as he shook his head. Alistair and Duncan exchanged a look which did not go unnoticed by Callum's parents. "Just what's going on here, Duncan?"

Duncan ignored the question, maintaining his eye contact with Callum's sister. "Was he alone?"

Davey snorted with derision. "What kind of a question is —"

"Was he alone?" Duncan repeated. Eilidh nodded. Duncan turned to Alistair. "He's gone to see Finn; I'd put my house on it."

Davey was about to protest, and Becky scoffed. "Just how in the hell do you think he's going to do that? We don't even know where Finn MacGregor is!"

Duncan looked at her. "I believe Callum knows exactly where he is."

Davey stepped between them, his face flushed. "And how is he going to get there, in this," Davey said, pointing absently behind him towards the window. "I mean… it's not like…"

Duncan watched as Davey's expression changed just as he stopped talking, mid-sentence. "What is it?"

Davey left the room, picking up the pace as he went through into the kitchen. Duncan followed, and then everyone else did too, apart from Eilidh whose movement was still impaired by her injuries from the previous November. Davey pulled a coat from a line of hooks by the back door, slipping his bare feet in a set of green wellingtons on a mat beside the door. He glanced at Duncan, and something passed unsaid between them.

Davey pushed open the back door and stepped out into the snow, Duncan a half-step behind him. The two of them hurried around to the front of the house, Davey almost breaking into a run. As much as he could do in wellington boots, anyway. They went to the edge of the drive and then Davey crossed the road and passed through an open five-bar gate, the entrance to another paddock of his croft.

An old stone barn with corrugated metal sheet roofing stood on the left and Davey made a beeline for it. Duncan didn't know what had possessed Davey, but he followed. Davey hauled open the barn door and stood in the opening, staring into the interior. Duncan came alongside, searching the barn as well. It was used for storage. There was a random assortment of equipment, tools and a stack of livestock feed, presumably for the sheep when he brought them down from the hills when the weather was too harsh to leave them out. There was nothing that struck him as odd, though.

"Davey?"

Davey Mcinnes stood stock still, shaking his head. He glanced at Duncan. "The little…"

"What is it?" Duncan asked, looking around, fearful of having missed something significant.

"He asked me this morning…" Davey stood with his hands on his hips.

"What?"

"Yesterday, I was working on my ATV," Davey said. "The injectors were sticking, and the fuel supply was erratic. The engine kept spluttering and I didnae want to get caught up on the hills…" He turned to Duncan, resignation in his tone. "This morning… Callum asked me if I'd fixed it? I told him it was all good, fully fuelled and ready to go."

Duncan looked around. The all-terrain vehicle was gone.

CHAPTER TWENTY-SIX

DUNCAN AND ALISTAIR stood in Callum's bedroom, Becky standing in the doorway, anxiously wringing her hands in front of her. His bedroom was much like any other teenager's room, a mess. Alistair sifted through the drawers next to the bed, picking through old comics, bits and pieces accumulated over several years.

Duncan opened the wardrobe and began looking through the clothes that were stacked on shelves or hanging from the rail, checking pockets of hoodies and jeans.

"What are you looking for?" Becky asked. Duncan glanced in her direction.

"We don't know."

The answer didn't satisfy her, and she exhaled loudly, clearly annoyed.

"I don't understand any of this!" she said. The detectives continued the search but having exhausted all potential places for possible concealment, they had to admit defeat. "What's going on?" Becky asked.

"I'll tell you what's going on," Davey said, coming to stand behind her. "Finn has got himself caught up in something and he's leaning on his best pal to help get him out of it." Duncan looked at Davey and their eyes met. He didn't say anything, but Davey was thinking the same as he was. His silence spoke volumes and Davey Mcinnes knew it. "Isn't that right, Dunc? Callum's being dragged into something?"

Duncan exchanged a glance with Alistair and nodded. "It looks that way."

"What's Finn done?" Becky asked.

"We don't know that either," Duncan said. Davey's eyes narrowed. He thought Duncan was holding back, which he was, but it was all just a theory at this point. "I think we're done in here," Duncan said to Alistair who agreed. They left Callum's bedroom, Davey steering Becky aside with a supportive arm around her shoulder. The four of them went through to the kitchen. The sound of social media shorts carried from the adjoining room, Eilidh streaming content loudly through her tablet. No one was feeling like sleeping just now.

"Can you turn that down a bit please, love," Becky said, and her daughter did so without argument.

"Where would he be heading on the ATV?" Alistair asked no one in particular. "Cross country, do you think?"

Duncan nodded. "That'd be my guess, aye." The Mcinneses had a map of Skye framed and mounted on the wall behind the dining table. They all turned to look at it, seeing a marker had been placed where they lived. Duncan paced back and forth, trying to make sense of everything they knew. He was confident they had all the right pieces, but he hadn't managed to bring it all together.

"Surely, you just need to know where Finn is?" Davey asked. Alistair looked at him, raising an eyebrow.

"Aye, that'd be a good start. I don't suppose you know where that might be, do you?"

Davey lowered his eyes and said nothing, not responding to Alistair's sarcasm. The DS returned his gaze to the map.

"What's the capacity of the fuel tank on your ATV?" Duncan asked Davey.

"Twenty litres. Why?"

"Thirsty, is it?" he asked, looking at the map.

"No, it's very frugal," Davey said. "Big engine, a bit of an old war horse."

"He could get quite far on it then?"

"Aye, as long as he's careful," Davey said. "The snow will help with visibility but it's not like it runs on tracks, you know?"

The fridge in the kitchen caught Duncan's eye. There was a magnetic wipe-clean weekly planner on the door. He looked at multiple entries written by different hands in different colours. Moving closer, he read one in particular, penned in purple and written into the box for Tuesday; *Pick me up, 5:30. C.* Duncan's gaze lingered on it.

"Duncan?" Alistair said sternly. Duncan looked over at him as he spread his hands wide.

"Sorry, Alistair. I was miles away there. What did you say?"

"What do you want to do?"

Duncan's eyes flicked to Davey who looked nervous under the scrutiny. "Davey, where did you pick Callum up from yesterday."

"What's that you say, Dunc?" Davey asked innocently.

Duncan crossed the room to stand in front of him, Alistair's body language changed as Duncan moved with purpose.

"Callum skipped school," Duncan said, glancing at Becky, "and the two of us were out looking for him. Everyone was looking for him right up until you phoned... and said you'd picked him up."

Davey shrugged. "I picked up my son, so what?"

"I was at the school with Rona MacAllister... and she saw you the day before. You had no idea Callum had missed school the first day, and likely not the second either because he was supposed to be staying at a friend's place."

"I don't think I like your tone, Duncan," Davey said, agitated and shifting his weight between his feet.

"I don't care what you do or do not like, Davey. Where did you find Callum?"

Davey glanced at Becky, and she inclined her head, encouraging him to cooperate. He relented. "He phoned, okay? Callum phoned me... and asked me to go and pick him up. And I did. Is that all right with the police... a dad collecting his son?"

"Oh, aye... that's fine," Duncan said. "Where was he when you picked him up?" Davey's eyes shifted towards Becky.

"Where was he, Davey?" Becky asked. "Tell him!"

Davey bit his lip and nodded. "Right... I'll show you—"

"You can just tell—"

"No!" Davey said, firmly. "If you're going..." he glanced between Duncan and then his wife, "then I'm coming with you." Duncan was about to object, but Davey held firm. "Do you want my help or don't you?"

Duncan sighed and reluctantly agreed. "As you wish."

"I'll go and get dressed properly," Davey said, moving off and affectionately grasping Becky's hand as he passed her. "It'll be all right. I promise."

Duncan took Alistair by the arm and led him away from the couple, out of earshot.

"I think you were right, he's gone to see Finn."

"Aye," Alistair said, "and Davey knows it too. How should we play it?"

"You take my car back to Portree—"

"Now, hold on a minute," Alistair said, protesting. "I told you not to go into McKinley's place without me and you didn't listen—"

"You go back to Portree," Duncan repeated, "and have everyone on standby. As soon as I know where they are, you can come in and close the place down. Until Davey opens up and we get there, we've no idea where they are, do we? We can't cover the entire island."

"I don't like it," Alistair said. Duncan understood. It went against any number of protocols, but he had another reason for approaching it this way; Callum was out there, and he was his son. Duncan was going to take it on himself to make sure Callum was safe. Alistair spoke in a low, conspiratorial tone, "Are you sure you can trust Davey... and his bairn?"

"It'll be grand, Alistair."

Alistair raised his eyebrows.

"Look," Duncan said, "I've never made two massive mistakes in one day before."

"Aye, there's a first time for everything."

Their conversation was interrupted by the return of Davey Mcinnes. He was dressed in multiple layers, kitted out for the conditions. He eyed Duncan coldly.

"Are you ready, DI McAdam?"

Duncan nodded. He looked at Alistair momentarily before walking across the room and falling into step beside Davey.

"I dinnae like this one bit," Alistair muttered as the two men left through the back door. Becky Mcinnes stood with her arms folded across her chest, fear in her eyes. She didn't like it either.

DAVEY TOOK great care as they drove out of Maligar and down into Staffin. Duncan was surprised when he turned left and headed north up the east side of the Trotternish rather than heading south towards Skye.

"Where are we heading then?" Duncan asked, trying to mask his surprise. Davey's eyes flicked across at him and then back to the road. He didn't answer. Despite being down almost at sea level now, the road was still treacherous. Davey drove through Staffin and then took the left turn as if they were heading for the Quiraing.

The road began climbing up into the hills once more, narrowing to a single track and Duncan was grateful they were in Davey's pick-up. There was no way this route would be passable in his car. They needed a four-by-four vehicle, and even in this it was still difficult. Their progress slowed further. One miscalculation and they would be hiking back to civilisation.

Soon they came upon the visitors' car park, where hikers would set off to walk up to the Quiraing. A lot of work had been done here in recent months to improve the amount of available space, lessening the impact of tourists blocking the road and using the verges. No one was here tonight though. No one was crazy enough to be navigating the pass in these conditions.

"So… where are we going?" Duncan asked, glancing at the screen on his mobile phone. He was down to one bar of signal. Davey snorted a laugh.

"You think I'm going to tell you now?"

"Well, seeing as we're in the car," Duncan said absently, gazing out of the window at the landscape. The snow had eased, thankfully. The mountains stood proudly around them, white peaks dominating the skyline with the pitch-black background. "I thought you might, aye."

"So that you can relay it to your pals at the station?" Davey said, smiling ruefully. "And then you'll have every man and his dog descend on my boy?" He shook his head. "No way."

"What do you think I want to have happen; get the lad hurt or something?" Duncan said. "I want him safe just as much as you do."

"He's my son, Duncan," Davey said, glaring at him briefly before being forced to look back to the road, his grip on the wheel tensing as the car slid momentarily before gaining traction once more. "I know what's best for him." Duncan snorted a laugh of his own. Davey snarled at him. "What do you mean by that?"

"Nothing."

"Go on, spit it out if you've got something on your mind, say it!"

"You think it's best for Callum to quit school?"

"Studying isn't for everyone."

"The boy needs an education… it expands his life options—"

"And what would you know about Callum? You've known him for five minutes," Davey said, shaking his head, "and now you think you can be a parent? Do me a favour, Dunc."

"Just because you were no good at school, it doesn't mean—"

"That's got nothing to do with it!" Davey snapped. Duncan let the matter drop. He was certain that Davey would oppose any rationale he brought to the conversation, whether it held merit or not. If it came from Duncan, it wasn't likely to fly.

"He seems like a nice lad," Duncan said. Davey glanced at him warily. Duncan noticed. "He does, honestly. That's a credit to…"

"His parents?" Davey asked, almost smug with his accompanying expression.

"I was going to say his mum," Duncan said, and then he met Davey's eye, "but that would be churlish of me. You must have had some influence."

Davey's gaze lingered on him for a moment, but Duncan wasn't going to add to what he'd said, and conversation dropped for a few minutes.

There were several points in the next mile or so that Duncan feared they might need to turn back. The heavy snow had not only settled deep on the high ground, but the wind had banked it up in places against the hillside, Davey struggling to get his vehicle past it. Just as they crested the high point to begin their descent, Davey lost control, and even though they were travelling at low speed the pick-up slid sideways and both men became passengers, Davey moving the steering wheel in vain, desperate to find grip.

The pick-up came to a stop with a thump, the engine stalling as Davey's foot slipped from the clutch pedal.

"Damn it!" he said, depressing the clutch and putting the gear stick into neutral. He turned the key and the engine turned over but failed to start. Cursing, he tried again, this time pumping the accelerator.

"Don't... you'll flood it," Duncan said.

"I think I know my pick-up better than you do," Davey said, looking at him just as the engine fired into life once more. "You see?"

Duncan inclined his head, happy to be wrong. Davey put it in gear and tried to move but they stayed put.

"You're stuck," Duncan said. Davey looked over at him begrudgingly, and he nodded.

"I've got some kit in the back," Davey said and both men released their seat belts and got out, thankful that further snowfall was still holding off. The wind was still bitterly cold though, sweeping across the open landscape and whipping fresh snow into the air before driving it at them. They moved to the rear and could see the nearside rear wheel as well as much of the rear quarter of the vehicle were buried in a snowbank.

Davey dropped the tailgate, reaching over and unhooking a canvas cover to reveal his tools. Davey pulled out a shovel and handed it to Duncan, having to shout to be heard above the wind.

"You make a start digging the wheel out," he said. "I'll make sure the front wheels have something to grip."

Duncan nodded, fastening his coat up to the neck and accepting the shovel. Davey had two short planks in with his tools and he dragged them towards him, hoisting them up onto his shoulder and moving past Duncan who set about digging the vehicle out. Seeing the snow blowing down the hillside towards them, he knew they had to get moving soon otherwise they would be going nowhere.

CHAPTER TWENTY-SEVEN

It wasn't long before Duncan was breathing heavily and sweating profusely. His fingers were numb despite wearing thick, water-resistant gloves but he continued labouring to dig the pick-up out of the snow bank. Once it was clear, he set about clearing compacted snow from the wheel arches. Even a pick-up like this with its raised suspension and ground clearance would still be stopped in its tracks once snow built up around the wheels.

Davey came to stand at his shoulder. "Are we good?" he shouted. Duncan nodded and gave him the thumbs up. Davey got back into the cabin while Duncan picked up the shovel and stepped back, ready to try and offer some more leverage if required. The engine fired up, Davey dabbing the accelerator causing thick plumes of smoke to be ejected from the rear. Duncan waited but he needn't have worried, for the pick-up edged forward, slowly at first, as Davey took great care, and then they were free and ready to go.

Duncan tossed the shovel into the back of the pick-up, retrieved the planks and put them in as well, lifting the tail-gate and dropping the latch into place. He hurried to the passenger door, clambering in, relieved to be back in the relative shelter of the cabin.

"Good work," Davey said, inclining his head towards Duncan who nodded.

"Same to you," he said, looking forward and seeing the Calmac ferry terminal of Uig in the stretch of water ahead. They'd be back on treated roads soon enough. They joined the A855, the coast road that wound its way around the Trotternish headland and descended further. A sharp hairpin bend was the last major obstacle to be overcome before they went down a steep stretch of road into Uig.

"We made it," Davey said, sounding relieved. Duncan was surprised because Davey hadn't shown any sign of concern on the drive, steadfastly tackling the route with apparent confidence.

"So… are you going to tell me where we're going yet or what?"

Davey glanced at him, casting an eye down him, possibly looking to see if he had his mobile in hand. He didn't. Davey relented.

"Yesterday, Callum phoned me and had me pick him up from Drynoch."

"Drynoch?" Duncan asked, his brow furrowing. "Is that where we're going?"

"Aye."

"Then why the hell did you take us up through the Quiraing?" Duncan asked. "We should have gone south to Portree and across to Sligachan—"

"Aye," Davey said with a mischievous smile, "and you'd have clicked where we were heading straight away." He glanced at Duncan, accelerating now they were on the better-quality road, his smile broadening. "Cutting across country threw you off, eh?"

"Too right."

"Some things you don't get from reading books, you know?"

Duncan scoffed. "Don't pretend I treat you like a fool, Davey. You're sharp enough."

"Thanks, Duncan. That's the nicest thing you've said about me in years."

"Ever," Duncan said, correcting him. Davey smiled. "He wasn't in Drynoch though, for the day I mean?"

Davey shook his head. "I doubt it. He was cold... wet... and I reckon he'd been walking for a while." He glanced at Duncan. "I don't know where he might have been. You got any ideas?"

Duncan was thoughtful, bringing the various threads together in his mind. "Archie was found at the side of the road out to Ardtreck."

"I hope you don't think my Callum had anything to do with assaulting McKinnon?" He was fearful of Duncan's reply, but he needn't have been. Duncan shook his head. "Good, because Callum would have none of it."

"I don't know how the assault fits into it," Duncan said. "Archie knew Ava... and had seen her recently, which brings him into it. He was found in the same area as we've been looking for both Finn and Callum..."

"Ardtreck, you say?" Davey said, thoughtfully. "I had an uncle who lived in Fernilea for a time. It was a while ago, mind you."

"Do you know the area?"

"As I say, it's been a while but, aye... fairly well. I doubt it's changed much."

"Aye, nothing changes much in these parts," Duncan said quietly. "Do you know anywhere out that way Finn might take shelter?"

Davey frowned. "There's no shortage of old working crofts… outbuildings, storage yards, that type of thing."

Duncan shook his head. "All searched recently. No sign of him." He thought about the beanie, Finn's beanie, and somehow thought that was relevant. "He's out this way… someplace."

"Did you look out as far as Dun Ardtreck?" Davey asked.

"The old broch?" Duncan asked. "That's just a ruin, surely."

"Aye, it is," Davey agreed, "but it's isolated, remote… and it was a fort for a reason. Much of the stone in the walls is still sound… it could offer some form of shelter, and… if Callum has been helping him…"

Duncan considered this. He had nothing to offer as an alternative. "Aye, okay. Head for Ardtreck." Duncan reached for his mobile.

"No!" Davey said and Duncan's head snapped up, looking over at him.

"Davey, Callum could be in danger!"

"Aye, and that's why you can't go in there with flashing lights and sirens, Duncan. What if Finn… what if he's lost the plot and your lot pile in on him, scare the daylights out of him. What will happen then?"

"You're talking like you think Finn MacGregor harmed Ava," Duncan said, seeing Davey recoil at the suggestion. "What do you know that you're not telling me?"

Davey was quiet for a moment, his lips pursed but Duncan knew he was mulling something over. Something he didn't want to share unless he had to.

"Davey… look, I know where we're headed and I'll call in the cavalry if I have to. You'll not be able to stop me," Duncan said defiantly. "Unless you give me a reason not to." Davey glanced at him and their eyes met. "Tell me now or I'll make this call." Duncan held up his mobile as if to emphasise the action.

"I don't know!" Davey said. Duncan sighed and made to dial Alistair's number. "No, don't," he said and his tone, the urgency made Duncan hesitate. Davey slammed on the brakes and the car came to an abrupt stop. He turned in his seat, looking at Duncan. "Look, Duncan... I don't know anything for certain, but I talked with Callum—"

"The other day when you picked him up?"

"Aye... he was upset, but not for himself," Davey said, pained. "As you said earlier, I knew he'd skipped school for the past two days. I hadn't told his mother, and I pressed him on it when I collected him. I was all ready to give him a right..." He must have seen Duncan bristle at the implication, and he took a deep breath before continuing, "telling off. But... he opened up to me... told me he had a good reason for skipping his classes."

"Which was?"

"He wouldn't say—"

"Och... come on, man!"

"He wouldn't, I'm telling you," Davey said. "Callum was helping a friend... he said he had to, and that we'd brought him up right; to look out for those he cared about. For those who couldn't take care of themselves."

Duncan was sceptical, especially considering how heavy Davey got with his hands towards his wife and children. The notion the man had any redeeming features, let alone being a positive parental role model, left him with a sour taste in his mouth.

"Go on," Duncan said, sensing he might be about to hear a bit of honesty from Davey Mcinnes for once.

"He asked me to trust him," Davey said, meeting Duncan's eye. "To trust him to do the right thing."

Duncan held the gaze for as long as it felt comfortable and then he looked ahead. It was snowing again. "And do you?" Duncan asked. "Trust him?"

"I do, aye."

Duncan took a breath, looking at his mobile in his palm, Alistair's contact displayed on the screen.

"I know you don't trust me, Duncan," Davey said softly. "But… can you trust your son."

Duncan looked across at him, annoyed that he was playing that card. "So, he's my son when you want him to be and nothing to me when you don't. Is that how it goes, aye?"

Davey exhaled, pensive. "I know what you think of me, Duncan." He shook his head. "And I deserve that. I've behaved… badly… unforgivably, in the past."

Duncan's eyes narrowed.

"But I'm trying to make a change," Davey said. "I'm going to counselling sessions… I'm trying to be a better man, husband and father." He angled his head towards Duncan. "You made that happen."

"Me?"

"Aye, you coming back… seeing how…" he closed his eyes, looking away, "*my wife* looks at you, just like she used to years ago. I realised I was going to lose everything that was important to me… if I didn't make a change." He opened his eyes and met Duncan's gaze. "I don't expect you to believe my words but judge me on my actions. I'm trying, I really am. If you won't trust me, then trust Callum."

Duncan exhaled heavily, putting his mobile back into his pocket, knowing in that moment that this was exactly what Alistair had feared might come to pass when they set off together earlier. Duncan hoped he was right and that this emotional connection to the players involved wouldn't come back to haunt him.

CHAPTER TWENTY-EIGHT

THE ROAD up through Ardtreck village was still passable, but even so, it was much trickier than it had been earlier when Duncan met Ronnie Macdonald at the scene of Archie's assault. The Defender still lay where Duncan had last seen it, half into the drainage ditch beside the road although the vehicle was now completely covered in freshly fallen snow. Ronnie had taped it off, but it was a half-hearted effort. Bearing in mind the conditions, and the unlikely interference from anyone locally, it was good enough. A forensic examination team was unlikely to be able to do anything until the weather eased at any rate.

They pressed on and as the tarmac road petered out, Davey brought the pick-up to a stop.

"We're walking from here," Davey said solemnly.

Duncan peered out into the darkness. "I've never been up to the dun. When was the last time you were up there?"

Davey thought hard. "It was a few years ago, right enough. Some archaeological team from one of the central belt universities came up to dig the ruins."

"They find much?"

"Nah… a few signs of burning," Davey said. "They think that's how it came down, in a fire."

"What can you tell me about the layout of it, what are we walking into?"

"Not much. It's small… maybe twelve or thirteen metres, stone walled. It backs onto the sea."

"Can we approach unseen, do you think?"

Davey grinned. "You're joking, right? It was a defensive position."

Duncan inclined his head and sighed. "Fair enough. Let's make a move."

The journey across the island hadn't been quick. On any given day – a normal day with clement weather conditions – they'd have made the journey in a little over an hour, but tonight it had taken them nearly two and a half. It was after three o'clock in the morning and Duncan felt his mobile vibrate in his pocket. He knew it would be Alistair, and that he couldn't answer it. He wondered how long it would be before his DS lost patience and had the mobile signal tracked. Not long, if he knew Alistair.

Davey directed them down what Duncan assumed would be a well-walked path, if they had been able to see it. His coat was done up to the collar, his hands thrust deep into his pockets and yet he still felt the cold. Within a couple of minutes, Duncan could hear waves breaking upon the coast-line, the sounds mixed with that made by the wind which was driving at them. His feet sank into the snow up to his ankles. By the morning it would be frozen solid and rapidly turning to ice where it would sit for days, perhaps a week or more until the temperature increased to aid the thaw.

The ground beneath the snow undulated and they had to take care where they placed their feet. They were climbing to a higher elevation but, looking ahead, Duncan could see a crest on the hill and then he assumed they would drop lower again as they reached the water's edge. The broch, *Dun Ardtreck*, would soon be visible and with the white landscape around them, so would they be to anyone watching.

As they walked, Duncan scanned the surrounding area in search of footprints or tracks, anything to indicate they were right, and Callum had made his way here. There were none though. The falling snow would quickly obscure any signs of his passing through and in this landscape, there were any number of routes he could have taken to make it here.

"Davey, wait there," Duncan called as they approached the top of the rise. Davey looked back at him, hunkering down as Duncan did so, mimicking his action. Together, they edged forward, ignoring the snow as they crept to the crest and looked down upon Dun Ardtreck. The broch was in a D shape, located on a rocky knoll with the straight edge backing onto the cliff face overlooking the water. It was raised on the outcrop by several metres. The footings of what Duncan guessed would have been a second wall circled the main building, and Duncan realised they would have to go down and then move up a fairly steep rise to gain access through the one doorway he could see.

The exterior wall of the main enclosure was roughly seven feet high. There was no way he'd be able to get over that without anyone inside knowing he was coming. They would have to approach the main entrance in full view of anyone who might seek to observe them. They were there, he knew it. An ATV sat at the base of the knoll, a light layer of snow lay on the seat although the engine housing must still be warm because the snow had melted there. Callum couldn't have been here for long.

"Anyone lost an all-terrain vehicle?" Duncan asked casually.

"Aye, that's mine all right," Davey said regretfully. He must have hoped he'd been wrong and Callum had no involvement in Finn's disappearing act. That hope was gone now.

"How did you know?" Davey asked. Duncan shot him an inquisitive look. "About Callum... coming out to meet Finn?"

Duncan pursed his lips. "I didn't, not really. Finn's mobile phone bounced off a cell tower near your croft and I put two and two together."

Davey searched Duncan's expression. "But you weren't expecting Finn MacGregor to be at our house though, were you?"

"No, I wasn't. The mobile received a call from Ava Caldwell's mobile phone, and Finn is linked to her. He must have her mobile, thinking we'd be monitoring his. He was likely banking on Callum keeping quiet for him, if asked by us."

"Callum is a loyal friend," Davey said. "Finn chooses good pals. How do we go in?"

"You... don't," Duncan said firmly. It was one thing to come all this way with Davey in tow, even taking the lead, but there was no way he'd allow a civilian to take an active role in this. "You stay here, and if you need to, then call in the reinforcements."

"Hey! Hold on a minute—"

"Davey, this is my job... it's not a measure of your..." Duncan sought the right word, "manhood. If you go in there as well, then who knows what will happen. I can't have it."

Davey looked ready to protest, but he relented and nodded. "How do I know if you're in trouble though?"

Duncan didn't have a clue. "If in doubt, call it in," Duncan said, passing his mobile to Davey who accepted it.

Alistair's contact details were open on the screen. "Don't hesitate."

"Aye, I won't." Davey held the mobile up and smiled. "I'm on it. Good luck."

Duncan eased himself up into a crouch and carefully descended the hillside, moving cautiously but with purpose. The wind was whistling around him, coming in off the water from the north. That would help, carrying any noise of his approach away from the two boys. They would have to look directly at him and as far as they were aware, they were alone and no one knew their whereabouts. It was also the middle of the night, not that Duncan felt any sense of fatigue. He was alert, his senses tuned to the landscape and what he was about to do.

Making it to the foot of the knoll unnoticed, he came to a rocky outcrop easily eight feet high. The ground at his feet rose to his left and he followed the contour of the land leading him up to a point where he could climb with relative ease up to the next level. This brought him in sight of the inner wall of the ruined broch, but the entrance was now on the other side, so he was confident he wouldn't be seen if he hurried to the wall. Angling the advance to his left, he hastened up against the massive stone blocks of the wall, pressing his back into it to become one with the structure.

The wind, funnelled between the hillside and the broch itself, drove fiercely against him along the course of the wall and Duncan felt his teeth chatter involuntarily. His fingers were numb now, despite the gloves. How could Finn have stayed out here for the last few days in these conditions? It was a miracle he was still alive.

Voices carried to him, drifting over the wall and across to him. He couldn't make out words, the details lost in the wind. Duncan looked back to where Davey should be, but he couldn't see him. Had he backed away out of sight or was he still hunkered down in the snow keeping a watchful eye? Having that particular man as his back up, responsible for calling for help if needed, unnerved Duncan. Despite what Davey said to him in the car, despite his apparent attempt at charting the right course, Duncan still couldn't bring himself to accept what he said as gospel. Men like Davey didn't change. Experience taught him that.

Setting aside those concerns, Duncan edged along the curved wall, making his way to the doorway. The door had long since disappeared and it was now an opening, the width of a heavyset man. The stone blocks of the wall came to above Duncan's head at this point. His assessment was accurate; there was no way he'd make it over them without a great deal of effort. Not impossible, but with frozen fingers and ice forming in the junctions where the blocks met, he'd likely fall as not.

He reached the entrance, his back against the wall. The conversation had stopped or at least he couldn't hear it now. The waves crashing against the cliff face roared below, the noise of them battering the rock carrying to him on the wind. He chanced a look around the corner and he glimpsed two figures standing just inside the broch. The height of the walls offered some respite from the wind, but it wouldn't be much.

Duncan looked past the doorway, across to the northern side and saw the snow banked deeply against it. Finn had chosen the only shelter available to him in the area, but it must have been through necessity rather than choice. He looked in on them again, seeing their body language as rigid, recognising Callum he could see he was animated. The other boy stood firm, his hands on his hips, defiant.

Duncan took a deep breath and entered. Conversation ceased as soon as he appeared, both boys turning to face him with a mixture of shock and surprise. Callum's mouth fell open whereas Finn MacGregor stood like a cat, poised and ready to move in an instant. He glared at Callum.

"You said you didn't tell anyone!" Finn yelled at Callum.

"I didn't... I swear!"

"Liar!"

Duncan held his hands up before him, showing them he meant no harm, doing his utmost to defuse the situation.

"Finn... my name's Duncan," he said calmly. Finn's eyes darted between him and Callum. "You've no need to be afraid of me—"

"I'm not afraid of anyone," Finn snapped. "Not any more."

"Whatever's happened, lad," Duncan said, "we can fix it."

"How?" Finn asked, anguished. Duncan could see tears welling and it looked like he'd been crying already, his eyes were red-rimmed and bloodshot.

"There's nothing that can't be resolved, Finn."

"I told you," Callum said, as much to Duncan as to his friend. "You should come home. It'll be all right, it will." He looked at Duncan, almost imploring him to reinforce the point.

Duncan nodded. "We just need to get you both safely inside first." Duncan could see a superficial wound on the side of Finn's face. It had been bleeding but had long since dried, the blood mixing with dirt by the look of it. Duncan took another step forwards, Finn immediately sidestepping to his right, closer to Callum but away from Duncan. "Come on, lad," Duncan said, forcing a smile. Finn reached into his coat pocket, taking out a small blade. He brandished it at Duncan.

"You keep back!" he yelled, eyes widening in shock and fear. Duncan stood still, keeping his hands out, palms up.

"I'm not here to harm you, Finn," he said calmly.

Callum shot Duncan a nervous glance and then stepped towards his friend. "Finn... don't be crazy—"

Before Duncan could react, Finn leapt towards Callum, grabbing him by the shoulder and spun him to face Duncan, wrapping an arm around him and bringing the blade up to Callum's neck.

"Finn!" Duncan said, raising his hands higher, fearful of antagonising the boy and making him react further. "Don't do anything... crazy." He regretted using that particular adjective. In a volatile, high-pressure situation the last thing you should do is accuse the aggressor of being mentally ill.

"Finn?" Callum said, almost whispering, the blade depressing the skin of his throat. "Don't... please don't hurt me."

Finn glared at Duncan. His expression was pure, unmitigated rage now. Duncan had miscalculated this entire situation and now it might cost his son his life. Instinctively, Duncan took a half-step forward and Finn responded by backing away, hauling Callum with him. The ground inside the broch was uneven and both boys slipped as they moved, Callum falling into Finn and they both stumbled. Duncan took the chance to bridge the gap between them, but Finn righted himself and tightened his grip on Callum, hauling him up and away from the advancing policeman.

He jabbed the knife in the air threateningly towards Duncan. "Stay back!" he screamed. Duncan stopped, now barely three feet away from the boys.

Finn had nowhere else to go. They were now positioned at the back wall of the broch, much of which was missing. The rear wall was the only straight edge of the structure and here, the dun was in the worst state of repair. Much of the wall had either been stripped for use in buildings elsewhere over the years or, which was more likely, had pitched into the foam sea below. The drop to the water was by way of a sheer cliff face, the perfect defensive position to keep attackers out and also, perversely, now kept Finn MacGregor hemmed in. Duncan was all that stood between him and escape.

Peering over the edge, Finn looked down into the boiling, frothing waters below, breaking upon the rocks. He turned back to Duncan, terrified. "I didn't mean it, none of it!" he screamed. "It wasn't my fault!"

"I know!" Duncan called back. "I know it wasn't your fault, Finn. None of this is your fault." Finn's eyes locked on Duncan's, staring at him, gauging his sincerity. Duncan reached out with his right hand, palm open. "Come on, Finn. You don't want to harm your friend."

Callum looked horrified, frozen in fear. Duncan extended his hand further towards Finn who seemed ready to respond. He looked at Duncan's outstretched hand, his eyes flitting between it and Duncan's face.

"Come on, Finn. It's time to go home," Duncan said. Movement in the corner of Duncan's eye made him look to his right, Davey Mcinnes stepping into view. Finn, the relinquishing of his blade forgotten, shoved Callum towards Duncan and turned away looking to climb the broch wall to escape. Callum clattered into Duncan who was knocked off balance momentarily, but he managed to stop Callum from falling and stay upright himself.

Releasing his hold on Callum, Duncan turned just in time to see Finn, attempting to climb out over the slippery rocks, lose his grip. For a moment, it seemed as if he was stationary in mid-air, but then he screamed and fell from the wall, pitching backwards and landing with a thump at the wall's base on his back before tumbling over the edge of the cliff. Duncan hurled himself forward, seeing Finn's frantic arms sweeping all around him as he desperately sought something to hold onto.

Duncan scrabbled with both arms and managed to grasp Finn's coat as he almost disappeared from view. However, Finn was a big lad and his momentum dragged Duncan with him. Duncan sought purchase with his feet, trying to wedge himself in place to arrest their fall, but he was going head-first, and he couldn't deploy any weight through his feet to do so. The cliff edge grew rapidly closer, like the view of an infinity pool across the ocean below. Only in this case, to follow Finn over the cliff would mean certain death for the pair of them.

A decisive action flashed into his mind; *let him go and save yourself* but, casting the thought aside, Duncan's fear quickly turned to panic. They were picking up speed towards the edge and even if Duncan maintained his hold as best he could, he was likely to lose his grip on the boy in any event. He couldn't let go despite his rational mind telling him not to do so would lead to catastrophe. Finn pitched over the edge and Duncan saw his own outstretched arms follow before the vista opened up before him and the roiling waves below were all he could now see. It was too late. He'd failed.

Their fall stopped suddenly, and Duncan gasped, not realising he'd been holding his breath. Finn dangled beneath him, looking up at Duncan and grasping at his forearms, terrified as he bounced against the cliff face, violently at first and then gently as his momentum slowed. Duncan felt weight across the backs of his legs, hands also held tightly around his ankles. He felt secure. As secure as he could hanging from the cliff face high above the raging waters below anyway.

With Finn holding onto him with a vice-like grip, born of abject terror, Duncan felt the strain in his muscles. Finn stared up at him, wide-eyed, pleading with Duncan not to let go.

Duncan glanced over his shoulder. He couldn't see them, but he knew they were there.

"Pull us up for God's sake!" he yelled. For a moment, which felt interminably long but, in reality, was little more than a few seconds, they stayed where they were, suspended in mid-air as the Atlantic winds buffeted them. Then he was moving, slowly at first but then with more surety. As soon as his waist was back over the lip of the cliff edge, Duncan was able to use his own body weight to assist in hauling Finn to safety.

Moments later, they were all back within the relative safety of the confines of the broch. Collapsing to the ground, no one spoke as they all caught their breath. The wind howled around them, the waves continuing in their vain attempt at punishing the cliff face and aside from their collective heavy breathing, the only sound was that of Finn MacGregor, quietly sobbing as he lay on the ground beside them, his knees brought up against his chest in the foetal position.

Duncan was the first to rise, crossing to the base of the wall where Finn had initially fallen from. He dropped to his haunches, retrieving the small knife Finn had dropped when he fell. He examined it. It was three inches long and slightly less than an inch wide where the blade met the hilt. The handle was fashioned from beautifully woven steel in a Celtic style, with a Cairngorm quartz stone set into the pommel. The blade had one sharp, cutting edge and the other was serrated for the first third of the blade and smooth for the remainder.

Both the blade and handle exhibited a high level of quality craftsmanship. Hefting the blade in his palm, Duncan felt the weight. It was one of the finest sgian-dubhs he'd ever handled. He reversed the knife, seeing an inscription on the blade; *air son gràidh do mhàthar*. His Gaelic wasn't great, but Duncan's grandmother had been a speaker, holding onto the language despite successive government's attempts at its suppression. He studied the inscription, glancing down at Finn. *For the love of your mother.*

Duncan felt immense pity for the teenager. Regardless of how the event came to pass, Duncan knew that Finn MacGregor was responsible for the death of Ava Caldwell, his biological mother. That fact would weigh heavily upon him for the rest of his life.

CHAPTER TWENTY-NINE

THE NURSE PULLED BACK the screen shielding Finn MacGregor from the open plan area of the Accident and Emergency triage area. She smiled at Duncan and he raised his eyebrows with an unasked question. Finn was behind her in the bed, looking very much the lost little boy, pale and frightened.

"He has the onset of frostbite in both his feet and was exhibiting symptoms of hypothermia," she said, glancing back at Finn who paid neither of them any attention. PC Fraser Macdonald stood off to one side of the bed as well, arms folded, tasked with keeping a watchful eye on the youth during treatment. Oftentimes, medics didn't care for a police presence while they worked, but under these circumstances no one had complained.

"Will he be okay?" Duncan asked.

The nurse smiled forlornly. "Physically, he will be fine. It's something of a miracle based on how long he's been sleeping rough, but he will recover." She glanced at Finn one more time and then smiled at Duncan. "He'll be transferred to a ward in a little while, and then likely discharged tomorrow morning, all being well. Then he's all yours, Detective Inspector."

"Thank you," Duncan said, walking into the cubicle. Fraser acknowledged him and Finn glanced up as well. "How are you feeling, Finn?"

The boy shrugged. "All right, I suppose."

"You've led all of us a merry dance these past few days."

"I'm sorry," Finn said, lowering his eyes. "I never meant to cause trouble." His eyes flitted between Fraser and Duncan. "Is my… are my parents here?"

Marsali MacGregor had turned herself into the station at Portree while Duncan and Davey were battling through the snowstorm to reach Ardtreck. Having arrived home and seen the massive police presence, she'd fled the scene, unsure of what to do. With nowhere to go, her beloved son still missing, she'd seen sense and driven herself to the Portree station and given herself up.

With the shocking discovery of the remains of their biological child, it would be some time before either Marsali or Anthony MacGregor would be allowed their freedom. They were yet to establish if the death had been, as Anthony insisted, via natural causes. Craig Dunbar's opinion that their story matched the physical evidence he'd evaluated thus far gave them some credibility, but there was no way they'd be allowed out of the police station until the procurator fiscal concluded what they may or may not be charged with.

An appearance in court was subsequently likely, either way, where bail conditions would be determined, or the couple could be held on remand. None of this would be decided within a matter of hours following such a grim discovery.

"I'm sorry, they're not here," Duncan said. Finn was disappointed. "I'm sure they are both keen to see you and they know you are alive and safe."

"Do I have to see them?" he asked, clearly reticent.

"Do you not wish to?" Duncan asked.

Finn shrugged. "I don't know what I'd say."

Duncan, not wishing to explain why the reunion would be delayed, "You don't have to worry about that just now." Finn seemed relieved. "And we can get into what happened tomorrow, once you're discharged from the hospital—"

"It's my fault," Finn said. He looked up at Duncan with a tired expression, dark circles hung beneath puffy eyes. He'd stopped crying once they began their journey away from Dun Ardtreck, settling into a withdrawn, uncommunicative state ever since. "That she's dead."

"Ava Caldwell?"

At the mention of her name, Finn fought back tears, swallowing hard. "She was... my mother."

Duncan nodded. "When did you find out? When she gifted you the sgian-dubh?"

Finn shook his head. "I was never very good with my Gaelic. Dad always said it was a nonsense... and should be allowed to die like all pointless languages."

"Well... it's an argument," Duncan said, sitting down on the end of the bed. "I can't say I agree." The formal interview would have to take place with a chaperone present and legal counsel for the boy, so none of this conversation would be admissible at trial.

"I met her online," Finn said, "in a chatroom." He pursed his lips. "We believed in the same things. Shared the same interests. I'd met an adult who listened to what I had to say," he said, sounding bitter and Duncan wondered which adults in his life didn't show an interest in his passions. Two names sprung to mind.

"When did you learn who she was?"

He shrugged. "I... I think she'd hinted at it loads, looking back. I probably should have known something was up when she kept giving me cash… saying she had plenty and just wanted me to be happy and that, you know?"

"Aye, no one gives anyone anything for nothing, do they?" Duncan said.

"She told me… when I met her that day, when we were supposed to be out keeping an eye on that sod McKinley and his diseased stock."

Duncan took a breath, the venom in his tone perhaps revealing the volatility of his temperament beneath the passion for a righteous cause.

"Where were you at the time?"

"We'd been out to Heath Falls… and then walked on to the coastal cliff overlooking the Talisker Stack, from above the bay." His eyes met Duncan's again, briefly, before he looked down at his hands cupped together in his lap. "She told me who she was then… and…"

"That must have been hard to hear," Duncan said, glancing at Fraser whose silent acknowledgement showed he agreed.

"I didn't want to believe it," Finn said, his eyes tearing, "but I knew it was true. It all made sense. I tried to walk away from her, but she followed, dragging me back. I just wanted to… to go—"

"Home?" Duncan asked.

Finn's face flushed then, a veil of darkness clouding his expression. "No! Why should I ever go back there. They lied to me… my mum and dad… but she's not my mum, is she? And Anthony MacGregor isn't my dad either."

Duncan pursed his lips, shaking his head slightly. "There's more to being a parent than biology though," he said quietly.

"My whole life… is a lie. Everything about me… is a bloody lie! I don't even know who I am any more…"

Duncan had no words of comfort to offer. The boy's life had been torn out from beneath him, the only constant figures he had in his life had deceived him since before he was old enough to know his name.

"It's a lot to take in," Duncan said.

"She could have left me alone," Finn said, pained. "I had a life. I was happy. I knew who I was…"

Duncan considered that point. It was true. What could Ava have hoped to achieve in her actions? Craig Dunbar's post-mortem findings came to mind. Ava was ill, her life expectancy diminished. Perhaps she thought she was running out of time. He looked at Finn, remembering what Craig had told him about Kearns-Sayre Syndrome and how it was hereditary and passed on from mother to child. Maybe, to give Ava the benefit of the doubt, she felt the need to see her child, to see if he'd inherited the syndrome, to enable him to get the treatment he needed at an earlier age than she had. Maybe she'd come back to him to try and make amends for abandoning him at birth.

There was no way of determining her motivations now, and there never would be.

"That day," Duncan said, "up on the cliffs. What happened?"

"I was so proud of the gift she'd got me," Finn said. "I carried it with me every day after I got it. I'd wanted one for so long, been saving up…"

"The sgian-dubh?"

Finn nodded. "I knew it was expensive."

"Which is why you hid it in your room, so your parents… so Marsali and Anthony wouldn't find out?"

Again, Finn nodded. "I asked her what the inscription said… and she told me: *the love of your mother.*"

"And you tried to leave," Duncan said.

"I did, aye." Finn stared at the foot of the bed, emotionless now. "She wouldn't let me leave… so angry and upset. She wanted to explain, to apologise… and to make it up to me. I mean…" he shook his head, "how can you abandon someone you claim to love. I pulled away from her… I just wanted to get away. She kept… she wouldn't let go of me, and I… I… just lashed out!" He looked up at Duncan, tears rolling down his otherwise expressionless face. "It was just the once… and she let go of me…"

"You stabbed her?"

"I didn't mean to! I swear to God, I didn't mean to hurt her…"

"What happened then?"

"She stood there… just looking at me," Finn said, staring ahead as if seeing something in the distance, "and then she staggered to her right. I went towards her, but she must have thought I was going to attack her again… and she slipped… and fell."

Duncan sat there in silence, Finn openly weeping now. Duncan glanced at Fraser whose stoic demeanour seemed moved. He shook his head, which was about as emotional as Fraser allowed himself to be.

"Did you go down to the beach?" Duncan asked.

Finn shook his head. "I looked down… and I saw her on the rocks. Her eyes were open, and I could see blood all around her, on the rocks and in the water. I was scared and so… I ran… and I kept running."

"Where have you stayed these past few days?" Duncan asked.

Finn shrugged. "Here and there. Outbuildings, sheds… wherever. I went out to Dun Ardtreck when I saw you lot searching the area for me."

Duncan's sympathies extended to the boy, for his loss, the confusion as well as the trauma surrounding what had happened. By all accounts, Finn MacGregor wasn't a dysfunctional child. He had never been in trouble, however, there was still one event that had to be discussed and Duncan knew that here was where his empathy would be at an end.

"Can you talk to me about Archie?"

Finn looked up at Duncan, saddened. "That was an accident... he... he wanted me to go with him to the police station."

"Archie did?"

Finn nodded. "He said it would be better for me to go in voluntarily... he said it would help me."

Duncan cocked his head. "Aye, he wasn't wrong. So, what happened?"

Finn shook his head. "He brought me food, a sleeping bag... he was Ava's... he was her friend. I don't know what he saw in me..." Duncan knew Archie would have been following his own moral compass, an act that so often put him at odds with everyone else, including Duncan. His heart was always in the right place though. "He talked me into going with him, back to Portree... but I got scared."

"You were with him, in the car?" Duncan asked.

"I was... I told him to stop, to let me out," Finn said, choking on his emotion, "and then the car just skidded and... we crashed. I got out and I ran... I didn't know where I was running to, but I took off. He came after me."

"And what happened?"

Finn fell silent.

"What happened to Archie, Finn?"

"I told you... I was scared," he said, lowering his head. "I just lashed out." It was a running theme with Finn MacGregor as far as Duncan could tell, the inability to control his emotions in tense scenarios. Firstly, with his biological mother and later, with Archie. "I'm so sorry. I never meant to cause so much trouble."

Duncan took a moment, letting the intensity of the moment pass. "I know what you did though, Finn."

The boy looked up, his eyes narrowing. "What do you mean?"

"McKinley's yard." Finn averted his eyes from Duncan's gaze. "I know you set it alight," Duncan said firmly. Finn shook his head but didn't verbally deny it. "I know you were angry... and upset at the injustice of what you've learned in this past week, but it wasn't right to take that out on Graeme McKinley the way you did—"

"He deserved it!" Finn snapped. "He's been cheating... raping the climate... and all for his own gain. He deserves everything coming to him."

Duncan inhaled through his nose and got up from the bed, considering whether Finn's medical condition could be a factor when it came to his apparent impulsiveness in his decision making. That wasn't for him to say though. There were medical minds who would have to make that assessment. "I'm sorry for your loss and for what you've been through, Finn, I really am," Duncan said, "but there are ways to cope with what comes at you in life, and you should have known better. Despite everything, you should have known better."

Finn glared at him but said nothing. Duncan glanced at Fraser who nodded to Duncan as he left the cubicle. The nurse Duncan spoke to passed by him and he drew her attention.

"When you come to move Finn onto a ward, can you make a note to have the doctors assess him for Kearns-Sayre Syndrome?" The nurse looked at him quizzically, and Duncan smiled. "It's a hereditary condition – passed on from mother to child – and the boy's mother suffered from it. From what his..." Duncan was about to say parents but didn't want to spend the rest of the night explaining the complexities of this peculiar case to the nurse, and re-framed his thoughts, "relatives and teachers tell me, he shows many of the symptoms."

The nurse nodded and went to continue with what she was doing.

"Oh, could you tell me where Callum Mcinnes is please?" Duncan asked. The nurse pointed to another cubicle on the far side of the department. Duncan thanked her and headed towards it. Davey appeared from behind the closed screen and Duncan stepped behind a supporting pillar to hide himself. Davey hurried past. Duncan made sure he'd gone, took a deep breath and stepped beyond the screen and into the cubicle.

CHAPTER THIRTY

CALLUM LOOKED up from the bed, surprised to see Duncan entering. Duncan forced a smile.

"How are you, lad?" he asked, searching for signs of injury. Callum had a small cut to the side of his head where he'd fallen during the struggle with Finn. Duncan hadn't seen it at the time, but it looked superficial, requiring only a good clean and some sterile strips to seal it. He looked at Callum's neck, where the point of Finn's sgian-dubh had been pressed against his throat but other than a reddened patch, the skin had been unbroken.

"I'm okay," Callum said, nodding. "How is Finn?"

Duncan wasn't sure if he'd be so quick to ask after someone who'd held a blade against his throat, but he admired Callum's loyalty. He cocked his head.

"Physically, he'll be fine, but he will have some harsh times ahead of him, that's for sure."

Callum's head dipped. "I know. I really wanted to help him… I tried," he said, almost apologetically. "I know I should have come to the police, but…"

Duncan held up a hand and smiled. "I know. You did what you thought was right by your friend."

"Aye," Callum said. "Fat lot of good it did though, eh?"

"You stood by your friend, Callum." Duncan angled his head. "I wish I had friends as good as you." Callum looked up and smiled weakly. "Or that I could be as good a friend myself," he said, thinking of Archie. He'd been so caught up in all of this that he hadn't checked up on his condition. He hoped he was doing all right. "We'll need to have a formal interview with you to go through all of this," he said, "once you feel up to it."

Callum nodded. "Of course. I... I'm sorry I caused so much trouble."

Duncan shook his head. "You're not to blame for any of this."

"No, I know that," Callum said, but lowered his eyes. "But I feel like I let him down."

Self-deprecation... perhaps that was a trait they had in common, but Duncan didn't know if that was genetic or a learned pattern of behaviour. Duncan looked around briefly, hearing some staff members pass the cubicle on the other side of the curtain screen. He didn't know how much time they'd have alone together.

"Callum," Duncan said, his brow furrowing, "when we found Ava Caldwell's..." he hesitated, deciding to soften his description. "When we found her, she had a handwritten telephone number on a slip of paper, and my name." Callum didn't look up. "I was a bit confused," Duncan said, sitting down on the end of the bed, hands clasped together casually in his lap. "You see, I'd never met her before... or even spoken to her as far as I know."

"Right," Callum said, still looking down. "I can see how that might be..."

"Confusing?" Duncan asked. Callum nodded. "It was. It had me stumped... until I was at your home and I saw the note you'd left your mum to remind her to pick you up on Tuesday. You remember?"

"Rugby practice," Callum said, his eyes flitting to Duncan and away again.

"You any good?"

Callum shrugged. "I'm on the school team."

"That's good."

"It's a small year group," Callum said, dismissing the achievement.

Duncan nodded. "Only... I recognised the handwriting. At least, the numbers. You write a six and an eight quite distinctively." Callum grew restless, shifting his position on the bed. "You gave it to her, didn't you?"

Callum looked up and briefly met his eye, frowning, before looking away again. He shook his head. "I gave it to Finn... and he must have passed it on to her, I guess."

Duncan found that plausible. "Why did you have my—"

"My mum gave it to me," Callum said, anticipating the question.

"Did she?"

"Aye, she gave it to me before Christmas... and she said if I was ever in trouble, like real trouble... and I didn't know what to do or who to turn to, that I should call you," Callum said, looking up at Duncan expectantly. "Why would she do that?"

Duncan felt his chest flutter, as if he'd been caught doing something he shouldn't be doing. His mouth was dry and he struggled to swallow all of a sudden. Bringing his hand up to cover his mouth, Duncan dragged it slowly down across his chin, trying to resist the urge to tell the boy the truth, to tell him everything. Callum stared at him and, despite nothing being said, it was the deepest moment of contact they'd ever had between them.

"Your mum and I... we go back a long way."

"I know that," Callum said, his eyes narrowing, "but why you... and not... Archie, or someone else?"

Duncan had been holding his breath and he slowly exhaled, his mind churning over the likely outcomes if he spoke his mind. He pursed his lips, coming to a decision. Looking at Callum, he reached out and gently touched the boy's left hand, lying flat on his thigh.

"Whatever happens in your life, Callum," he said calmly, holding the boy's attention, "you can always come to me and... you can trust me, you know?"

Callum stared at him for a moment, something unsaid seeming to pass between them, an understanding perhaps. The teenager nodded slowly. "Okay."

Duncan patted the back of his hand, returning the nod, trying his best to appear casual. "Okay."

The curtain was thrown back and Becky hurried through, pulling up as she clapped eyes on the two of them. She looked at Duncan, wide-eyed, and then bypassed him to reach Callum's side before throwing her arms around him and hugging him fiercely.

"Callum, I've been so worried about you, are you okay? Are you—"

"Mum, I'm fine," Callum said, smiling affectionately as his mother clasped both his cheeks and stared into his eyes. "I promise, I'm okay!"

"Good," Becky said, then leaned back from him a touch. "What were you thinking, going off like that? You could have got yourself killed—"

"Mum!" Callum said, placing his hands over hers and squeezing them. "I'm okay... it's all okay."

Becky's anger, born of fear and frustration, dissipated and she stroked her son's cheek affectionately, her eyes gleaming. "Don't ever do that to me again," she said quietly.

Callum smiled. "I won't. I promise."

"I'll... er... leave you to it," Duncan said, feeling awkward and desperate to extricate himself from this moment. He felt something new watching Becky share such an intimate moment of joy with her son, their son... an emotion he wasn't used to, it was envy. He slipped out from the cubicle, keen to find out the nature of Archie's condition. It would be a welcome distraction as long as his friend was out of danger, at any rate.

"Duncan!"

He turned at hearing the call, seeing Becky hurrying after him, glancing nervously about her as other people also looked to see who was making the noise. He waited for her. She came to stand before him, glancing around, presumably to ensure no one else was standing within earshot. She lowered her voice.

"What did you say to him?" She glanced over her shoulder towards the cubicle and then across to the double entrance doors. Was she fearful of seeing Davey return, and therefore him seeing the two of them talking?

"Just..." Duncan shrugged. "Nothing much, why?"

"Davey told me."

"Told you what?"

"That you want a relationship with... with your son, with Callum?" She almost hissed the question. He didn't pick up any hostility in her tone or judgement, but he did detect a note of fear. "Did you tell him?"

Duncan shook his head. "Callum? No, of course I didn't. What do you take me for?" Now it was Duncan who looked around, sensing that somehow everyone in Accident and

Emergency knew they were discussing the shared secrets of their past life together.

"I'm… sorry," she said, her demeanour shifting, her face flushing red.

"No… I'm sorry," Duncan said, biting his lip. He closed his eyes, quelling the rising emotions within. "Look, there might come a time when… Callum gets…" he shook his head, struggling to find the right words. *What were the right words?* "That time might come but it's not today," Duncan said, looking around them, "and it's not here, not now." Ava Caldwell came to mind, followed closely by the haunting image of Finn MacGregor's expression as he recounted learning that his entire life had been built on secrets and lies. "If I told him now, then I'd be doing it for me… and certainly not for him."

Becky searched his eyes. Was she assessing him or judging him, Duncan didn't know. She slowly reached up and placed her palm against his cheek and smiled, glassy-eyed. "You have changed, wee Duncan McAdam."

"I have?"

She nodded. "You're not the selfish man you used to be."

"Thanks… I think," he said, unsure of her meaning. As a compliment, at best, it could be seen as a backhanded one. She withdrew from him, taking a half-step backwards.

"It's a good thing… you've grown up."

Before he could respond – not that he was sure what to say anyway – she turned and briskly walked back to her son's cubicle. She didn't look back at him and Duncan felt a curious mix of emotions at that point. Davey Mcinnes came through the entrance alongside Alistair, both men's eyes sweeping the room. Davey paused, glancing sideways at Alistair, who nodded, and then Davey crossed to Callum's cubicle while Alistair came over to join Duncan. Davey had seen him,

Duncan was certain, but he hadn't seen fit to acknowledge him in any way.

Whatever passed between them earlier was all that would be said, that was clear. Alistair came up to him.

"You made a meal of that tonight by all accounts?" Alistair said.

Duncan bristled. "What do you mean by that? I saved the lad's life?"

"Aye, and very nearly at the cost of your own," Alistair said, frowning. He read Duncan's expression. "Sorry, were you expecting to be hailed as a hero or something?"

"Well... a hero might be an exaggeration... but..."

Alistair clapped him on the shoulder, sporting a big grin beneath his moustache. "It's all in a day's work, isn't it? No thanks necessary or sought for that matter."

Duncan smiled. "If you put it like that..."

"You impressed your man over there, though," Alistair said, inclining his head towards Callum's cubicle where they could just about see the family through the gap between the curtain and the wall, Davey and Becky taking turns to hug Callum who was still sitting on his bed, looking uncomfortable with all the fuss.

"Who, Davey?"

"Aye."

"He said that?" Duncan asked, surprised.

"Well, no... not in so many words." Alistair shrugged. "Let's face it, the man hates you."

Duncan laughed. "Aye, true."

"He must know you well," Alistair said, drawing breath and straightening his back. "Where are you off to now?"

"I was going to look in on Archie."

"He's in fine fettle, is young Mr Mackinnon," Alistair said. Duncan looked at him inquisitively. "I figured you'd want to know. Surgery was a success, and the staff tell me he is comfortable. Asleep as well, which is a good thing seeing as it is the middle of the night." Alistair looked Duncan up and down. "Decent people are asleep at this time, Duncan."

"I notice you haven't got your head down, Alistair."

Alistair grinned. "Come on. I'll give you a ride home. You can get some sleep before you need to come back into the station and explain all of this to big trousers upstairs," Alistair said, referencing the detective chief superintendent.

"How long do I have, do you reckon?"

"At least an hour, maybe two," Alistair replied, grinning as he checked his watch. "Enough time for forty winks, a shower and a change of clothes, I suspect. And if you can see your way clear to not finding any deceased people for a day or two, I'd appreciate the respite. Things were much quieter before you came back to the island."

"I'll see what I can do, Alistair, but no promises."

Duncan looked past Alistair and towards the cubicle. He could see Becky fussing around Callum as well as a doctor scanning a clipboard, discussing something with Davey but, as for the teenager himself, Callum was looking out across the medical department at Duncan. Their eyes met and Duncan didn't look away.

Only when someone distracted Callum did the eye contact break, and Duncan was left feeling hollow. The day would come. Everyone had a right to know who they were and where they came from. The boy was bright. Duncan found himself wondering whether Callum was already asking the same questions of himself.

FREE BOOK GIVEAWAY

Enjoy this book? You could make a real difference.

Because reviews are critical to the success of an author's career, if you have enjoyed this novel, please do me a massive favour by entering one onto Amazon.

Type the following link into your internet search bar to go to the Amazon page and leave a review;

http://mybook.to/JMD-skye3

If you prefer not to follow the link please visit the sales page where you purchased the title in order to leave a review.

Reviews increase visibility. Your help in leaving one would make a massive difference to this author and I would be very grateful.

THE CUILLIN DEAD
PREVIEW

THERE IS A GENTLE BREEZE tonight which I am thankful for. My skin is still clammy to the touch and I've got this headache that I've been unable to shift for the last two days. It's this damn heat. There are two to three weeks a year where we have weather like this and every time it feels like a personal torture. I'm not prepared for it. It's something to do with the genes, I reckon. Fair enough if I'm deployed in Afghan or Iraq because you expect it there, but not here.

I'm grateful that we're not out on exercise somewhere but, then again, having something useful to be doing would help focus the mind as well as help pass the time. Instead, I'm standing here in this little box on the main gate, alone. At least during the daytime there would be someone else to speak to along with the comings and goings of daily activity as people pass in and out. No one comes through here in the wee small hours, though, unless it's after the pubs have kicked out on the weekend. No, this night is going to drag. I know it.

I can feel the sweat inside my shirt running down my back. What would I give for a cool shower now? This is my third rotation where I've pulled guard duty overnight and I know full well why that is. I'm not going to give him the satisfaction of showing my displeasure though. He'll be looking for it, looking for that chink in the armour that he can exploit. However, I'm not confident I'll win through when all is said and done. I'm stubborn, certainly, but I'm not stupid. One thing I do know is that I'll go down fighting. I've been up against the likes of him before and I'll stand my ground even if I have to take a kicking every once in a while. My old man taught me that. It's arguably one of the few things he did teach me, that and not to accept drinks from strangers in foreign climes, although that also works when you're back home too.

No one gives you anything for nothing. There's always a cost... and the payback can be painful.

Stepping out of the gatehouse, I look up at the stars. They're dimmed by the light pollution from the nearby town and the base lights along the road don't help either, but I can still make out the familiar families of the constellations. They are the same here as they were in the night sky back home, but they were more plentiful and vivid on the island once the sun goes down. Here, they are muted. In Afghan, once out beyond the wire, the sky was wondrous to behold. The patterns above us were different obviously, and I'd love to go back one day and take the time to view them properly. Out on patrol was not the time, but when we laid up for a bit and I wasn't on watch, I used to take in what I could.

Being out there, so far from home, and seeing the vastness of the universe made me realise just how insignificant we are. *How insignificant he is.* He can do his worst, but he'll not beat me down. Pulling in a deep breath of warm air, I feel the skin on my arms prickle and as I stare out into the darkness, along the fence line and into the trees beyond. *What is it that's caught my eye?* Tensing ever so slightly, I narrow my eyes as I peer into the gloom wishing I had a set of NODs to help. I've learned to trust my instincts over the years, instincts honed in several conflict zones in faraway lands I never knew existed let alone could point to on a map.

A flash of light from deep within the trees followed by a familiar crack splits the peace of the humid night and I'm diving for cover, hitting the ground hard and scurrying to get my back up against the wall of the gatehouse. There was no whistle though... no fizz of a passing round.

Now, there is only silence. Was I mistaken? No... I know what I heard and it was unmistakable. A second crack. Another round discharged, but not towards me. Keeping low, I crawl back inside the gatehouse and reach blindly for the telephone receiver on the desk above me whilst gathering my service rifle in my hands. I'm breathing heavily, but muscle memory takes over, phone clamped between my shoulder and the side of my head. I don't have to think as I check the magazine is in place, the safety catch is to the right, and I pull the cocking handle back then release it, chambering a round. Just in case.

But I know what this is. When I saw them earlier, I had a thought that something was wrong. I hope, for their sake, I'm wrong this time too...

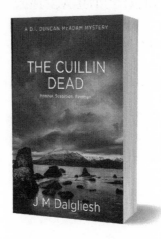

Publishing 2024

ALSO BY THE AUTHOR

In the Misty Isle Series
A Long Time Dead
The Dead Man of Storr
The Talisker Dead

In the Hidden Norfolk Series
One Lost Soul
Bury Your Past
Kill Our Sins
Tell No Tales
Hear No Evil
The Dead Call
Kill Them Cold
A Dark Sin
To Die For
Fool Me Twice
The Raven Song
Angel of Death
Dead To Me
Blood Runs Cold
Life and Death**
**FREE* EBOOK - VISIT* jmdalgliesh.com

In the Dark Yorkshire Series
Divided House
Blacklight
The Dogs in the Street
Blood Money
Fear the Past
The Sixth Precept

AUDIOBOOKS

In the Misty Isle Series
Read by Angus King

A Long Time Dead
The Dead Man of Storr
The Talisker Dead

In the Hidden Norfolk Series
Read by Greg Patmore

One Lost Soul
Bury Your Past
Kill Our Sins
Tell No Tales
Hear No Evil
The Dead Call
Kill Them Cold
A Dark Sin
To Die For
Fool Me Twice
The Raven Song
Angel of Death
Dead To Me
Blood Runs Cold

Hidden Norfolk Books 1-3

AUDIOBOOKS

In the Dark Yorkshire Series
Read by Greg Patmore

Divided House
Blacklight
The Dogs in the Street
Blood Money
Fear the Past
The Sixth Precept

Dark Yorkshire Books 1-3
Dark Yorkshire Books 4-6